It's Your Party, Die If You Want To

Also by Vickie Fee

Death Crashes the Party

It's Your Party, Die If You Want To

Vickie Fee

KENSINGTON PUBLISHING CORP.

http://www.kensingtonbooks.com

KENSINGTON BOOKS are published by

Kensington Publishing Corp.
119 West 40th Street
New York, NY 10018

All Kensington Titles, Imprints, and Distributed Lines are available at special quantity discounts for bulk purchases for sales promotions, premiums, fund-raising, and educational or institutional use. Special book excerpts or customized printings can also be created to fit specific needs. For details, write or phone the office of the Kensington special sales manager: Kensington Publishing Corp., 119 West 40th Street, New York, NY 10018, attn: Special Sales Department, Phone: 1-800-221-2647.

Kensington and the K logo Reg. U.S. Pat & TM Off.

ISBN-13: 978-1-4967-0064-3
ISBN-10: 1-4967-0064-3
First Kensington Mass Market Edition: October 2016

eISBN-13: 978-1-4967-0065-0
eISBN-10: 1-4967-0065-1
First Kensington Electronic Edition: October 2016

10 9 8 7 6 5 4 3 2 1

Printed in the United States of America

33614057746488

*For Daddy Richard Blair
and "Mom" Dorothy Fee—
gone too soon*

Chapter 1

I entered Town Square Diner and spotted Morgan Robison, who despite my druthers was meeting me for lunch. My dining companion, a thirtyish blonde with artificially plumped lips, was strategically positioned in a corner booth licking her chops, peering over the top of her menu at a well-built, younger man seated at the counter. If he was typical of Morgan's usual choice in men, he was also married.

I was seemingly invisible until I cleared my throat and spoke her name.

"Liv McKay," she said, lifting her butt just high enough off the red vinyl seat to give me a limp shoulder hug. "Sit down. I've been waiting for ages."

"Am I late?" I asked, knowing I wasn't.

"No matter. You're here now, and we have so much to talk about."

Morgan is president of the Professional Women's Alliance of Dixie. The group's unfortunate acronym is commonly pronounced *pee wad*. Despite the group's laughable moniker, the association of women professionals in a male-dominated business landscape had been a big help to me when I launched my party-planning venture three years ago. Fellow members had provided a wealth of practical information on permits and taxes, as well as sent clients my way. Even Morgan, who makes a habit of tap dancing on my last nerve, helped me fill out the paperwork for a loan from the Small Business Administration.

The waitress brought our orders. I had the homemade turkey potpie. Health-conscious Morgan ordered a spinach salad with vinaigrette on the side.

Our conversation mostly consisted of Morgan giving me marching orders for PWAD's annual retreat, set for the coming weekend.

"You're just a doll for taking care of this for me, Liv," Morgan said, answering the buzz of her cell phone as she leapt up from the table and hurried on her way—leaving me with the bill. But I figured picking up the check was a small price to pay for her to go away. Morgan left behind the salad she had taken only a few bites of. I devoured the rest of my potpie before settling the bill.

I strolled back to the office on the opposite side of the square, from which I operate my party-planning business. The October air was crisp, and the red maples in front of the courthouse dabbed flames against a cloudless sky. Hay bales, gourds, and scarecrows decorated several storefronts.

Dixie has a quaint town square with a courthouse in the middle and one-way streets on three sides. While big-box stores now dominate the highway, the square is still the heart of our little town. A diner, beauty salon, drugstore, and bakery draw a steady stream of customers each day. The fancy hat shop I remember from my childhood has morphed into a thrift store, and the former grand movie palace is showing its age. But childhood memories of the annual Christmas tree lighting and waiting in line in front of the courthouse to share my secret wishes with Santa mean Dixie's town square will always hold a special place in my heart. Some days after school when I was little, if Mama didn't expect to be home by three o'clock, I'd walk to my dad's insurance office here. A gift shop now occupies that space, but I can still almost smell the Old Spice aftershave of my dearly departed daddy when I walk past.

Before going up to my office, located above Sweet Deal Realty, I tucked into the real estate office to chat with Winette King, who works there as an agent. The bell on the front door jingled as I entered.

"How was lunch?" Winette said.

"I had lunch with Morgan Robison."

"You have my condolences," she said. "I suppose Morgan issued your assigned duties for the retreat. She e-mailed my to-do list."

"What's she dumping on you?" I asked.

"Cleanup. I'm sure she thinks my people are well suited to cleaning. I probably remind her of the mammy she had as a child."

"No, she didn't," I said.

"Oh yes she did."

Since Winette is the only active member of PWAD who's African-American—not to mention that she stands head and shoulders above Morgan in intellect, heart, and moral fiber—it really chapped my hide that Morgan would ask her to do the cleanup. I can't say, however, that it came as a complete surprise. Morgan was raised with a silver spoon, the only child of one of the wealthiest families in the county. She's a vice president of Dixie Savings and Loan. Her major qualification for the job is that her daddy owns the bank.

After standing with my mouth agape for a moment, I said, "I'll help with the cleaning up."

"You bet you will," Winette said, matter-of-factly.

"Better yet, if you'd like, I'll swap jobs with you. Morgan wants me to babysit our guest speaker, Lucinda Grable."

"That ghost woman on TV?"

"Yep."

"No, thank you. I'd just as soon hang on to my broom and dustpan," Winette said.

Unless you count the lady who won a set of luggage on *The Price Is Right*, Lucinda Grable is the only celebrity that the town of Dixie, Tennessee, can lay claim to. She hosts a "paranormal reality" series on cable, called *P.S. Ghost Encounters*. The P stands for *psychic* and the S stands for *scientific*. I'm not sure how much of the show qualifies as scientific, or reality, for that matter. But it is entertaining.

Lucinda provides the psychic element as she senses and sometimes even talks to ghosts. She works with a team of investigators who use infrared cameras and other special equipment to demonstrate that some otherworldly phenomena are present.

"This may be a silly question, but is there any

practical or sane reason that we're having a psychic as the guest speaker at our professional women's retreat?" Winette asked.

"Lucinda's supposed to tell us how she built her local ghost hunting business into a television empire. But she's also going to try to make contact with ghosts in that little family cemetery down the hill from the lodge. It might be fun, with the retreat being held just before Halloween."

"Lord, help us," Winette said.

"Okay, I'm headed upstairs. Do you know what Mr. Sweet is up to? I haven't seen him at all today, or yesterday for that matter."

Nathan Sweet is my landlord and the "Sweet" of Sweet Deal Realty.

"He's involved in the development of that new shopping center they're building up on the highway. He spends more time investing in new development these days than he does in selling existing properties," she said. "The old coot's probably still got the first dollar he ever made, but he's busy making more money. You'd think at his age he'd want to retire and enjoy spending some of that legal tender before he kicks the bucket."

"Are you kidding? I bet he outlives both of us."

"You're probably right," Winette said, tossing her head back and letting loose a room-filling laugh.

Although my office is directly above Sweet Deal Realty, I had to exit through the front door and walk a few steps down the sidewalk to access the stairs that lead up to my office. The street door is topped with a green awning that displays the name of the business, Liv 4 Fun. I had to choose a short business name, since the width of the glass door is the entirety of my street frontage. There's no restroom upstairs, so my rent includes use of the facilities in the real estate office. Not completely convenient, but the rent's cheap and the location on the square is primo.

I had settled in at my desk, caught up on some paperwork, and touched base with a couple of vendors for an upcoming engagement party I was planning when my cell phone rang. I knew from the ringtone that it was my mother, but I answered anyway.

"Liv, jump in your car and get over here right this minute," she said in a panicked voice.

"Mama, what's happened? Are you okay?"

I heard some kind of tapping sounds.

"Oh, dear Lord," Mama said in a breathy voice before the phone went dead.

I grabbed my purse and raced down the stairs, hurrying to my car without even taking time to lock the office door.

My mom lives in a neighborhood just east of the town square, so I was in her driveway within five minutes of backing out of my parking space.

I rushed in through the kitchen door, which is never locked, and started calling for her. I ran through the house worried I might find her unconscious—or worse.

I finally found my mama, who stands almost six feet and weighs well over 200 pounds, cowering in the doorway to the back porch, her eyes transfixed. Her one hand was clutching her chest and the other was holding a hoe.

I grabbed her arm. "Mama, maybe you should sit down," I said. "Are you having chest pains?"

"No," she said in a quiet voice.

This worried me, since my mama never talks in a quiet voice.

"I'll be fine just as soon as you kill that snake over there," she said as she nodded toward a corner of the porch and shoved the hoe in my direction.

I took a closer look at the brick floor of the porch and spotted a good-sized snake coiled up near the steps to the backyard.

"Why in the world did you call *me*?" I said, feeling more than a little irritated. "Why didn't you phone Earl?"

Earl Daniels is Mama's boyfriend, although she'd never call him that.

"I tried, but Earl's out in a field somewhere helping his brother-in-law get soybeans loaded for market," she said.

"You're the one with the hoe," I said, pushing it back in her direction. "You kill it."

"Don't be ridiculous," she said. "You know I was traumatized as a child when I saw my brother get bit by a snake. The bite ended up leaving a big hole in his leg."

She nudged my shoulder and gestured in the direction of the reptile, which had raised its head and was looking our way.

"But you'll be fine, hon," she said. "I don't think this one's poisonous."

"You don't *think* so?"

"Pretty sure," she said. "If you keep an eye on it, I'll go look up pictures of poisonous snakes in the encyclopedia just to be sure."

She was serious.

"Oh, just give me the freaking hoe," I said, ready for this to be over.

I took the garden implement and stepped haltingly toward the hissing creature, which suddenly looked much bigger than before.

"Hold the hoe out away from you, Liv," Mama said. "Don't get too close. I don't know what I'd do if something happened to you like it did to Junior."

I briefly thought about *accidentally* hitting her shin with the wooden end of the hoe. But I knew if the snake slithered away into the vegetation and she didn't know where it had gone, she'd refuse to stay in the house by herself.

I closed my eyes and slammed the metal edge of the hoe several times against the brick in the vicinity of the snake and then raked it off the side of the porch.

"Is it dead?" Mama asked from a safe distance.

"Yeah, it's dead," I said, without knowing if it was dead or not.

Chapter 2

Even though I hadn't accomplished as much as I had hoped at the office, I just couldn't face work after the whole snake-wrangling episode. Dealing with Morgan *and* Mama was about all the drama I could handle for one day. I pulled up to the building and left the car idling while I locked the front door. I got in the car, but instead of backing out of the space I switched off the engine.

I decided to leave my car parked in front of the office and walk the eight blocks to my house instead. The weather was perfect—in the seventies with a light breeze—and my fatted calves needed the exercise.

It wasn't exactly an aerobic workout, as I kept stopping to chat with people along the way. One of the perks—or problems, depending on how you look at it—of small-town life.

Deputy Ted Horton emerged from the sheriff's office just as I stepped onto the sidewalk in front of it.

"Evenin', Ms. McKay," Ted said with a courteous nod.

Ted's a nice guy and thoroughly dedicated to his work, but he got slighted a bit in the looks department, mostly on account of an overly long, skinny neck and weak chin. Although he does have a nice smile thanks to the braces he wore as a kid.

"Evening, Ted. Are you heading home or out to keep the peace?"

"Neither, I guess—unless a fight breaks out at the diner," he said with a broad smile. "I'm going to grab some supper, then come back to finish up some paperwork."

"Things could get rowdy if Mabel runs out of pie," I said, referring to the diner's owner, Mabel Cross, whose pies have been known to incite tussles as customers vie for the last piece.

"I might have to arrest her for disturbing the peace if she runs out of pie—especially if she runs out before I've had a slice."

"'Night, Ted," I said. "Try not to work too late."

I had made it about a block before Nell Tucker hollered at me from the doorway of Dixie Dolls Hair Salon.

"Hey, Liv, is it true Lucinda Grable is coming to our PWAD retreat?

"It's true," I said. "I'm supposed to pick her up at the airport."

"Well, ain't that something. That's what I'd heard through the grapevine, but I don't put much stock in gossip. See you this weekend," the hairstylist said before ducking back into the beauty shop.

It was a triumph of self-control that I didn't burst out laughing when Nell said she didn't put much stock in gossip, since she spreads rumors thicker than jam on biscuits.

Leaves crunched underfoot as I strolled through my neighborhood. Neighbors raking leaves and checking mailboxes waved as I walked by.

As I rounded the corner onto Elm Street, about half a block from home, a noisy, old Buick pulled up alongside me and the driver asked, "You need a ride?"

"I think I can make it from here. Thanks."

"All right, I'll meet you there," she said, hitting the gas pedal and speeding ahead before whipping into my driveway.

Our house is a grand old Victorian lady, although she's showing her age. If you squint and don't look too closely at the peeling paint or crumbling chimney, you can get a glimpse of her former glory, which my husband and I hope to restore—possibly even in my lifetime.

When I walked up to the house a couple of minutes later, Di was leaning against the trunk of her car, flipping through a magazine.

"This was in your mailbox," she said, handing it to me, along with a couple of envelopes.

"Isn't it a federal crime to tamper with other people's mail?"

"I just deliver it," she said, which is literally true. My best friend, Diane Souther, is a mail carrier who covers a walking route in Dixie. In fact, she was still wearing her uniform, which let me know she hadn't been home yet.

"Come on in. I'll treat you to the beverage of your choice."

"Rum?"

"Help yourself."

"Naw, I think I'll stick with iced tea for now."

I poured us each a glass of sweet tea over ice.

"Let's sit on the patio," I said, and Di trailed me through the garage to the backyard. My husband and I had the kitchen of our old house remodeled before we moved in a little more than two years ago. Most of the rest of the interior was in a state of disarray due to the never-ending remodeling, which Larry Joe insists on doing himself. The living room was basically the staging area for other projects.

"What time do you expect Larry Joe home?" she asked.

"Around two in the morning. He had to run a load of freight to St. Louis."

My husband and his dad own McKay Trucking. Generally, my father-in-law oversees shipping and administrative matters while Larry Joe handles sales and clients. But in a pinch they both do whatever's necessary, like most small business owners.

"Are they still short-handed?"

"Not so much with drivers, but they're still short a mechanic," I said.

A couple of months back, the FBI had discovered a drug ring operating through McKay Trucking, unbeknownst to Larry Joe and his dad. They were still dealing with the aftermath, including staff shortages due to two employees who were killed and a couple more who were now in jail.

"The driver who was scheduled for the St. Louis run was involved in a motorcycle accident last night."

"Was he hurt bad?"

"He should be okay, but he has some broken bones and a dislocated shoulder."

"Ouch," she said. "I guess it could've been a lot worse."

Di leaned back on the chaise longue, stretching out the full length of her frame, which is several inches taller and several pounds lighter than my own.

"So how was your day, honey?" Di asked.

"I had lunch with Morgan Robison."

"I'm sorry to hear that."

"That's just what Winette said. The annual PWAD retreat is this weekend and Morgan gave me my to-do list."

"So what's your assignment?"

"Basically, I'm supposed to babysit our guest speaker, pick her up at the airport, chauffeur her around, and make sure she has everything she requires."

"And who is this VIP?"

"Lucinda Grable," I said.

"That woman who talks to dead people on TV?"

"That's the one."

"Lucky you," she said.

"Yep."

We both spent a quiet moment sipping our iced tea and enjoying the stir of a fall breeze that shook a few spent leaves from the trees and gently ruffled Di's shoulder-length, strawberry-blond hair.

"So what's the story with Lucinda Grable? Didn't she grow up around here?"

Having lived in Dixie more than six years now, Di was pretty well acquainted with the locals. But since she's not a lifer like me, she occasionally asks about the more distant past.

"She did, indeed," I said. "She and Morgan were

a few years behind me in school. They were both cheerleaders at Dixie High School and went on to be roommates at Ole Miss."

"You mean Morgan actually has a friend? One who pees sitting down?"

"Hard to imagine, but it seems so."

"So will Miss Grable be staying at the big house with Morgan and her parents?"

"No. She's staying at the hotel."

"If they're such old, dear friends, why isn't Morgan picking her up at the airport or having her as a guest at her own home?"

"I don't know," I admitted. "I didn't ask. Not that Morgan gave me the chance. But from my experience, it's probably easier to be friends with Morgan if you don't spend too much time with her. Besides, Lucinda is going to be spending the night out at the retreat center with Morgan and the rest of the PWAD members on Friday. And her camera crew is also staying at the hotel. Maybe it's just more convenient."

"Her camera crew, huh? So are the women of PWAD going to be featured on TV with the ghost whisperer?"

"I don't think so, or at least not according to Morgan. She said they're filming footage of Lucinda in her hometown and such, and they might include a scene from that little family cemetery behind the retreat center."

"Do Lucinda's folks still live around here?"

"Actually, her parents died in a car accident when she was quite young. Her grandmother raised her, but her granny passed away a few years back."

"Maybe she developed a morbid fascination with

ghosts because her mom and dad died when she was a kid," Di offered.

"Could be," I said, wondering just what would entice someone into stalking cemeteries for a living.

"I wonder if she collects men the way Morgan does," Di said.

"I'm not sure even Morgan gets around with as many men as local gossip would have us believe. How could she possibly have the time?"

"It doesn't necessarily take that much time—depending on the man, of course," she said.

"Speaking of men . . ."

"Don't ask me about Sheriff Davidson," Di said. "I've put the lawman on probation."

Di left for her weekly yoga class. I had quickly dropped the conversation about Dave. From her tone I knew better than to pursue it any further.

Sheriff Eulyse "Dave" Davidson and Di are two people who obviously have feelings for each other, but just can't seem to get on the dance floor at the same time. Dave's a widower who lost his wife to cancer a few years ago. Di suffered through an ugly divorce from a man who had left her in dire straits financially, as well as emotionally.

I made myself a turkey wrap for dinner and tossed a load of laundry into the washing machine. During the wash cycle, I logged onto the computer to see what I could dig up about Lucinda Grable and what she's been up to since she moved away from Dixie and became famous. Since I would be stuck in a car with her all the way from the Memphis airport to Dixie, I thought it might be easier to make conversation with the woman if I had a bit of background information.

After graduating from Ole Miss, Lucinda had started her own business as an event planner. A ghost tour of Oxford she had organized and led for a group of tourists was such a hit that ghost tours soon became the cornerstone of her business. Apparently, traipsing through cemeteries "awakened" some latent psychic abilities.

She drummed up funding to shoot a documentary of her ghost tour. The short film traded on the atmosphere of Oxford's ancient cedars, the provenance of William Faulkner's purportedly haunted home, Rowan Oak, and a fog machine to ratchet up the spooky factor. The documentary was so well received that it had garnered an offer for her own show on cable, which is wildly successful.

After moving my freshly washed clothes over to the dryer, I checked out the celebrity gossip sites to see if anyone was airing Lucinda's dirty laundry. It seemed she had developed a reputation for being quite the diva with her staff, changing personal assistants almost as often as most people change socks.

If rumors were to be believed, Lucinda had been through a series of romances involving a jazz musician, a movie producer, and a talk show host, none of which lasted very long. There was also talk that she and her hunky personal trainer were up to more than Pilates lessons during their private sessions.

My cell phone buzzed, and I answered the call.

"I just finished supper at the diner with a couple of women from my yoga class," Di said. "I'm buying a pie to take home. Since you mentioned Larry Joe wouldn't be home til late, I thought I might stop by on my way. If you have any interest in pie, that is."

"You're always welcome to come over with or without pie," I said. "But I certainly wouldn't turn up my nose at a slice."

I put on a pot of coffee, unlocked the kitchen door, and reached in my purse to press the button on the garage opener. I saw the headlights flash across the windows as Di pulled into the driveway. I was retrieving plates from the cupboard when she slipped in through the door from the garage.

Di unboxed the pie, and I grabbed a pie server from the drawer.

"*Mmm*, peach pie," I said. "Do you want me to warm up your slice in the microwave, too?"

"Yeah, that sounds good."

We filled our coffee cups and sat down at the kitchen table. The peachy, cinnamon scent of the warm pie was intoxicating. I savored the aroma and flavor as the first bite melted in my mouth.

"Do you want a scoop of vanilla ice cream on top of your pie?" I asked.

"Naw. I don't think you could improve on this," she said.

Di told me about yoga class, and I filled her in on what I'd discovered online about Lucinda.

After a beat, Di blurted out, "Liv, do you believe the theory that there's someone for everyone?"

"I don't know, I suppose so. Why?"

"I've been thinking about Ted."

"Really?" I said, my voice involuntarily rising half an octave.

"Not for me, you idiot," she said, giving me the evil eye times two.

"Okay," I said, throwing my hands up into a "don't shoot" posture. "I get it." Then, in a cringe-worthy homage to Bob Marley, I began singing, "Di likes the sheriff, but she does not date the deputy."

"Sometimes I have to strain to remember why I'm even friends with you," she said, trying hard not to smile. "It's just, I've been thinking how Ted is such a nice guy, but he has absolutely no clue when it comes to women. He's bound to get lonely. I'm convinced that's why he joined my class—he certainly has no affinity for yoga. But none of those women will give him the time of day."

"I agree," I said. "It's too bad Ted can't find a girl-friend. His job can be pretty stressful. It'd be nice if he at least had someone to hold his hand and listen to him after a rough day. Of course, in a town as small as Dixie there's a limited pool of prospects."

"Hmm, I wonder. . . ." Di mumbled, staring into space.

"You have someone in mind, don't you?" I said, dying to know who she thought might be a good match for our lovelorn deputy.

"Maybe," she said. "There's a woman who recently moved to town. She's renting the Woodleys' house over on Willow Street."

"They went to live with their daughter somewhere in Kentucky, didn't they?"

"Yeah, but they didn't want to sell the house in case it didn't work out, so they put it up for rent. Anyway, a couple of weeks ago, their tenant joined my yoga class."

"What makes you think she'd be a good match for Ted?"

"She seems as shy and awkward as he is. And it could be my imagination, but I think I've seen her stealing glances at Ted. Then again, he is the only straight man in the class."

"What does she look like?"

"Short, mousy. Kinda cute, in a pixie sort of way. She's at least as good looking as Ted, and she doesn't have a bad figure," Di said. "Here's the thing: Even if they're perfect for each other, they're both so shy I don't think they'll ever get together without some outside help. Would you be willing to help me work a little matchmaking magic?"

"Sure. I'm a hopeless romantic," I said. "But I'm a little surprised you'd be willing to dabble in matchmaking. It's a bit out of character for you. No offense."

"None taken. I know I'm not a hopeless romantic, as you say. But I do occasionally have a compassionate streak. Dave mentioned that Ted's seemed pretty down lately. And when a man actually notices someone else's feelings, especially another man's, I figure it must be pretty serious. Dave would never come up with the notion that a girlfriend is what Ted needs—he'd more likely just take him out for a beer. So it's pretty much up to you and me to cheer up Ted, or at least give him a shot at finding happiness with someone."

"I'm on board. What did you have in mind?"

"Well, I'll try to find out more about the new kid in town," Di said, "what she does for a living and if she has any outside interests, besides yoga.

"Since Ted eats lunch at the diner most days, I

thought you could stake out a table and ask him to join you one day this week. Just casually try to find out what kind of movies and music he likes and inquire about the yoga class to see if he mentions anyone in particular, like the new chick. Once we have some background information, we can cook up a plan to bring them together."

"Okay, I'm game."

Di took the rest of her pie and headed home. I wondered if she'd be sharing some peach pie with a certain handsome sheriff later on.

Chapter 3

After Di had gone, I glanced at the clock and noticed the time. It was only a little after seven PM, but that made it after eight Eastern time. I decided to give my sister a call before it got too late. She was well into her third trimester and tended to go to bed pretty early these days.

She answered on the third ring.

"Hey, Liv," she said, followed by a labored sigh.

"Hey, little sister. Are you okay?" I asked. "You sound a little pained."

"I was just sitting down," she said. "Everything's awkward and uncomfortable when your stomach's the size of a watermelon."

"Aw, Emma, it won't be much longer now until you're carrying that baby in your arms instead of your belly."

I asked her what my adorable three-year-old niece, Lulu, was up to these days. She's becoming quite the little diva.

"Lulu never wants to wear any of the clothes I

pick out for her," Emma said. "She's got her own fashion sense. Something best described as gaudy sparkle.

"I'd been keeping some of Lulu's out-of-season clothes in the chest of drawers that I'd moved into the nursery. I had cleared out a couple of the drawers and started putting some of the baby's clothes in there. Lulu went through those drawers and tossed all the baby clothes onto the floor. When I got onto her about it, she told me I'd have to find somewhere else for the baby's clothes because she couldn't spare the drawer space."

Emma and I both laughed, and I asked her if Lulu sounded like Mama when she said it.

"Don't even go there," Emma said. "Although I might as well accept it. She's definitely got Mama's eyes, so I shouldn't be surprised if she's got some of her meemaw's attitude, too."

"Speaking of attitude . . ." I said, and proceeded to tell Emma about Mama calling me to kill a snake for her.

"I rushed over there like a crazy woman, thinking she was dying," I said. "Of course, by the time I left I was ready to kill her."

"That's Mama all over," Emma said, laughing. "Dear one minute and deranged the next. You remember at family reunions how she always made Uncle Junior roll up his pant leg and show everybody the hole in his calf?"

"Then she'd tell everyone what a traumatic ordeal it had been for *her*," I noted with a giggle.

"Liv, you have to promise me that when I have this baby you'll make the trip up to Charlotte with

Mama. I know she can handle watching after Lulu and helping with the baby, as well as doing the cooking and the cleaning. But I need *you* to take care of the more complicated job of handling Mama—so Hobie doesn't kill her and so I can get some rest."

"That depends somewhat on when you have this baby, little sister," I said. "I can't possibly leave town until after Halloween."

"I feel pretty confident, and so does my doctor, that this baby won't make his or her debut until after Halloween."

"In that case, you couldn't keep me away," I said.

Emma sounded tired, so I encouraged her to get some rest while Lulu was asleep.

I had planned to stay up until Larry Joe made it home. About midnight, I propped myself up on a pile of pillows against the headboard and started reading Lucinda Grable's book, *Ghost Encounters*, which I had downloaded to my Kindle. I fell asleep while reading, but woke up screaming and leapt out of bed when Larry Joe kissed me on the forehead.

"Whoa, there. It's just me," he said, standing on the other side of the bed already stripped down to his plaid boxers.

"I'm sorry, honey. I was reading ghost stories before I went to sleep. I guess I'm kinda jumpy."

Truth is, I never used to be jumpy in my own home. But during all the unpleasantness surrounding the murders and drug smuggling, two men had broken into our house. The intrusion had left a lingering uneasiness that was going to take some time for me to get past.

My husband got into bed and I snuggled up next to him, nuzzled my nose into one of his irresistible dimples, and traced a line through the cleft in his chin with my finger.

"Since when do you read ghost stories?"

"Since Lucinda Grable is going to be the guest speaker at our retreat this weekend. I'll tell you all about it tomorrow."

We cuddled and nuzzled and more before drifting off into a contented sleep.

When I woke up Thursday morning, Larry Joe had already left for work. I wished he would have slept in after getting to bed so late, but I can't trust him to take care of himself when it comes to business. Things have gotten even worse since his dad had a heart attack a couple of months ago. Larry Joe tries to head off any problems at the office before his dad has time to worry.

Since I had left my car parked at the office the day before and I didn't get up early enough to catch a ride with Larry Joe, I had to depend on my feet to get me to work. I poured some coffee in a travel mug, slipped on a light jacket, and headed out.

A few minutes before nine, I walked into Sweet Deal Realty. Winette was making coffee, both high-octane and decaf varieties. We chatted as I placed information packets at each seat around the conference table.

Members of the planning committee for a charity fund-raiser began arriving one or two at a time. We were there to iron out the final details of an ambitious Halloween event to raise money for Residential Rehab, which provides house repairs for the elderly and disabled in our community.

Nearly everyone in town was pitching in to make this fund-raiser a success. People's excitement about the project could be attributed to the fact that it's a worthy cause and to the hard work and enthusiasm of RR's director, Winette. At least those are the reasons I had agreed to sign on as chairperson.

On Halloween night, there would actually be a series of fund-raisers happening simultaneously. A haunted hayride and bonfire for the teens would be held at a farm just outside town, with some parents for chaperones. A local church with a large hall and gym would be hosting children's activities. Parents could drop off their kids, who would enjoy games and candy under the reliable supervision of local teachers and church workers.

With the big and little kids taken care of, parents and grandparents could participate in the main event of the night—a Clue-themed murder mystery dinner, followed by a dance at the country club.

Everything for the event would be donated, from local farmers and grocers sending the food to local chefs preparing the dinner to a local band playing at the dance. At twenty dollars a head for the dance and one hundred dollars a plate for the dinner, we hoped to raise a whole lot of money for Residential Rehab.

"Hi, Liv. Here's an updated printout from this morning," Bryn Davenport said, handing me a short stack of papers. Bryn is the director of the Dixie

Chamber of Commerce and had been kind enough to allow people to register for the fund-raiser events via the chamber Web site.

"Thanks, Bryn," I said. "I can't tell you how grateful I am to you and the chamber board for letting us use the Web site for registrations. It's definitely made my life easier."

"Just about all our chamber members are involved with the fund-raiser, including you," Bryn said. "So we're glad to help."

Winette placed boxes of doughnuts and a stack of napkins on the table before we got down to business. Dorothy, the mayor's secretary, immediately scooped up three doughnuts and piled them on a napkin in front of her.

As chairperson, I brought the meeting to order just after nine. Everyone was present except Morgan, who was reliably late.

"I have a concern," Pastor Bryce Downing said. "There's a cash bar listed here. When was that added? I mean, wine with dinner is one thing . . . but I don't think an open bar is appropriate. I think most of my congregation would be uncomfortable with that."

"Only wine will be offered during dinner. The cash bar will be set up at the dance afterward," I said, surmising that Pastor Bryce and the more conservative members of his congregation weren't likely to bust a move or pay to watch other people move their bodies in a rhythmic fashion. "So those who might be uncomfortable with the cash bar may want to opt out of the dance portion of the evening."

He grunted and looked sullen, but let it go.

Morgan swept through the front door like an ill wind, chattering away about how unbelievably busy she was while her high heels clicked loudly against the tile floor.

As soon as she sat down in a chair that one of the men had jumped up to pull out for her, she began her tirade without waiting to be recognized by the chair.

"I see on the mockup for the ad and the posters that Dixie Savings and Loan is *way* down on the list with all the other contributors for the fund-raiser. While we really should be listed above all the names as a primary sponsor, I'm not asking for that. Daddy's a very humble man, and we don't want to put the spotlight on us. But I think it's only reasonable to put the bank name at the top of the list. Can you take care of that, Liv, when you talk to the printers?"

The bank wasn't "way down" on the list. The sponsors were listed in alphabetical order.

"Morgan, it's already been printed," I said, with as much kindness as I could muster. "The committee voted at the last meeting to list the sponsors in alphabetical order. I believe you had to miss that meeting for some reason."

"Whatever," she said, waving her hand dismissively. "I should know by now that things are going to get overlooked when I'm not able to make it to a meeting." She pulled a bottle of mineral water from her large purse and took a sip. She shot a look of disapproval at a man across the table from her who had just stuffed a jelly doughnut in his mouth. He froze for a moment, like a deer in headlights.

"Liv, I think providing a fruit platter at these meetings would be a better choice than these artery-clogging pastries. Anyway, moving on," she said without pausing for comment. "Just who are you thinking about asking to judge the costume contest at the dinner?"

I explained that the judges had already been approved by the committee and had already accepted our invitation to judge the contest. The judges were Mayor Virgil Haynes; Mrs. Cooley, the high school drama teacher; and Hayley Wright, who was crowned Miss Dixie during the annual Dixie Fourth of July celebration.

"Oh, that's just ridiculous," Morgan said, scanning the faces of those seated around the table and looking at us as if we'd lost our minds. "I understand that you asked the mayor as a courtesy. But Mrs. Cooley and Hayley know nothing about fashion or style—it's obvious by the way they dress. I know I'm probably a teensy bit biased, but Daddy is by far the best-dressed man in town. I don't think any sensible person would argue that point. And Rowena Whitby, who owns Glad Bags and Fine Rags, sells the only clothing in town that could be described as fashionable."

Rowena Whitby also just happens to be Morgan's cousin.

"Morgan, we clearly can't withdraw our invitations," I said. "They've already been asked and have accepted."

"I don't know why I bother. I really don't,"

Morgan said before springing up from her chair and storming out the front door.

After a moment of stunned silence, I smiled, raised my eyebrows, and said, "So . . . is there any other business before we adjourn?"

Everyone laughed and shook their heads as they began gathering up their meeting notes.

I helped Winette clear the food debris off the table before heading up to my office.

Tossing the doughnut remains and Styrofoam coffee cups reminded me that I needed to check the catering contract for my clients' upcoming engagement party. Sometimes the host or venue handles trash removal and in other cases the caterer handles it. Even though we were using a caterer I had worked with often and one that generally handled trash removal from parties at private residences, I've learned never to take anything for granted. The person responsible for cleanup and trash removal should always be clearly spelled out— or things can start to stink pretty quickly.

Just after lunch I had a meeting scheduled with my clients to go over some details for the engagement party.

I stood to greet recently engaged Rachel and her mother, Jo Ann Dodd. At Rachel's suggestion, her parents, who were hosting the party, had requested a riverboat gambler theme. Her fiancé, Mark, works in marketing for one of the casinos in Tunica—the Las Vegas strip of the mid-South— and the theme was intended to be a surprise for

him. Since this would be the first opportunity for
the Dodds' extended family and all of Mark's kin to
get acquainted, they wanted to create a relaxed
atmosphere.

Like many couples, Rachel and Mark were planning a more traditional wedding and reception, so
the engagement party presented the perfect occasion to have some fun with a theme.

Mrs. Dodd seemed pleased with the details for a
whiskey and cigar "lounge" area at the party. I had
to play peacemaker at our previous meeting when
Mr. Dodd announced that he wanted to pass out
cigars at the party like he did when his beautiful
daughter was born. Mrs. Dodd had become quite
upset and told him that handing out cigars would
look as if he were celebrating having finally found
a man he could unload their daughter on.

I had diplomatically suggested a whiskey and
cigar lounge, where drinks and cigars distributed by
a bartender, rather than by Mr. Dodd, would work
perfectly with the riverboat gambler theme.

Jo Ann and Rachel left smiling—always the
hallmark of a successful meeting.

After seeing my clients out, I gathered up my
things to drive to the airport to pick up our
celebrity speaker for the PWAD retreat.

I allowed plenty of time to navigate heavy traffic
on Interstate 40 coming into Memphis and made it
to the Memphis International Airport well before
Lucinda Grable's flight was scheduled to arrive.
The lighted arrivals/departures board indicated
that her flight was running on time.

I had made a little sign that read GRABLE to hold

up so my VIP could find me. Spotting her was easy enough. A contingent of fans enveloped her as she stepped off the escalator, taking photos with their smartphones and waving bits of paper for her to sign.

I approached the circle of adoration and held my little homemade sign aloft to draw Lucinda's attention. She posed for a few photos, but brushed off requests for autographs.

"I'm sorry, y'all. But I can't stay for any more photos or autographs. I'm on a pretty tight schedule, and it looks like my driver has arrived."

I didn't remember ever hearing her say "y'all" on her TV show, so I assumed it was an affectation for the benefit of the locals. I introduced myself as she approached, but she just kept walking. I hurried to catch up with her.

"Where's the car?" she asked as we passed through the automatic doors into the sunlight.

"I lucked out and snagged a spot in the first lot, just across there," I said, motioning toward the parking lot directly ahead of us.

Lucinda sighed deeply and stopped dead in her tracks. When she remained motionless for a long moment, I gathered that was my cue to fetch the car and pull around to pick her up.

"Do you have any luggage I need to retrieve?" I asked, since she was holding nothing but a small designer handbag.

"My staff handles that sort of thing," she said, pausing before adding "Thank you" with a forced smile that looked as if it hurt her face.

I drove the borrowed Bentley, belonging to

Morgan's parents, around to the curb. Morgan had insisted that Lucinda would be more comfortable in the Bentley than in my SUV. When Lucinda remained statuelike, I jumped out of the car like a good little chauffeur and started around to open the door for her. A curbside porter beat me to it, opening the door to the backseat and telling Lucinda how happy he was to welcome her to Memphis. She flashed him a million-dollar smile and slid gracefully onto the seat.

The moment I pulled away from the curb, she pulled her cell phone out of her purse and started punching in numbers. She talked all the way to Dixie—but not to me.

When I delivered her to the hotel, her personal assistant was waiting for her in the lobby. I was more than happy to pass off the thankless job of tending to Lucinda to someone else.

I called Larry Joe on my cell phone and told him supper tonight would be restaurant or takeout, his pick. He said Mexican sounded good to him. I wrapped up a few things at the office before heading out to meet him for dinner.

Taco Belles serves an intriguing menu of "Southernized" Mexican fare. Around six PM, Larry Joe pulled into the restaurant parking lot right behind me. He caught up to me in the lot and gave me a quick kiss just before opening the door to the eatery.

"Table for two?" Miss Maybelle Wythe said, grabbing a couple of menus and walking toward a table near a window without waiting for an answer.

"So, how are the McKays doing today?"

"Can't complain," Larry Joe said. "How about you, Miss Maybelle?"

"I shouldn't complain, but I don't let that stop me," she said with a mischievous twinkle in her eyes.

Maybelle and Annabelle Wythe never married and, now in their seventies, own and operate Taco Belles, a local institution.

"Will you and Miss Annabelle be coming to the PWAD retreat this weekend?" I asked.

"We're planning to. I always enjoy it, and I think it's a treat for Annabelle. You know her mind's just getting worse all the time."

"Oh, I'm sorry to hear that," I said.

"The doctor says it's not Alzheimer's, still it's hard to take her places these days—she sometimes wanders off and gets confused. But the retreat should be a safe environment. Everybody knows her, and she can't get into too much trouble. Is it true that Lucinda what's-'er-name will be leading us on some kind of ghost hunt?"

"That's what I hear."

"Oh, goody," she said, before buzzing away to welcome another customer.

"Oh, goody," Larry Joe said, mimicking Miss Maybelle. "So is Lucinda Grable going to be taping your group for her TV show?"

"Lord, I hope not. If she does, I'll be the ghostly figure standing behind a tree."

"I can't believe grown folks are going to be standing out in a graveyard trying to conjure spirits," he said.

"It might be fun. Everyone enjoys a good ghost story. You're just jealous because I'll be spending the weekend with a big TV celebrity. By the way, what are you going to do with yourself while I'm at the retreat?"

"I'm going to work on the house, of course. I did promise you a working shower in the upstairs bathroom by Thanksgiving."

It was my turn to say, "Oh, goody," knowing the ongoing renovations on our fixer-upper house weren't likely to be completed by Thanksgiving—or ever.

Chapter 4

Morgan had asked me to accompany her to the retreat venue on Friday morning to make sure everything was in order before the retreat attendees arrived that evening.

There are three lodges scattered over forty wooded acres at the St. Julian's Retreat Center. It was originally founded as a church-affiliated property, but was now open for bookings for civic and professional groups as well. The main building, Eagle Lodge, was the biggest, with more private rooms. Lark Lodge, where PWAD was booked, was a bit smaller and less luxe, with mostly dormitory-style rooms. Sparrow Lodge was the smallest and by far the most rustic, with an attached bunkhouse.

We met Tammy Gray at the main lodge, who gave us the keys and the security codes—one for the lodge, one for the front gate. She and her husband, Keith, managed the retreat center and lived in a log cabin behind the main lodge.

Tammy, a sturdy woman wearing an oversized flannel shirt, drove us to our lodge in a golf cart to ensure everything was in order. Naturally, Morgan sat in the passenger seat next to Tammy. I perched on the narrow rear bench, facing backward with my legs dangling, enjoying the scenery of where we'd just been. I bounced along with my fanny spending as much time in the air as on the seat as Tammy navigated a road that was mostly dirt with a bit of gravel mixed in.

Tammy parked in front of Lark Lodge, which would be our home for the weekend. The log building, framed by large sweet gum trees ablaze with color, was picture-postcard perfect.

"It's a busy weekend," Tammy said. "In Eagle Lodge, three Pentecostal churches are holding a joint choir retreat, so you may hear some Amens and Hallelujahs wafting from that direction. I also wanted to let you know there's a group of pagans or some such called Sisters of the Full Moon staying at Sparrow Lodge. They said they plan to do some kind of outdoor ritual, and I'm not altogether clear on whether or not this ceremony involves wearing clothes. They paid cash; I didn't ask. So if you ladies go out for a walk, I'd suggest strolling toward the lake instead of in the other direction."

Morgan seemed unsettled at the thought that there might be a group of naked pagans staying at the neighboring lodge. This struck me as a bit ironic coming from a woman who's president of a group called *pee wad* that had booked a psychic ghost hunter as its guest speaker.

After we had finished our inspection at the retreat center, Morgan dropped me off on town square, idling her Corvette just long enough for me to disembark before she sped away.

After grabbing a quick lunch at the diner, I had a conference call scheduled for an upcoming event. I had recently been hired by a nearby community college to handle plans for its December graduation reception.

My conference call was a joint meeting with the director of marketing and the director of student services. I always prefer to meet in person, but they had said they couldn't work it out with their schedules—even though I would have gone to them and their offices are in the same building. My suspicion, which was pretty much confirmed by the phone call, was that there was some marking of territory going on between the two. Unfortunately, I was the one mostly getting tinkled on.

I'm accustomed, however, to dealing with husband-and-wife clients who are often at odds over party plans. I get to play mediator and try my darnedest to make everyone happy. I can usually figure out pretty quickly which one of the pair I really answer to and which one I merely need to humor. In the case of *Who's the Boss?* at the community college, I was able to ascertain that the marketing director was the one who would be authorizing my payments. This moved her directly to the top of the totem pole.

I wrapped things up at the office a little early and headed home to pack my overnight bag for the retreat before picking up our guest of honor at her hotel.

I drove the Bentley while Lucinda sat in the backseat like a head of state attending to business on her cell phone. Bits and pieces of her side of the conversations led me to believe she was conferring in turn with her agent, her boyfriend, and her personal trainer. It wasn't completely clear whether her boyfriend and personal trainer were the same person, although the celebrity gossip sites had suggested they were. She finally spoke to me after losing cell phone reception in the hinterlands of Delbert County.

"Darlin', how much farther is it? I never knew Delbert County was *so big*."

I couldn't help thinking that since she grew up in Dixie, she should have had some idea of how large and rural Delbert County was. I also couldn't help noticing how she always addressed me as "darlin'" or "hon." Presumably, this saved her the nuisance of having to remember the names of us little people.

"It won't be long now," I said, speaking to the rearview mirror with a forced smile. Her breast implants seemed to leap out at me. I wondered if the car's center mirror created an optical illusion in reverse of the "objects may be closer than they appear" way that the exterior side mirrors do. As we approached the driveway to the retreat center, I struggled to remember the gate code Tammy had given us. Fortunately it was a moot point, since the gate was open when we arrived. I drove slowly down the bumpy gravel road. As we approached the main lodge Lucinda said, "This looks nicer than I expected."

"That's not where we're staying," I said, quickly adding, "but Lark Lodge is very nice, too—a bit more intimate."

Lucinda let out a doubtful sigh.

A couple of skirt-clad women with gravity-defying hairdos waved as we drove past.

"Are those members of your women's group?"

"No. I think they're part of a choir group that's staying at the main lodge."

Lucinda sighed loudly. I had the distinct impression she felt very much out of her big-city comfort zone. And I couldn't help but wonder how Morgan had persuaded her to condescend to speak at our little retreat.

Lucinda seemed relieved when we arrived at Lark Lodge, a building with both electricity and indoor plumbing. I opened the trunk and fumbled with the luggage—my overnight bag and Lucinda's two large suitcases and cosmetics bag—while the star greeted her public.

Miss Maybelle, who was parked beside me, was helping her sister get out of their minivan. Bryn Davenport pulled in behind me. She retrieved an overnight bag from the back of her SUV and waved as she walked briskly past me.

Winette came over and took one of the suitcases and a small bag. "Us cleaning women and Sherpas have to stick together," she said with a smirk.

Everyone buzzed around Lucinda while Winette and I passed unnoticed through the great room. The main room of the log building, dominated by a massive fieldstone fireplace, had soaring beamed ceilings and clerestory windows that funneled sunlight into the space. The west side of the structure housed the kitchen and two small, private bedrooms, which shared a bathroom. The east side housed three dormitory-style bedrooms, each furnished with bunk beds. The hallway on the dorm side led to a large communal bathroom with toilets and shower stalls.

We dropped off Lucinda's luggage in one of the private rooms. Morgan, of course, would be staying in the other private room, already strewn with her belongings.

"Is there still space in your bunkroom for me?" I asked.

"Sure," Winette said, "as long as you don't mind taking an upper berth."

We walked to the dorm side of the building. I slung my overnight bag onto the top mattress to stake out my territory and looked around at the luggage and purses on the two other bunks.

"Do you know who else is bunking in here with us?"

She said Miss Maybelle and Miss Annabelle Wythe had each claimed a lower berth.

When we returned to the great room, we saw that the crowd had dispersed. Some women were still gathered around Lucinda, while others were taking their seats on love seats and club chairs scattered about in conversation groupings. Flames were crackling in the fireplace, filling the room with a mild smoky scent. The caterer brought out platters of Brie, Gouda, and cheddar, along with grapes and crackers, to tide us over until supper. I was more interested in the man at the kitchen counter who was uncorking a bottle of wine. After retrieving a glass of Merlot I sat on a love seat next to Bryn Davenport. Her bleached-blond locks stood in contrast to my own cocker spaniel blond hair, as my mother had dubbed it. Sporting a lavender cashmere sweater and precisely creased canvas slacks, Bryn looked refined even when deliberately dressed down.

"I see Lucinda's still holding court," I said, glancing over my shoulder.

"I suppose we are acting a little celebrity crazed," Bryn said, with a well-rehearsed giggle. "Morgan's not exactly one of my favorite people, but I have to give her kudos for snagging Lucinda Grable as a guest speaker. This weekend should be a lot of fun."

"Yeah, Lucinda's something else, all right," I said. The more time I spent with Lucinda, the less I liked her, but I was betting she performed better with an audience and I didn't want to dampen Bryn's enthusiasm.

"I am a bit embarrassed that Billy Tucker and his Grills on Wheels crew are doing the catering. I think Morgan could have come up with a classier menu for our special guest than stew cooked in vats and pans of corn bread. And cheese and crackers for appetizers? I mean, really," Bryn said, casting a look of disdain toward the cheese platter on the coffee table in front of us.

I eyed the piece of Brie on my cocktail napkin before taking a dainty bite.

"Since Lucinda's originally from Dixie, maybe Morgan thought she'd enjoy some down-home cooking. Anyway, I just assumed she was trying to economize on food to offset the cost of bringing in Lucinda."

"We haven't spent a dime on Lucinda, at least not from PWAD funds. I know because all checks require two signatures—mine and Morgan's—as treasurer and president."

"You mean we didn't even pay for Lucinda's airfare?" I asked.

"Not unless Morgan paid for it out of her own pocket, which I doubt very much."

I felt the weight of someone plopping down on the arm of the sofa, pushing against my arm with her hindquarters. I looked up to see Miss Annabelle Wythe's dewy blue eyes gazing down at me.

"You're Virginia Walford's girl, aren't you?"

"Yes, ma'am. I'm Liv McKay, used-to-be Walford." I knew Miss Maybelle had said her sister's memory was really starting to slip. It made me a little sad that someone who had known me all my life couldn't remember my name. But she did remember who I was, or at least who I was related to. Then again, my mama is hard to forget.

"Are they going to feed us anything besides cheese?" she said loudly.

"Yes, ma'am. We're having Brunswick stew and corn bread in just a bit."

"Good. Cheese makes me constipated," she said before wandering off.

I was beginning to hanker for something other than cheese myself. *More wine*, I thought.

"I think I'm ready for a wine refill," I said. Bryn said she was a bit thirsty, too, so we headed toward the beverage area.

As we approached the bar, Jasmine Green called to us from a nearby table that was laden with pitchers and glasses filled with ice. Morgan spoke to us as she buzzed away from Jasmine's table with a glass of something.

"If you've had your fill of wine, try one of these floral-and-fruit-infused herbal teas," Jasmine said.

I hadn't exactly had my fill of wine yet, I thought to myself. But she looked lonesome standing at the table by herself—the bartender was definitely getting more business. And I figured I should probably pace myself with the alcohol consumption.

"Sure, what do you recommend?"

"My favorite is blueberry with almond and sweet hibiscus," she said, pointing to one of the pitchers. "But this lavender sage with orange and pineapple seems to be popular, too."

"I'll try a glass of the blueberry, please," I said. Bryn said she'd take the same.

The tea smelled a bit like cough syrup, but actually tasted pretty good.

"*Mmm.* Did you make these yourself?" I asked, knowing perfectly well that she had.

"Yes. Morgan thought we should have some healthy nonalcoholic beverage choices, and these are some of my own blends."

"How nice," Bryn said, before excusing herself to mingle.

Jasmine Green, who could be described as an aging hippie, grows organic plants and sells medicinal herbs, as well as herbal teas and beauty products. She definitely stood out from most of the other women in her tie-dyed dress and hemp cardigan. Usually her most attractive accessory was her much younger boyfriend, Dylan, who was not in tow tonight. Not that she isn't attractive in her own right, with a peaches-and-cream complexion and naturally curly hair.

"So, Jasmine, what do you think of our celebrity guest?"

"I think she's awesome. I sense a blue aura around

her, which is very spiritual. I hope she's able to connect with some spiritual energies tonight. Wouldn't that be exciting?"

"That would be something," I said.

"Oh, your aura seems a little gray around the edges, Liv," Jasmine said with a look of concern. "You're a skeptic, aren't you. Don't worry, even skeptics can experience psychic energy."

"I'll try my best to keep an open mind," I said with what I hoped was a hint of sincerity.

I sipped my tea, stopping to chat a moment with those I hadn't had the chance to connect with. Billy, our caterer, came in from outside and walked into the lodge's small kitchen to retrieve a pan of corn bread from the oven.

"That Billy must work out. It takes a lot of effort to maintain a physique like that. I should know," Morgan said in a whispery voice as she grabbed my forearm. "It's a shame his wife doesn't take more pride in her own appearance. She really should join an exercise class. And maybe you could go with her," Morgan said, giving me an up-and-down glance before walking away to spread joy to others.

I tried to shrug it off, but felt my face flush red. *She makes me so mad.* Winette, who had obviously overheard the remark, stepped over and tried to impart a calming influence. But I wasn't in the mood.

"Winette, where's the broom and dustpan? There's some trash in here I'd like to sweep out."

"Now, Liv," Winette said quietly, "just leave the broom by the door and maybe Morgan will climb up on it and fly away."

She always knows how to make me smile.

As I made my way back to the seating area, Morgan clapped her hands and began to shush everyone.

"Okay, ladies, may I have your attention, please. I'd like to officially introduce our very special guest, television star and renowned psychic Lucinda Grable. Let her give you some information about tonight's proceedings."

After a few moments of effusive applause, Lucinda gestured for us to stop.

"Thank you so much for your gracious welcome. It does a heart good to be embraced so warmly by the hometown folks. I have so many fond memories of growing up in Dixie and very much wish I could visit more often."

Shifting from her gushing schoolgirl voice to a down-to-business demeanor, Lucinda continued. "After dinner we will be walking just down the hill toward the lake to the small nineteenth-century family cemetery beside the woods to see if we can detect any paranormal phenomena. There are release forms on the counter; please sign one if you'd like to witness our psychic investigation, as we will be filming the proceedings. This is not planned to be a regular episode of our show, but I think you'd agree that if we discover a presence we'd certainly want to be able to share it with the world."

Back to her gushing schoolgirl routine—maybe she really was channeling spirits, after all—"I hope y'all are looking forward to our little adventure as much as I am. Now I do hope you'll excuse me if I don't join you for dinner, but I need a little alone time to summon my psychic energies before we begin. However, I promise there will be plenty of time to ask questions tomorrow morning when I share information about the business side of producing our show. Thank you."

Lucinda disappeared into her room as the group gave her another thunderous round of applause.

"I've just been advised that dinner will be served in a few minutes," Morgan said. "So if you ladies would like to freshen up or grab a sweater, then make your way out back, we have tables set up to dine al fresco to enjoy the wonderful fall weather. And please take your beverage of choice along with you."

My beverage of choice was another glass of Merlot.

The thermometer on the back porch registered 65 degrees, and three cloth-draped tables for six were set up in a semicircle around a blazing fire pit. The mild winters and pleasant autumns almost made up for the miserable southern summers—almost.

Bryn sat down at the center table with Jasmine Green and the two Misses Wythes, Morgan predictably gravitated to the table where Lucinda's three-man production crew—*man* being the operative word—was sitting, and Winette and I joined Nell Tucker and Sindhu Patel at the third table. The light from the porch, the glow from the hurricane lanterns in the center of each table, and the fire created a pleasant ambiance.

The Grills on Wheels guys placed baskets of hot corn bread on each table and began ladling steaming Brunswick stew into each of our bowls.

"So is everyone planning to go along for the ghost hunt?" I asked.

"Oh yes," Sindhu said, her eyes flashing with excitement. "Did you see the recent episodes of *P.S. Ghost Encounters* filmed in England? Those were very good. My mother loves watching the ghost-hunting show. Amma was so excited when I told her Lucinda Grable would be speaking to our group."

"I wouldn't miss it for the world. But I'm hoping we don't come across any ghosts," Nell said before knocking on the wood table for good luck.

I looked at Winette.

"I'm going along, too. Against my better judgment, I signed one of those release forms," she said.

Nell, a hairdresser, and Sindhu, who owns and operates the local hotel along with her husband, couldn't look more different from each other. Nell is tall and fair-skinned, with hair dyed an unnatural shade of red—magenta, really. Sindhu is shortish, with an olive complexion and long black hair. Nell is a brash, gregarious woman who is devoid of tact. Sindhu is soft-spoken and never utters a harsh word.

Still, looking across the dinner table at them I couldn't help but ponder the one thing they had in common. According to local gossip, both their husbands had succumbed to Morgan Robison's seduction. I don't know for certain that it's true, especially of Sindhu's husband, Ravi. But my intuition told me it probably was true of Nell's husband, Billy—the well-built hick Morgan had been salivating over in the lodge.

Billy came by offering refills on our drinks.

"This wine sure hits the spot," Nell said after draining nearly half of her just-refilled glass.

"The teas that Jasmine made are quite tasty, too," Sindhu said.

"That Jasmine's a wonder, all right," Nell said. "Have any of y'all tried that anti-aging cream of hers?"

"No, I haven't," I said. "I know Miss Maybelle and some other folks swear by it, though."

"Me too," Nell said. "It's turned back the clock several years for me. She uses some special ingredient that's available only from Europe. Even Miss Uppity Morgan uses it. Morgan actually talked to Jasmine about trying to work out a deal to manufacture it with some big cosmetics company—with a fat cut for herself, of course. But Jasmine prefers to keep her business local and personal."

Billy joined us at the table, leaving his catering assistants to look after the diners. He sat down next to Nell and gave her a peck on the cheek.

"I hope you ladies are enjoying your supper."

We all *mmm*'d with mouths full of Brunswick stew, a feed-a-crowd dish that's popular across the South for fall cookouts at political rallies, church suppers, and football tailgate parties.

"Are you coming along on our ghost hunt to protect us from angry spirits?" Nell asked her husband, leaning over and playfully touching her head to his shoulder.

"Naw, I think I'll pass. Me and the boys will work on cleaning up while you gals have your little adventure."

"I haven't seen Naomi," I said. Naomi Mawbry is PWAD's secretary and she never misses a meeting or event. "Does anybody know where she is?"

"Oh, hon, didn't you hear?" Nell said. "Her sister passed away just this afternoon. Naomi's gone down to Mississippi, near Jackson I think, to be with her mama and help make arrangements for the funeral."

"Oh no. I'm sorry to hear that."

I suddenly felt a presence over my shoulder, which fortunately turned out to be Annabelle Wythe once again.

"What do you need, sweet lady?" I said, clasping her hand.

"I want some more stew," she said bluntly.

"Well, I'll get that for you right now, Miss Annabelle," Billy said, jumping up from the table.

"Are the Wythes staying in the same room with the two of you?" Sindhu asked, looking to Winette and me.

We nodded.

"I would be worried that she might wander during the night," she said.

"I'm a pretty light sleeper," Winette said. "Hopefully, we can keep her from straying too far."

"I think it's admirable that Miss Maybelle is taking care of her sister at home—it can't be easy," Nell remarked.

I looked around and noticed that Morgan's table was empty. I guessed that the camera crew had gone to set up at the cemetery and Morgan had gone inside to check on our star.

Chapter 5

Morgan emerged from the lodge and positioned herself just beyond the fire pit, where she was bathed in golden light. "Lucinda is going down to the cemetery, where her crew is setting up for filming. She would like us to start heading that way in about ten minutes. So everyone please finish up dinner and make any necessary pit stops," Morgan said. "Following our expedition to the cemetery, we'll gather here to toast marshmallows and make s'mores by the fire pit and chat about the experience."

We started clearing the table, but Nell said, "Just leave the dishes. The boys will take care of all that. Now I think I'd better make a stop at the little girls' room so I don't pee my pants if a ghost turns up."

We all trudged down the hill behind Morgan, like a bunch of Girl Scouts following their troop leader. Bryn and Winette, like any good, prepared scouts, were wielding flashlights. Lucinda stood with her back to us as the camera crew divided us into two groups behind the lichen-encrusted tombstones and adjusted the lighting equipment. A boom microphone with a furry covering they referred to as a "dead cat" hovered above our heads. There were two video cameras—a larger one on a tripod and a smaller one that a technician held on his shoulder, allowing him freedom to move about. One of the crew called for quiet before saying, "And we're rolling."

Lucinda turned to face the camera and began her usual spiel to introduce the show. I don't know if it was the effect of some special makeup or just her love affair with the camera, but Lucinda absolutely glowed in the spotlight.

"This is a very special occasion for me," she said. "We're filming in western Tennessee with a group of businesswomen from my hometown. What you are seeing here is a small cemetery, a long-forgotten and neglected family plot from a bygone era.

"My team's preliminary investigation of this little graveyard has already uncovered some exciting phenomena. Digital photography captured the presence of a rather large orb of light, and our EMF meters, which measure disturbances in the electromagnetic field, have detected anomalies in the graveyard area.

"But most exciting, our recordings have captured a Class A category electronic voice phenomenon. Class A EVP recordings are those that can be clearly heard without any sophisticated noise filtering equipment. Listen closely. One of our investigators is about to play back the voice that was recorded just a short time ago in this very cemetery. I should add that this will be the first time that the seekers here with me this evening will hear this. Are we ready, ladies?" she said, turning to us.

We silently nodded in unison. She cued her tech to play the recording.

There was what sounded like static, followed by a high-pitched, otherworldly voice saying, "Danger. Go back." In a few seconds, the technician played it again, static followed by a female voice clearly saying, "Danger. Go back."

For a moment I wasn't sure if I was holding my breath or if I had stopped breathing. I heard gasps and murmuring around me. The eerie spell was broken when Miss Annabelle suddenly walked up to Lucinda and said, "Was that the dead cat talking?"

Someone yelled "Cut!" and Lucinda's face withered into a scowl. She threw her hands in the air and walked over to her crew.

Miss Maybelle took Annabelle by the hand and said, "I'm sorry, maybe we'd better go back to the lodge. I think Sister is getting tired."

We were trying to encourage her to stay. Lucinda came over to the group—Mr. Hyde had disappeared and she was wearing her Dr. Jekyll face again.

"No one needs to leave," she said graciously. "We never record a whole episode in a single shot. I think we all needed to catch our breath after hearing that recording, don't y'all?"

The women started chattering about how spooked they were.

"I may not have seen a ghost, but I tell you, icy fingers ran up my spine when you played that recording," Nell said.

I noticed the tech with the camera on his

shoulder was quietly circling us just outside the pool of light, trying to capture the moment unobtrusively.

"Lucinda, was that voice one of the people buried here? Can you make a psychic connection to find out who she is, or was?" Jasmine asked.

"I'm certainly going to try," Lucinda said. "There are only two female names listed on these seven tombstones: Millie and Agatha. The voice sounded young to me, so it may have been Agatha, who was only fourteen when she died. We'll see if we can make contact with her in just a few moments," she said, gazing directly into the camera.

After her announcement about making contact, both Lucinda and the cameraman walked away from our group. Most of the group paid little notice to the camera, but Lucinda certainly never lost track of it.

During the lull, I pulled my smartphone out of my jacket pocket and shot a few photos with the camera, hoping to capture one of those orbs Lucinda had mentioned.

A member of the crew called for quiet as Lucinda returned to her host position. "And we're rolling," he said.

"The voice on the recording caused some excitement here in our group. It would seem that one of the spirits in this little cemetery has something to say. I will try to build a bridge between this world and the next by focusing my psychic energies or vibrations so that this spirit may communicate with us, if she wishes to do so."

Lucinda closed her eyes, tilted her head back slightly, and held her hands out.

"Agatha, are you here?"

After a moment, Lucinda clasped her hands together and said, "I'm sensing something hot, very hot. Perhaps a fire or a high fever. Agatha, yes, Agatha suffered a high fever. I sense she and another member of her family died of yellow fever.

"Agatha, was it you who spoke on the recording? Is it your voice speaking of danger?"

Lucinda contorted her face and tilted her head slightly. "I see a girl with long brown hair wearing a white nightshirt. Agatha, is that you?"

After a moment, Lucinda said, "Yes. I sense strongly Agatha is the young girl in my vision. Agatha, do you wish to say something to us? Are you speaking of a present danger?" She paused. "Do you need our help?"

Suddenly, a desperate voice from behind me cried out, "Yes, please help me!"

I nearly jumped out of my skin before realizing it was the voice of Miss Maybelle.

"Annabelle's gone. We have to find her," she said with a note of panic.

I wasn't thinking about it much at the time, but I'm pretty sure the cameras continued to roll, at least for a while, as our little drama unfolded.

A moment of chaos ensued before Winette took things in hand.

"Miss Maybelle, she couldn't have gone far. Bryn, you and Nell take your flashlight and search in that direction. Liv and I will search over this way." Winette motioned to indicate directions. "Someone better take Miss Maybelle back to the lodge to see if her sister is there. And some of you should stay here in case she comes back."

We made our way into the woods, and Winette was walking so fast I could barely keep up.

"Shouldn't we slow down and search this area more carefully?"

"The first thing we're going to do is hurry down to the lake and pray to God that Miss Annabelle hasn't fallen into the water," she said.

"Oh, Lord. That thought hadn't even occurred to me. I hope it hasn't occurred to Miss Maybelle, either."

"Me too," Winette said.

The small flashlight brightly lit the path for about six feet in front of us, even in the dense woods. The trees thinned into a clearing, and I could see the light of a full moon reflecting off the water at the bottom of the hill. Reflective tape ran along the side of a small wooden pier.

We walked beside the lake, Winette shining the flashlight along the edge of the inky water, looking for footprints or any evidence that would indicate someone had been here recently. Then we walked onto the pier, looking for the same.

On a sunny day, standing on the pier or floating lazily in a canoe, the lake was lovely and welcoming. But here in the darkness searching for a missing person, it took on a sinister appearance.

"It couldn't have been more than moments before Miss Maybelle realized her sister was missing," I said. "And we practically ran down to the lake. I don't believe Miss Annabelle could have made it here ahead of us."

"We'll hold that good thought," Winette said.

"There's nothing more to see here, anyhow. Let's start walking back and look more closely among the trees. She could have tripped over some brush and fallen."

Winette scanned the flashlight once more over the surface of the lake before we started up the hill.

We made our way slowly through the woods, shining the flashlight in every direction and calling out her name. We heard a chorus of cicadas and other woodland noises I couldn't identify and tried not to think about. In a few minutes, we heard the other voices calling "Miss Annabelle" moving closer to us, and we emerged from the trees about the same time as Nell and Bryn. We could see the pool of light cast over the cemetery by the television lighting equipment just a few yards away.

As we neared the graveyard I thought I saw movement along the edge of the woods. I clasped Winette's hand and guided the flashlight toward the movement. The light fell on a pale figure. It was Miss Annabelle. She looked disoriented as she stumbled out of the woods and into the clearing.

"Oh, sweet Jesus," Winette said, handing off the flashlight to me and rushing to take charge of our missing person. Miss Annabelle was visibly shaking. Winette peeled off her cardigan and wrapped it around the elderly woman's trembling shoulders.

The man with the camera on his shoulder scanned to follow her.

Winette looked over to Lucinda and said firmly, "I don't think there's anything going on here that needs to be filmed for public viewing."

"Jeff, I think that's a wrap," Lucinda said.

The crew started disassembling the lights and

cameras from their frames. Nell, Bryn, Winette, and I started walking with our lost lamb back toward the lodge.

Winette's sweater hung generously from Miss Annabelle's slight frame, the hem falling at her knees.

"Where's my sister?" Miss Annabelle said, her eyes filled with bewilderment.

"She's up at the lodge," Nell said. "We've all been looking for you. Where did you get off to?

"I don't know where I was, but I met these Sisters of the something-or-other holding a service by the fire. I thought it was odd they were *nekkid*, but since they were nuns I figured it must be okay," she said. "Maybe their habits were in the wash."

"Miss Annabelle, I don't think they were that kind of sisters," I said.

"Where's my sister? Are we going to my house?" Miss Annabelle was obviously confused and shivering in the night air.

"We're going to the lodge to see Miss Maybelle," I said. "Remember the log building with the fire out back where we ate that good stew and corn bread for supper?"

"Could you get me some corn bread? I'm a mite hungry."

"Sugar, I'm sure we can find you some corn bread. Don't you worry," Nell said, reaching over and putting her arm around Miss Annabelle's slender shoulders.

The lodge was clearly in view, illumined by the porch light and the flames dancing in the fire pit, when the beam from the flashlight skimmed across something large lying on the ground several feet ahead of us.

As we neared the spot we suddenly realized the "something" was a "someone."

"Oh, my God," Bryn said. "It looks like someone has fallen."

I hurried ahead and scanned the flashlight over the body and onto the face of Morgan Robison. Her glassy eyes were staring up blankly, and her lips were fashioned in a contorted smile. She was obviously dead.

Chapter 6

We all stood deathly quiet for a long moment, taking it in.

"Isn't that the bank girl who can't keep her hands off other people's husbands?" Miss Annabelle said. Her memory, at least about some things, wasn't failing her.

"Miss Annabelle, you and I need to go on in the lodge and find your sister. She's worried about you," Winette said. She began walking to the lodge, leading Miss Annabelle by the hand. "And somebody better call the sheriff," Winette called out, glancing back over her shoulder.

I pulled the phone from my pocket. "Oh, I forgot, I can't get cell reception out here."

"I'll go call from the landline in the lodge," Bryn said.

"I'll stay here with the, er . . . with Morgan," I said.

"I'll stay with Liv," Nell said, much to my relief.

Even though we were close to the lodge, I didn't

relish the idea of holding vigil over a dead body by myself.

"Why does she have that awful look on her face?" Nell asked after the others were gone. "Do you think she was trying to say something or call out for help?"

"I don't know. If she had screamed, surely one of the guys would have heard her, since they were outside clearing up after dinner."

After what seemed like forever, but was actually only about ten minutes, Sheriff Davidson and Deputy Ted Horton arrived. As sheriff of Delbert County, Dave is responsible for all the unincorporated areas of the county, along with contract coverage of the municipalities, like Dixie, that are too small to have their own police department. The county is sparsely populated, but it's a lot of ground to cover for Dave and his small band of deputies.

Dave came around the side of the building. I waved the flashlight in his direction. I could see through the lodge windows that Ted was in the great room, apparently giving instructions.

"Nell. Liv," Dave said, nodding to each of us. "Has anyone touched the body?"

"I don't think so," I said. "Nell and I discovered the body, along with Winette, Bryn, and Miss Annabelle. None of us touched Morgan. She looked so obviously dead—with her eyes and mouth fixed like that."

"When was this?"

"Bryn went to the lodge to call you just moments after we found her," Nell said. "It couldn't have been more than five minutes before you got the call. And it's been, what?" she said, looking to me, "maybe ten minutes or so since then?"

I nodded.

"Dave, you got here awful quick," I said. "You didn't drive all the way from Dixie, did you?"

"No, Ted and I were answering a domestic disturbance call over on Franken Road. Neighbor called and said somebody was screaming bloody murder. Turned out to be the neighbor's goat making all the racket."

One of the Grills on Wheels guys came out of the lodge and started walking toward us.

"Here's one of our reserve deputies," Dave said, nodding toward the young man.

"Deputy Horton said you wanted to see me, Sheriff."

"Yeah, Eric. I want you to stay with the body until the medical investigator arrives. Make sure no animals, or people, interfere with the scene."

"Yes, sir."

"Ladies, why don't you come back to the lodge with me so we can start taking statements."

"Sheriff, I guess it drives you nuts when you have to drive halfway across the county for a noisy goat," Nell said.

"I'd rather have a call turn out to be nothing than turn out to be a dead body any day," he said.

The sheriff, with his long strides, reached the lodge before us.

"Nell, I didn't know Eric was a reserve deputy. Did you?"

"Yeah, Billy had mentioned it. But I think he's only been on the force a few months."

Dave was holding the screen door open for us.

The mood in the lodge was decidedly somber. It was also unusually quiet.

"Okay, folks," the sheriff said, addressing the group. "We need to take individual statements, and we'll try to move things along as quickly as possible. Like Deputy Horton has explained, we need y'all to refrain from talking amongst yourselves until we have statements from everyone. When someone starts talking about what they saw or what they heard, it's easy for others to get mixed up about exactly what *they* saw or heard. We need to get the facts straight."

"Sheriff," Nell said, "do you think somebody killed Morgan?"

"We don't know what happened here, and until we find out, we have to be open to all the possibilities. Now I'm going to start with statements from the caterers and the camera crew, since I understand they're not spending the night on the premises. We'll set up a couple of chairs in the hallway back here and call you back one at a time. Thank you for your patience."

After Ted and Dave moved a couple of chairs to the hallway, Ted showed Dave a list of everyone who had signed up for the retreat, plus the names of Lucinda's crew and the catering staff. "Okay, Billy, let's start with you."

Billy Tucker and Dave left the room and closed the door.

Ted suggested that since we weren't supposed to talk, maybe we'd like to turn on the television that was sitting on a stand in the corner.

"It's not hooked up to cable or anything. The

only thing you can do is play DVDs on it," Nell pointed out.

Ted walked over to the cart and pulled some boxes off the shelf next to the DVD player.

"Let's see what we've got here," he said, shuffling the boxes in his hands. "Looks like *Groundhog Day, Hot Buns Aerobic Workout,* and *Texas Chainsaw Massacre.*"

There was unanimous agreement on *Groundhog Day.*

We watched the movie in silence, except for an occasional question or comment from Miss Annabelle and an intermittent eruption of giggles from the rest of us.

Every few minutes, someone would exit the back hallway and Ted would send in the next person on the list.

After talking with the first member of Lucinda's camera crew, Dave emerged from the hall and walked over to Lucinda, who was sitting alone on one of the love seats with a bored look on her face.

"Ms. Grable, as we're investigating a suspicious death, we're going to need to look through all the footage your team shot tonight. Your guy here says he'd need your permission to hand it over."

"Of course, Sheriff, we're more than happy to co-operate with the authorities any way we can. Jerry, give the sheriff whatever he needs," she said.

"Thank you, Ms. Grable," Dave said, before saying something privately to Ted and then returning to the hallway with the next person on the list.

"Folks, I need to go out to the van to collect the video evidence. I'm going to leave you on your honor not to talk about the case," Ted said.

I'm not sure if Ted was that naïve or just overly optimistic, but whispered conversations began as soon as the front door closed behind him.

"Miss Maybelle was an emotional mess, practically hysterical, by the time we brought her sister into the lodge. I think she would have needed medical help if Miss Annabelle hadn't turned up when she did," Winette said in a hushed voice.

"She had us all worried. I'm glad, at least, Miss Annabelle's story had a happy ending tonight," I said.

Sindhu leaned across from her club chair and touched Winette on the arm. "Do you think we stirred up some wrathful ghost that brought harm to Morgan?"

"I don't want to speak ill of the dead, but I think Morgan did a pretty good job of stirring up wrath among the living," Nell interjected, in a voice louder than a whisper. "Karma, or whatever you call it, eventually bites you in the butt."

"I don't believe in ghosts," Winette said, responding to Sindhu. "But I do believe in spirits, both good and evil."

"Which do you think we're dealing with?" Sindhu said.

"Well, since a woman is dead, I'm going with evil," Winette said, eliciting silence from the group.

Dave walked into the room, along with another member of the camera crew.

"Can I go next?" Lucinda asked. "I'd like to catch a ride back to the hotel with my crew. I really don't want to stay here tonight, under the circumstances."

"I suppose that would be okay, just don't leave town," Dave said.

"Anybody else thinking about going home instead of staying the night here? I should mention that one of my deputies will be here until morning if that influences your decision."

"I think I'd feel safe here with the deputy nearby," Sindhu said. "Besides, I don't want to drive on these back roads in the darkness."

I didn't say so, but I tended to agree with Sindhu. The thought of driving the Bentley, an expensive car that didn't belong to me, on dark, winding roads was unsettling.

"I think we're safe as long as long as no one wanders off on their own and we stay inside," Bryn added.

This seemed to be the general consensus.

"Fine, then. If you'd come on back, Ms. Grable," Dave said.

Headlights flashed across the front windows. A moment later, Deputy Ted walked through the great room and out the back door, followed by an older man I presumed to be the medical examiner.

Ted returned, knocked, and then opened the door to the hallway and said something to Dave. In a minute, the sheriff emerged and followed Ted out the back door.

Winette leaned toward me. "Oh, Liv, in all the confusion I didn't get a chance to tell you. After we came back to the lodge with Miss Annabelle, one of those Sisters of the Full Moon showed up. She said she just wanted to make sure the elderly lady was all right. They didn't mind Miss Annabelle joining in their ceremony, but after a bit they realized she seemed confused and something wasn't quite right. The woman—her name was Astrid—said she walked a few steps outside the fire circle to grab her robe so she could escort Miss Annabelle back to wherever she was staying. But when she turned back around, Miss Annabelle had disappeared into the woods. Astrid said she drove a golf cart Tammy had left for their use up to the main lodge looking for Miss Annabelle. They told her she must be part of our group, so she came over here. This Astrid seemed like a reasonable, normal person to me, but then she was wearing clothes when I talked to her."

"Did Miss Annabelle remember her?" I asked.

"She didn't see her. Miss Maybelle had taken her sister back to the restroom to wash up. I just thanked Astrid for her concern and told her we were in the middle of dealing with a situation here."

"You'll need to tell Dave about her," I said.

Winette nodded.

The sheriff and deputy entered through the back porch, and Ted went into the hallway. Dave glanced at the list, then said, "Liv McKay, come with me, please."

I started toward the hallway, but Dave nudged my shoulder, pointing me toward the back door, and we stepped onto the screened-in back porch. We sat down in two of the four rocking chairs. I pulled a plaid blanket off a bench and wrapped it around my shoulders.

"Hope it's not too chilly out here," Dave said. "Ted's in Lucinda's room with her, looking over the contents of her suitcase before she leaves, so you and I wouldn't have privacy in the hallway. Since she was in such an all-fired hurry to go, I wanted to make sure she's not hauling away evidence. She agreed to the search voluntarily, of course."

"Actually, it feels good to get some fresh air," I said. "Ted might be awhile going through her stuff. She had two huge suitcases and a cosmetics bag. I know because Winette and I carried them in for her."

"So who do you think might have had reason to kill Morgan?" he asked, as if I keep tabs on everybody in town.

"Are you sure it was murder and not some kind of seizure? She did have that weird look on her face."

"The investigator from the M.E.'s office thinks it's foul play. We'll know more after the autopsy."

"Dave, I honestly have no idea who killed Morgan."

"I'm not asking you who killed her. I'm asking you who you think might have had a motive to kill her."

"Well, she certainly had a reputation for running around with married men. If it's true, I'm sure some of their wives held it against her. And I don't think she was generally monogamous with any of her beaus, so I would think some of the men she was involved with wouldn't like that much, either."

"Any wives or husbands in particular?" Dave asked.

"I don't know anything for a certainty, just gossip."

"I understand that. But I'm not grafted onto the grapevine the way you are. Now dish me some dirt so I can start digging."

"Oh, okay. There's gossip about Billy Tucker and Morgan—and I tend to believe it. They seemed to be carefully avoiding eye contact during supper tonight. And Nell is definitely a wife who would care about that sort of thing."

"Anybody else?"

"There's plenty of gossip about Morgan and Pierce Davenport."

"Bryn Davenport's husband?"

"Yes. I think it might be true because it's a persistent rumor going back at least a couple of years—not just your flavor-of-the-week gossip. And Pierce has an ego as big as all outdoors, so I have no difficulty seeing him as easy prey to her attentions."

"Well, that's two of the women from our cast of suspects. Give me a rundown on the others."

"I have heard a remark or two about Sindhu's husband, Ravi. But I'm not sure I buy it. He seems like a sensible man, and completely devoted to his wife and daughter."

"But he does have quite a few beds at his disposal," Dave interjected.

"He'd be taking a big chance having a tryst at the hotel with his wife on the premises. Not to mention, one of the employees would be bound to notice."

"Okay, go on."

"I haven't heard any rumors about Jasmine's boyfriend, Dylan, but that doesn't mean there aren't any.

"I don't know anything about the men in Lucinda's life, but presumably that would be a long-distance commute for Morgan. The Wythe sisters don't have husbands, and neither does Winette for that matter."

"That just leaves you," Dave said, his gaze focused on me like a laser beam.

"If anyone thinks Larry Joe was fooling around

with Morgan, they haven't said so to me. And if I believed for a minute he'd been knocking knees with Morgan, you'd be arresting me for Larry Joe's murder—not hers."

"So you're definitely the kind of wife who would care about that sort of thing."

"Damn skippy," I said, my face feeling hot despite the night air.

"So the medical examiner must be thinking poison," I said, a lightbulb suddenly going on in my head. "I've read mysteries where the killer used a poison that caused some kind of death smile."

"Strychnine," Dave said. "Only problem with that theory is that Morgan didn't seem to show any other symptoms of strychnine poisoning in the time preceding her death. At least according to the witness statements I've taken so far. Did you notice Morgan displaying any symptoms, like muscle spasms or difficulty breathing?"

"No, nothing like that."

"After the autopsy and toxicology results, we should know if it was poison, and what kind, how it was ingested, and about how long before her death the poison was administered. Until then, we've gathered food and drink samples. Unfortunately, the caterers had already washed up all the glasses from cocktail hour by the time we arrived, and all but three of the bowls from dinner. We'll also go over all the video footage from the cemetery. Do you know if anyone was alone with Morgan during the evening?"

"Well, during cocktails I think she was in the great room most of the time—not that I was monitoring her. She did go into that little hallway at least once that I noticed, so I guess she could have been alone with Lucinda. And Morgan went outside to check on dinner. I don't know if she was alone with Billy then or not."

"What about after Miss Annabelle went missing? That kind of chaos could have provided cover for someone who was up to no good, including murder."

"You can't seriously think Miss Annabelle was involved."

"No, but someone could have lured her into the woods and left her there, knowing the rest of you would start a search for her. Tell me what you remember about who went where after you realized Miss Annabelle was gone," Dave said.

"Let me see. Winette and I went down to the lake. Nell and Bryn went into the woods in the opposite direction. I remember Sindhu was trying to comfort Miss Maybelle, so I assumed she walked back with her to the lodge. We got back to the cemetery about the same time as Nell and Bryn, and Miss Annabelle stumbled out of the woods just after that. Lucinda and her crew were still there, but Jasmine and Morgan were gone. I don't know if they walked back toward the lodge together or not," I said.

Dave looked at the list of names registered for the retreat and asked, "What about Naomi Mawbry? You haven't mentioned her, and I don't remember seeing her in the lodge."

"She didn't make it tonight," I said. "Her sister passed away this afternoon."

Dave scribbled something on his notepad.

"Okay, so Jasmine may have been the last one to see Morgan alive," Dave said, pursing his lips and squinting his eyes as if he were mulling something over.

"And she certainly would have knowledge of plants—and poisons," I suggested.

Dave asked me to keep any mention of poison under wraps for the time being. We went back inside the lodge. Miss Annabelle lay back on the sofa, snoring, and Miss Maybelle was asleep with her head on her sister's shoulder. An antlered deer head trophy looked down on them from its lofty position on the log wall.

Dave suggested we put the elderly sisters to bed and then asked Winette to join him on the porch.

Nell helped me get them to bed. I was keeping my fingers crossed that Miss Annabelle would sleep through the night—judging from the near-constant snoring, I'd say she did. On the other hand, after changing into my pajamas I don't think I slept more than fifteen minutes at a stretch all night. Every time I started to doze, the unsettling image of Morgan's twisted face popped into my head.

A few minutes after five AM, I decided to go ahead and get up. My bunkmates were still asleep when I grabbed my overnight bag and slipped out, quietly closing the door behind me. After brushing my teeth and getting dressed, I headed to the kitchen, where I found Jasmine making coffee. Deputy Ted was sitting on a barstool at the counter.

"Mornin'," Ted said.

"I guess it is morning, although I didn't sleep much," I said.

"Me either," Jasmine said. "I usually sleep like a rock."

The gurgling of the coffeemaker was music to my ears.

"Fortunately, we had an unopened bag of coffee, since the sheriff took all the opened containers of food and drink as evidence," Jasmine said.

"Morgan said . . ." I paused for a moment, thinking about the deceased. "Well, someone from the doughnut shop is supposed to deliver breakfast this morning."

Jasmine poured coffee into three Styrofoam cups, and we each doctored our brews with packets of sugar and creamer from a basket on the counter.

We took our cups and walked to the seating area by the fireplace, which still had a couple of dying embers flickering among the ash.

"Ted, have you been up all night?" I asked.

"No, I caught a few winks. Eric and I slept in shifts."

I was on my third cup of coffee when Winette and Sindhu emerged from the sleeping area, followed by Nell, Bryn, and Miss Maybelle. Jasmine put on a fresh pot of coffee.

"Looks like everyone else is up," Miss Maybelle said. "I'm going to let Sister sleep in. She probably needs it after all the excitement last night."

Our group perked up a bit when Renee from Dixie Donuts and More delivered doughnuts at six-fifteen.

"*Mmm*, these are good and fresh," Nell said. "I think the iced chocolate ones are my favorite."

Miss Annabelle tottered in, wild haired, still in

her flannel pajamas. "Why are you eating without me? I'm hungry, too," she said with a pouty look.

"I was just letting you sleep in, Sister," Miss Maybelle said.

"What kind of doughnuts would you like, Miss Annabelle, glazed or jelly filled?" I asked.

"Both."

"All right, then," I said, putting two doughnuts and a napkin on a plate for her.

"Pace yourself, Sister. I'll get you some coffee," Miss Maybelle said.

After she had gobbled down most of one doughnut, Miss Annabelle brought the quiet conversations around her to a halt when she blurted out, "I had one of those crazy dreams last night, you know, where you're naked in public. Only I had all my clothes on and these nuns were naked and dancing around a campfire."

We all shared a knowing smile.

"Well, you're just fine now," Nell said, reaching over and squeezing Miss Annabelle's arm. "I think we all had some crazy dreams last night."

Sheriff Davidson tapped on the lodge door about ten minutes to seven. Deputy Ted walked over to let him in. After conferring quietly for a moment, Dave joined the group around the fireplace.

"Mornin', ladies. I hope y'all were able to get some sleep last night."

"Dave, do you know yet if Morgan was murdered or died of natural causes?" Sindhu asked.

"We won't have any answers until after the autopsy. Until then, we have to treat this as a suspicious death. Some reserve deputies will be here soon to help Eric and Ted do a daylight search of the grounds."

"Do you need anything else from us, or are we free to leave?" Nell said.

"I need to get statements from Miss Maybelle and Miss Annabelle, since I didn't talk to them last night. The rest of you are free to go—just don't take any out-of-town trips without checking in with me first.

"Ted, I'd like you to go over to the small lodge and talk to the ladies that Miss Annabelle ran into last night. The church group up at the main lodge is scheduled to be here through tomorrow, so I'll interview them after I finish up here. You can join me when you've finished up at Sparrow Lodge," Dave said. "Miss Maybelle, I'd like to talk to you first, then we can talk to your sister together, if that's all right?"

Dave and Miss Maybelle stepped into the hallway and I sat down next to Miss Annabelle.

"Could I have another doughnut?" she asked.

"You've already had two. Are you sure you want another one?"

She nodded emphatically. "Where did Sister go?"

"She's talking to Dave. She'll be back by the time you finish eating this," I said, handing her a smaller cake doughnut. I didn't think she needed all the sugar, but I figured I'd chance it to keep her content until Miss Maybelle returned.

The woman with elegant manners I remembered from my childhood tucked into her breakfast with childlike abandon, leaving her chin dotted with crumbs. I gave it a quick swipe with a napkin, eliciting a smile from her.

Dave and Miss Maybelle emerged from the hallway. I left them to join Winette in the bunk-room and pack my things. I wondered how much of the previous night's events Miss Annabelle would remember, secretly wishing I could forget most of it.

I found Winette wiping down the counter and sinks in the bathroom.

"What are you doing?"

"The sheriff said it would be okay for us to clean up."

"I doubt Tammy and Keith are concerned about a bit of dirt in the lodge, what with a dead body and deputies combing the grounds," I said.

"I told Morgan I would, and I intend to keep my word," Winette said resolutely.

I filled the bucket from the broom closet and started mopping.

"I think the caterers left the kitchen in good shape. I'll just go wash the coffeemaker," she said.

The other women packed up and said their good-byes. Lucinda had been scheduled to talk to the group this morning, but she had taken off with her crew last night after the sheriff finished inter-viewing her. Although PWAD had booked the lodge through Sunday afternoon, none of us felt much enthusiasm for hanging around after what hap-pened to Morgan. After tidying up to Winette's exacting standards, we loaded the trash bags into the trunk of the Bentley. I told Winette I'd drop them in the Dumpster beside the main lodge.

She started toward her car, then stopped and turned to me. "Liv McKay, you go home. Keep your nose out of this business and leave it to the sheriff."

I started to say something, but she waggled her index finger at me and added, "I mean it."

She needn't have worried. I wasn't ready to fully accept that Morgan's death was murder, and I was too tired to think about it at the moment.

Besides, the one time I did get involved in investigating a murder was under different circumstances. FBI suspicions had fallen on both Larry Joe and my father-in-law. I had to do something before someone near and dear to me ended up getting arrested or possibly even killed. I wasn't pleased by Morgan's death, but she was neither near nor dear to me.

Chapter 7

When I arrived home, I could hear Larry Joe banging on some pipes upstairs.

"Honey," I called out from the top of the stairs.

He peeked his disheveled head out of the bathroom door.

"I thought you weren't coming home until tomorrow. What happened? Did the ghosts run you off?"

"Kind of," I said. "Morgan Robison is dead."

"Oh," Larry Joe said, followed quickly by "What?" He stood stunned for a moment, a monkey wrench dangling from his right hand.

"Several of us found her lying dead on the grounds behind the lodge. Dave said the medical investigator thinks she was probably poisoned. He won't know for sure until after the autopsy."

"That's rough," Larry Joe said. "I guess there are plenty of people who won't really miss Morgan, but still . . . Her daddy worshipped the ground she walked on."

"Yeah, I do feel sorry for her parents."

"There's still coffee. Why don't you come on down to the kitchen and tell me the whole story."

I recounted the previous night's events to Larry Joe.

"Wow. Naked moon dancers, a talking ghost, and a dead body. You've got yourself a made-for-TV movie there."

"I wish it was just a bad movie. My head is killing me. I barely slept last night. I might take some aspirin and lie down for a bit."

"Would you rather I didn't work on the plumbing?"

I knew better than to give him an excuse to put it off.

"No. I'm so tired it won't matter. I'll stretch out on the sofa in the den."

"Okay," Larry Joe said. "I've got to run to the hardware store for a couple things. Maybe you can catch a few winks while I'm gone," he said before planting a kiss on the top of my head.

Despite the headache and the copious amounts of coffee I'd consumed, I fell asleep quickly. Visions of Morgan's contorted face and glassy eyes invaded my dreams. I can honestly say she had never made an appearance in my dreams while she was alive. Our obnoxious little Morgan with the great big mouth had been a party on heels, always looking for some other woman's man to park next to. Now she was lying all by herself under a sheet at the morgue. No matter how much and how often she had annoyed me, it was still upsetting to think of her lifeless body laid out on a cold slab awaiting an autopsy.

I was awakened a little over an hour later by the noise and vibrations of what sounded like a jackhammer upstairs. I didn't want to know, so I decided to seek refuge at Di's place. I texted Di, who told me to come on over. Too lazy to walk up the stairs and too afraid to see what he was actually doing to the house, I texted Larry Joe to let him know where I was going. I wondered for a moment if I should go ahead and return the Bentley. But since the Robisons had expected it to be gone all weekend and since I didn't want to face Morgan's parents just yet, I decided it could wait. Besides, it wasn't beyond the realm of possibility that Lucinda would call up demanding a chauffeur.

I tapped on the door as I entered Di's trailer. She was seated at the dining table with her checkbook open, apparently paying some bills.

"There's nearly a full pot of coffee if you want some," she said.

I opened the cabinet above the coffeemaker and grabbed a mug that read MAIL CARRIERS DO IT FIRST CLASS.

"So," Di said, without looking up from her paperwork, "somebody killed Morgan."

"Word sure gets around quickly," I said.

Di's knowing smile made me suspect she'd heard about Morgan's death from Dave, but she didn't say so.

"I'm determined to remain hopeful that the autopsy will show she died of a seizure or an allergic reaction—anything other than murder."

"*Hmm.* Hate to undermine your hope, but of all the people I know, Morgan Robison is probably the least likely to die of natural causes. Making enemies was practically a hobby for her."

Di scooped up her paperwork and stuffed it in a manila envelope labeled BLOOD-SUCKING LEECHES.

"I'm going to make some scrambled eggs and toast. Want some?" Di said.

"Yeah, that sounds good. I had a pretty early breakfast."

Di gathered supplies from the fridge and placed bread in the toaster.

"I'm surprised you're not all over this murder investigation like fuzz on a peach," Di said. "If it was murder, it almost certainly was committed by one of the people at the retreat. That gives you a handy list of suspects."

"That's the problem," I said. "I know all the people who were there—some of them I know really well. A lot of them didn't care much for Morgan, including me. But I can't imagine any of them actually killing her. . . . I'm leaving this one completely up to Dave."

The toast popped up. I buttered the bread while Di scrambled the eggs.

I had hoped Sunday would be a quiet day of rest, but no such luck. My mother insisted Larry Joe and I join her and Earl for lunch at her house. She said she wanted to see with her own eyes that I was all right. I knew what she really wanted was to hear with her own ears every detail about the events surrounding Morgan's demise.

Mama's a good cook, so I didn't have to talk Larry Joe into going. Of course, it was painless for him. He ate a big meat-and-potatoes meal and then disappeared into the family room with Earl to watch football. Mama's "good friend" Earl makes repairs around her house, escorts her to events, and takes her grocery shopping. She cooks supper for him most evenings, but his truck is never parked in her driveway overnight. I have my suspicions that there may be more to their relationship, but Mama would certainly never admit it—and frankly, there are some things I'd rather not know.

My mother, on the other hand, felt entitled to know every detail of my life and Morgan's death. She grilled me while we were cleaning up in the kitchen. I wrapped the pot roast in aluminum foil and put it in the fridge while she loaded the dishwasher.

"It was real nice of Lucinda Grable to agree to speak to your business group," Mama said. Her dangly purple earrings were the exact color of her plus-size purple pants suit, a striking contrast to her emerald green eyes.

"Too nice. As far as I know PWAD didn't pay her a cent to come—or even pay for her airfare."

"You're thinking Morgan blackmailed her into coming?" Mama's psychic abilities spooked me even more than Lucinda's.

"Blackmail certainly wouldn't be out of character for Morgan," I said. "And I don't know Lucinda well, but the little time I've spent as her driver hasn't shown me that she's a kind and generous soul."

"I suppose Lucinda could be the one who killed Morgan," Mama said. "Lord knows celebrities do crazy stuff all the time—and even get away with it. But my money's on Nell Tucker. She's always had a temper. I once saw her fling a hot curling iron at another beautician. Fortunately it was still plugged in, so it didn't go very far. In fact, it swung back at Nell and she had to jump out of the way to keep it from smacking her. I had to bite my lip to keep from laughing out loud.

"Anyhow, if she believed Morgan was messing around with her precious Billy, I don't think she'd be long-suffering about it."

"If she believed Billy was fooling around, why wouldn't she kill him instead of the other woman?"

"Now, that's what any reasonable woman would do," Mama said. "But Nell Tucker isn't a sensible person like you and me. Besides, she's got Billy Junior to think about, and that boy worships his daddy."

"How old is their son now?"

"I'm guessing about thirteen. And he looks more like his daddy every day," Mama said.

The men were both snoring in front of the TV, with Larry Joe stretched out on the sofa and Earl laid out in a leather recliner. I woke up Larry Joe and told him it was time to go.

On the drive home, all eight or nine minutes of it, I told Larry Joe how Mama had pegged Nell as Morgan's killer and how she thought any sensible woman would have killed her husband instead of killing his mistress.

"I don't know if I agree with your mama on either point—but don't tell her I said so," he said with the wisdom of experience. "Throwing a fit or a hot curling iron, as the case may be, is one thing. But it doesn't sound like Morgan was killed in a blind rage. Her murder was obviously planned. I'm doubtful Nell has the patience or the smarts to pull that off.

"By the way, Earl told me your mama asked him to handle disposing of the snake that afternoon after you had taken a hoe to it," Larry Joe said.

Apparently Earl found a snake in the bushes. It wasn't dead, but it also wasn't poisonous. He told Larry Joe it was a black rat snake, which are good snakes, if there is such a thing. He said they help keep the rodent population in check.

"They can get to be fifteen or twenty feet long, according to Earl," Larry Joe said. "But the one in your mama's yard was bigger than he's usually seen."

"What did Earl do with it?"

"He tossed it in a box in the back of his truck and let it loose out in the country. But he let your mama go on thinking it was dead."

"Earl's a smart man," I said.

Late Sunday evening, the Robisons' housekeeper called me to ask if I would drop off the Bentley and the keys at the hotel for Lucinda's use. Our star had apparently decided to stay in town until after Morgan's funeral. So Monday morning, Larry Joe followed me to the hotel to deliver the Bentley and then dropped me back off at the house to pick up my car a little before eight AM. Though I usually don't go to the office until nine, focusing on work would be a relief. I patently refused to let my mind dwell on Morgan's death. It was less than two weeks until the Halloween fund-raiser for Residential

Rehab, plus I had an engagement party to put on in just five days.

I hit the phones, or tried to. I kept getting interrupted every few minutes.

Lucinda's assistant, Mitzi, called me just after nine. I foolishly imagined she might be calling to thank me for delivering the car. Not even close.

It seemed some local ladies were "stalking" Lucinda and she wanted me to "take care of it."

"They're probably just starstruck fans," I said. "Surely Lucinda is used to getting this kind of attention."

"Miss Grable already graciously talked with these women and gave them free autographed photos. They still won't go away. They hang around in the lobby. They even followed her yesterday when she went out with the camera crew to shoot some footage around town, distracting her and getting in the way of some of the shots. Would you please talk to them? You really are Miss Grable's only contact in town besides the Robisons, and I'm sure you understand that she doesn't want to disturb Morgan's parents."

"Do you know who any of these women are?" I asked.

"One of them has an accent. I think she's probably a maid at the hotel. One looks like an aging hippie, and the other one is tall with . . . unusual hair."

"I'll see what I can do."

I had a pretty good idea who the stalkers were.

I decided "the maid" who wasn't really a maid was

probably the most sensible one of the threesome, so I rang Sindhu on her cell phone.

She answered in a whisper. "Yes, Liv, what do you need of me?"

"Why are you whispering?"

"I'm keeping my eye on a situation," she said.

"Would that situation be named Lucinda Grable?"

"Why do you ask?" she said nervously.

"Because her assistant just called and asked me to talk to the women who are, in her words, 'stalking Lucinda.'"

"Oh." She paused. "We have been trying to not be conspicuous."

"It's not working," I said.

I tried to imagine in what universe a hippie, a garish hairdresser, and a short Indian woman would be inconspicuous—certainly not in a town as small as Dixie.

"Are you three really that starstruck over Lucinda?"

"Oh, we're not watching her as fans. We're keeping an eye on her, as I told you."

"I don't understand," I said.

"We think it is too much of a coincidence that Morgan was killed just as Lucinda arrived here and stirred up some ghost," Sindhu said with all sincerity.

"Look," I said. "The sheriff will find out who killed Morgan. Since the three of you were at the retreat when Morgan died, y'all are suspects, too, you know. So you probably shouldn't be drawing attention to yourselves. The sheriff may decide to haul you in on suspicion. More important, if there's even a slim chance Lucinda really is a murderer, you, Jasmine, and Nell should try to stay off her radar. So back off, okay?"

"I will tell the others what you said." *Click.*

About ten AM, I came very close to actually getting some work done when my phone rang again. I feared it was Mitzi or the three stooges, but this time it was Winette. She wanted to know if it was a good time to come up and talk to me. I thought it might make for a nice change to talk to someone who was sane.

She came in and sat down in a chair facing my desk.

"Liv, Mayor Haynes has been getting phone calls from folks who think we should cancel, or at least postpone, the Halloween fund-raiser."

"Why on earth would we do that?" I asked in disbelief.

"Apparently some people are saying it would be in poor taste to have a city-wide party, especially one that includes a murder mystery dinner, so soon after Morgan's death. Dorothy called and asked me to get back to the mayor with my thoughts. What do you think?"

I took a moment to gather myself.

"While it is a party and we hope that people will have a good time, it's also a fund-raiser for a worthy cause. Why would we call that off? Half the people in town are involved in some way, either volunteering or donating services or goods. If we cancelled, I think all those people would be really disappointed— and RR would miss out on badly needed funds. The mayor's not up for reelection anytime soon. Why do you think he's worrying over what a few people might think?"

"I don't know if it's a few people or a lot," Winette said. "I've gotten a couple of calls myself— one from Bryn at the chamber and one from Trudy, the loan officer at the bank. That's two people who think we should at least postpone the fund-raiser. Trudy mentioned that, for one thing, they don't know yet when Morgan's funeral is going to be. They don't even know when the medical examiner will release the body. No one wants to expand Residential Rehab's work more than I do, but I also want to be sensitive to what Morgan's family is going through right now. I just don't know. . . ."

We sat silent for a moment, lost in our thoughts.

"Well," I said. "We can't realistically postpone a Halloween-themed fund-raiser until Christmas. And I don't think we can turn around in a couple of months and ask people who have already put a lot of time, effort, and donations into this fund-raiser to start over with a new theme. If we don't go ahead with it, we probably won't be able to put it on for another year, if ever."

"If that happens, I guess we could ask the local churches to take up a special collection to help fund RR," Winette said.

"Most of them already do that periodically anyway."

"I know," she said, then sighed deeply.

"Look, my opinion is that pulling together for charity is just what the town needs right now, especially after a tragic death. It'll boost morale," I said. "Besides, Morgan was a member of the planning committee, so we should soldier on in her memory. I think *that's* what you should tell the mayor."

"I agree," she said.

She got up to leave, but paused in the doorway, turned toward me, and said, "But it certainly wouldn't hurt matters if the sheriff arrested somebody for Morgan's murder sooner rather than later. Let's just pray he's able to catch a killer this week."

By the following evening, it seemed as if Winette's prayers had been answered.

Chapter 8

Tuesday, on my way to the office, I decided to stop by the hotel to see if the stalkers were behaving themselves. That was wishful thinking on my part.

Jasmine and Nell were across the street, peeping over some shrubbery and wielding binoculars.

I parked and walked over to their stakeout.

"What are you two doing?" I asked, taking a seat on the grass next to where they were kneeling.

"You know good and well what we're doing," Nell said.

Sindhu's eight-year-old daughter, Darsha, suddenly popped up from behind Jasmine.

"We're playing Harriet the Spy, Miss Liv," she said, her big, brown eyes wide with excitement.

"And who are you spying on, sweetie?"

"We're just watching all the hotel guests come and go, and taking notes," she said. "It's my job to count the number of men and women and kids. It's just for fun. But Mommy says it might help our hotel give better service if we learn more about our guests."

"I see."

Nell stood up and brushed off her pants.

"Darsha, honey, we'd better go check in with your mama now."

Little Darsha skipped across the street holding Nell's hand. Nell stopped by the columns on the portico of the hotel—no doubt trying to keep out of sight of Lucinda's entourage and Sindhu's husband. When she had made sure Darsha was safely inside the hotel lobby, she headed back across the street.

"I can't believe y'all are dragging that innocent child into your stakeout," I said. "Why isn't she in school today, anyway?"

"There's a teachers' in-service today," Jasmine said. "And besides, it's just a game for her. She doesn't know who we're really keeping an eye on."

Nell rejoined us behind the shrubbery.

"We're keeping an eye on Lucinda 'the killer' Grable, that's who. We can see into the sitting room of her suite from here," Nell said, raising a pair of binoculars to her beady eyes.

"We don't know that Lucinda had anything to do with Morgan's death," I said. "For that matter, we don't even know for sure that Morgan was murdered. The medical examiner hasn't determined the cause of death yet."

"Who are you kidding?" Nell said. "Morgan may have been sickening, but one thing she was *not* was sickly. Somebody whacked her, all right."

"I agree," Jasmine said in her usual placid tone. "You could tell from Morgan's complexion and healthy pink gums and clear eyes that she was in very good health."

"Okay, I agree Morgan's death is suspicious. Although you do hear about perfectly healthy people, even athletes sometimes, dying unexpectedly of a seizure or some unknown heart defect. At any rate, don't you think the sheriff is checking up on Lucinda and any other suspects?"

"That's just the point, Liv," Nell said. "All of us who were at the retreat are suspects."

"But you're convinced it was Lucinda who killed Morgan. Why?"

"It does make sense," Jasmine said. "If the murderer was someone here in Dixie, they could have killed Morgan anytime. They certainly could have picked a better time—sometime when they wouldn't automatically make themselves one of a handful of suspects."

"Right. Instead it happened right after Lucinda rolled into town," Nell said, arching one expertly plucked eyebrow. "We're just gathering intel. Dave's eventually gonna arrest somebody, you know. The more facts he has, the more likely it is he'll arrest the right person."

"He could arrest you two right now for stalking," I said. "I spotted you as soon as I drove up. Don't you think Lucinda or a member of her entourage is bound to see you?"

Jasmine looked at her watch.

"Nell, I have to go mind the shop for a while," she said, standing up and brushing off the knees of her jeans. "I'll check in with you later."

"All right, hon. I think I'm going to go sit in my

car for a while. Sindhu will text me if Lucinda leaves the building."

Jasmine walked toward the end of the block, while I walked across the street with Nell to the parking lot.

"Why does Jasmine have to hurry off to the nursery?" I asked, thinking how the greenhouse was usually open limited hours by October, mostly just on weekends.

"She's not going out to the greenhouse, hon. She's going to the store in town," Nell said. "Belinda lets her have some shelf space for her products in one corner of the shop. She doesn't charge Jasmine for it, says it draws more customers in. But in return Jasmine minds the store a couple of hours a week so Belinda can run errands."

Belinda Gosner runs a small stationery and gift shop. My best guess is that most of her revenue comes from wedding invitation orders, but she also sells a variety of gift items, such as scented candles, collectible Christmas ornaments, porcelain statues, and plaques displaying inspirational sayings. Jasmine's cosmetic creams are actually a good fit for the store.

Nell opened her car door and said, "I know you think we're crazy, but I have to do something. I can't just sit around waiting for someone I know to get arrested while the ghost whisperer in there gets away with murder."

I drove to the office, pondering whether the insistent stalkers were conspiring to frame Lucinda for murder or if they were nuts. I decided on the latter. Or maybe they wanted to hand the sheriff a suspect to get their own names off the list. Either way I hoped they would at least keep a prudent distance so Lucinda wouldn't have them arrested.

When I arrived at the office, I returned some phone calls and sorted through the jumble of papers on my desk before making out a deposit slip for the bank.

I had received a few client payments that I really needed to deposit if I was going to pay the bills on time.

I drove to the bank and snagged a parking space near the door. When I got in line, I was a little surprised to see Naomi Mawbry at the teller's window, since her sister had passed away Friday afternoon. She had a pin fastened to a navy blue blouse that recognized her thirty years of employment with Dixie Savings and Loan.

"Naomi, I'm so sorry for your loss," I said as I stepped up to the counter.

"Thank you. But my sister didn't actually pass away," Naomi said. "In fact, she's doing much better."

"Oh, hon, I guess I got the wrong end of a rumor," I said. "I apologize for speaking out of turn."

"That's okay, Liv. I actually did get a phone call at the bank Friday afternoon from the hospital saying that my sister had died," Naomi said. "I hurried home and packed a few things and took off to Mississippi crying my eyes out, wondering if my mama's heart would hold up to the strain of losing a child.

"I ran into the hospital and asked at the desk if

they'd taken my sister away yet, and they told me she was still in her room. I raced down the hall, thinking Mama would be holding vigil and wondering if anybody else was with her. When I got to the room, Ruth was sitting up in the bed eating her supper. I about fainted."

"How in the world could something like that happen?" I said, trying to imagine how I'd react if I received such a call about my own sister.

"I don't know," Naomi said. "Either the hospital made a huge mistake and got their patients mixed up, which they deny, or it was some kind of horrible prank call, which is even harder to believe. Ruth had undergone heart bypass surgery over a week ago, but seemed to come through it just fine. So I was shocked when I got the call. I'm just thankful she's alive and that nobody had called my mama and told her Ruth was dead. In fact, it upset Mama so bad when I told her what had happened that I stayed through yesterday just so I could take Mama to her doctor for a checkup."

"Oh, my goodness, Naomi. I just can't imagine," I said. "I'm so sorry you had to go through that."

"Thank you. Since it turned out to be a false alarm, I'm actually kind of glad I wasn't at the retreat anyway. I knew Morgan her whole life. When she was little, she'd come visit her daddy here at the bank. While he'd be meeting with somebody, she'd sit on the floor in the lobby and count out Monopoly money to her little Cabbage Patch doll," Naomi said.

She teared up before turning away from the counter to blow her nose, honking loudly into a wadded tissue. It was actually kind of nice to know that someone other than Morgan's parents was grieving for her.

I drove back to the square and parked in front of my office. I waved through the window of Sweet Deal Realty to Winette, who was on the phone, before walking across the square to the diner. I nabbed a table in the seat-yourself restaurant and faced the window so I could watch for Winette, who was joining me for lunch.

I ordered a glass of sweet tea and looked over the menu. I waved to Winette as she came through the door.

"I'll have some coffee, please," Winette told Margie, who was walking past as Winette sat down in the chair facing me.

"It's getting chilly with that wind kicking up out there," Winette said, briskly rubbing her upper arms to warm up.

We both ordered catfish chowder, one of the daily specials featured on the chalkboard by the front door.

"Well, I talked to Dorothy this morning and fortunately the mayor's gone off the idea of postponing the mystery dinner," Winette said.

"Thank goodness."

"In fact, at the town council meeting tonight they're supposed to vote on moving trick-or-treating in town from Halloween night to the thirtieth to keep trick-or-treating from interfering with the fund-raiser, or the fund-raiser from interfering with trick-or-treating, depending on how you look at it," Winette said.

"That's probably not a bad idea," I said. "I don't

know how it will sit with folks, though. Most people don't like change."

"Dorothy said a number of people had actually requested that the mayor change the date. She asked around, and most people seem to like the idea, in light of all the other stuff already going on Saturday night. Plus there is precedent. Delbert County moved the date for trick-or-treating to a different date four or five years ago when the weather service was predicting that ice storm moving in on Halloween. People had been worried about kids trying to get around on icy roads and sidewalks."

"That's right, I'd forgotten about that," I said.

Margie set our steaming bowls of catfish chowder in front of us and slid a basket of hush puppies on the table between us.

"*Mmm,*" Winette said. "This chowder really hits the spot."

"And the hush puppies are piping hot," I said.

Relieved that talk about postponing the fundraiser had died down, Winette and I went over a few details for the Halloween events.

After lunch I made a quick stop in the ladies' room before driving over to pick up my part-time assistant, Holly. She lives in an impressive Tudor home on the edge of town. As the widow of a retired general, Holly is the kind of employee most party planners can only dream about. She has experience entertaining military brass, government officials, and diplomats around the globe. Most fortunate for me, she does the work because she enjoys it. If I had to pay her based on her résumé I'd never be able to afford her. She has a quirky sixties' fashion sense and refuses to work on Elvis's birthday or the anniversary of his death. But I can live with that.

Also fortunate for me, Holly was generally up for a road trip. Today we were driving to Jackson, Tennessee, to see a man about a screaming old lady.

Actually, it was an animated Halloween prop we were checking out for the teen bonfire and hayride set for Halloween night. Homer Crego, who was hosting the event at his farm, had come up with several homemade thrills and frights to strategically place along the hayride route. But he wanted a real showstopper, and I had told him I'd see what I could come up with.

Had we been holding the event anytime other than the week of Halloween, I could have borrowed, or at least rented inexpensively, a top-notch scare-the-dickens-out-of-you animated prop. But Halloween is when people who own such devices are making use of them.

I talked to someone from the Junior Chamber of Commerce in Hartville, which holds a haunted house fund-raiser each year, about helping me locate such a prop. I had high hopes when he called to tell me he had tracked down a Jaycees chapter in Arkansas that wasn't running their haunted house this year. But we soon discovered they had already sold off all their prime scream inducers.

Then yesterday the Hartville Jaycees president called to say he had found a guy in Jackson who collected and sold used Halloween and movie props. He thought the man would give us a good deal on an animatronic screamer. I had called the collector, who then e-mailed me a few photos. Holly and I were going to look at the props in person and see if we could rent something at a good price.

The business wasn't in an area of Jackson I was familiar with, so I had punched the address into the GPS. We found it without any trouble, but as we drove into a run-down part of town with several boarded-up buildings we began to feel a little uneasy.

"Slow down, darlin'," Holly said, the rough edges of her *r*'s polished smooth by a proper Southern finishing school. "Are you sure this is the right address?"

I double-checked.

"Yeah, this is it," I said.

"Perhaps the scary appearance of the place is for the benefit of customers," Holly suggested.

"I think he lives here," I said.

"Oh."

We pulled up on our respective door handles, opened the doors a crack, and then sat motionless for a moment, waiting for the other to get out first.

Finally I said, "There's two of us and I've got some pepper spray in my purse that Di gave me."

"I think you should put the *pepuh* spray in your pocket—just in case," Holly said.

I did, and we proceeded to the front door.

The doorbell screamed when I pressed it. A man with wild eyes opened the door and said, "I've been expecting you. Come inside."

I took a deep breath and stepped across the threshold. I looked over my shoulder to see that Holly hadn't moved an inch. I reached back, grabbed her hand, and pulled her up beside me.

Cobwebs festooned the corners of the room. The

eyes of a painting over the fireplace followed us, and eyeballs floating in liquid in a jar on the mantle stared back at us. I told myself they looked fake.

Holly and I were still lingering near the door, which had creaked closed behind us without any visible assistance. The sun was shining outside, but the room was dark, dimly lit by just a few flickering gaslights.

"Please, come on in. I'm Lucien. Which one of you is Mrs. McKay?"

I glanced over to see Holly nodding her head sideways toward me. I hesitantly raised my hand.

"Would you like me to give you a demonstration?" he said.

"Of the props?" I asked in a shrill voice. "Sure, I suppose."

"Excellent," Lucien said. "Watch the door beside the fireplace."

We turned a half step in that direction. In a matter of seconds, the door flew open and a witch with glowing red eyes flew up from the closet floor with a horrifying laugh, hovered near the ceiling for a moment, and then retracted into the closet.

Her laugh was masked by the sound of our screams. I must have jumped a foot backward. By the time the witch retreated into the closet, Holly was behind me, her head buried between my shoulder blades and her arms locked around my waist.

Lucien took a step toward me and said, "Was that what you had in mind?"

Pull yourself together, I thought. *You're acting ridiculous.*

I peeled Holly off me and said, "I'd like to get a

closer look at her with some lights on. Could you show us how it works?"

"Certainly," he said.

He walked to the wall and flipped on an overhead light, along with a light in the closet.

"Come closer," he said, moving over to the closet.

I followed him, and Holly followed closely behind me.

He explained how pneumatics propelled the figure forward. "It can be activated by a motion sensor or by a controller, like this one," he said, pulling a remote control from his pocket.

I explained how the figure would be set up in front of an outbuilding along a trail for a teen hayride.

"Ah, I have just the thing," he said. "Follow me into the study."

Holly whispered, "I'm not going into another room with that man."

"Fine, stay here on your own," I said quietly, trying to keep my voice from quivering.

She came along, as I suspected and hoped she would.

He stepped inside a book-lined room while we hovered in the doorway. He turned the dimmed lights up slightly, revealing an old woman in a rocking chair with her head down, straggly gray hair obscuring her face. The rocker began to rock with an eerie creak. In a moment, she slowly lifted her head, unveiling a skeletal face and glowing eyes. Then she leapt up screaming and sprang forward three or four feet.

"I like this one better," I said. "Holly, what do you think?"

"Me too," she croaked, before clearing her throat and saying, "Yes, I like this one, as well."

He turned up the lights so we could take a better look at her.

"It's a used prop, but in excellent condition, as you can see," he said.

"I'm sure it would work nicely, Lucien," I said.

"I'll let you have it for twelve hundred dollars," he said.

That was the scariest thing I'd heard all day. I think he noticed I had stopped breathing.

"It sells for more than two thousand new," he said.

"I'm sure it does. But we just want to rent it for one night," I said, "not buy it."

"Oh, I'm sorry. I misunderstood you on the phone. I don't generally do rentals," he said.

"Does *generally* mean never?" I asked in my sweetest voice. "It is for a charity fund-raiser."

"I don't know. . . ."

"Darlin', let me tell you about our charity," Holly said, looping her arm through his and walking him over to the fireplace.

Over the next few minutes Holly employed her considerable talents of persuasion to impress upon him the worthiness of our charity and the joy and excitement this prop would bring to our young people.

After some haggling, he agreed to rent it to us for $200. It was a bit more than I wanted to spend out of our cash donations. But unlike the children's festival that was basically a break-even affair to provide childcare for those attending the dinner, the teen event was a fund-raiser. They were paying twenty-five dollars apiece for a bonfire, roasted hot dogs and s'mores, a haunted hayride, and a cheesy horror movie under the stars. Since the food, the cost of showing the movie, and the firewood were donated, I thought the frightening prop was a worthwhile investment.

I even managed to talk Lucien into letting us take the prop with us after promising to recommend his wares to the Dixie and Hartville Jaycees as a haunted house resource and assuring him that the expensive prop would remain locked up in a secure place. I was extremely happy we wouldn't have to make a return trip.

He showed us how to use the controller and how to use the prop with a motion sensor. He said Mr. Crego could phone him if he ran into any problems getting it set up.

Lucien refused, however, to help Holly and me load the heavy prop into my SUV. I had a feeling that not going out into the sunlight was part of the creepy mystique he put on for effect. At least I was pretty sure it was just a put-on.

Back in Dixie, Holly and I lugged the old lady into Holly's house. I didn't have room for it in my office and figured it would be safer at her place than in the construction zone I called home. Lucien had made me leave a $500 deposit with him, in addition to the $200 rental fee. If we ended up damaging the animatron, I'd pay him the 500 bucks. But I planned to put a stop payment on the check just in case he happened to decide the rental fee we had agreed upon wasn't enough for his mint-condition prop.

* * *

After a busy day, Larry Joe and I had just finished our homemade Taco Tuesday supper. I was putting away the leftovers while Larry Joe stacked the dishes in the dishwasher when we heard a tap at the back door. It was Di. She opened the door and stuck her head inside.

"Oh, I'm sorry," Di said. "I didn't mean to interrupt your dinner."

"We're done, just clearing up," Larry Joe said. "Come on in."

"We've got leftovers if you want me to fix you a plate," I said.

"No thanks, I've eaten already," Di said.

"What'cha know?" I said.

"I know that Dave arrested Jasmine Green for Morgan's murder today," she said.

"What? Really? Did Dave say why?" I said.

"I haven't talked to Dave. I heard from someone else."

"A reliable source?" Larry Joe asked.

"Yep. Doug, the UPS driver. He was dropping off a package at the sheriff's office when they brought Jasmine in. I ran into him on my route."

"Well, I wouldn't have thought she had it in her," Larry Joe said. "But I'll sure be glad if Dave is able to wrap up this case quickly. If you ladies will excuse me, I'm going to chain myself to the computer and go through McKay's third-quarter financials."

"I'm sure Dave wouldn't arrest Jasmine unless he had evidence against her, but I'm still having a hard time believing Jasmine could have killed Morgan. Maybe I'm just as crazy as Nell and Sindhu," I said.

"Nell's definitely a nut, but Sindhu strikes me as

reasonably sane by Dixie standards," Di said. "What craziness do they have in common?"

"They're convinced Lucinda killed Morgan. They may even believe she used her psychic energies or ghost connections to do the deed," I said.

"That's pretty crazy, all right."

I filled Di in on the stalkers, which until her arrest included Jasmine.

"I don't want to get your hopes up," Di said, "because Dave obviously thinks Jasmine is his prime suspect. But they did run across a connection between Morgan and one of those Sisters of the Full Moon who were staying at the neighboring lodge the night Morgan got killed."

"Really? What's the deal?"

"It seems one of them had a very public altercation with Morgan a couple of weeks ago."

"What was it about?"

"Dave didn't say," Di said. "But I mentioned it to Trudy, who works at the bank. She goes home on her lunch break a lot, and sometimes I chat with her for a minute as I'm passing through her neighborhood. Anyway, she said she didn't know the details, but it sounded like maybe the bank was going to foreclose on Astrid's house or business or whatever. Morgan said something like, 'You better start packing, or you'll be out on the street by the end of the year.' And Astrid was yelling, 'You can't throw me out and you better not try it.'

"According to Trudy, Astrid got all up in Morgan's face and threatened to do her bodily harm. Her name is Astrid Caine. She lives over in Hartville and runs a little gift shop of some kind."

"Did Trudy actually witness this argument?" I asked.

"Apparently everybody who was in the bank at the time witnessed it," Di said.

"Oh, speaking of the bank," I said, "I went to the bank today to make a deposit and talked to Naomi Mawbry. She wasn't at the retreat because she got a phone call Friday afternoon telling her that her sister had passed away."

"I'm sorry to hear that," Di said.

"The thing is," I continued, "it turns out her sister isn't dead. Apparently, it was a huge mix-up or someone's sick idea of a prank call. Can you imagine?"

"That's awful," Di said.

"Anyway, back to this Astrid person, she could have lured Miss Annabelle away to create a distraction. That would have given her the perfect opportunity to kill Morgan," I said.

"Or it could be a complete coincidence that the two groups were at St. Julian's at the same time. At least, that's what Dave seems to think. He pointed out it was a full moon Friday night and that PWAD holds its retreat on the same weekend every year," Di said. "Of course, Dave also admitted that, as a cop, coincidences give him indigestion."

I offered Di a glass of wine and poured myself one, as well. Since Larry Joe was camped out in the den, we walked through to the living room and sat down on the drop-cloth-draped sofa.

Di stood and peeked through to the kitchen.

"What are you doing?" I asked.

"Making sure Larry Joe isn't within earshot," she said quietly. "This is for your ears only."

After making sure the coast was clear, she continued, "I managed to glean a bit of information today about Ted's potential soul mate."

What's her name, anyway?"

"Daisy," Di said.

"That's a good name for a wallflower, I suppose. What did you find out?"

"Either she works from home or she's independently wealthy," Di said. "I'm guessing the former, because she rarely leaves the house. That's according to her neighbor, Mrs. Roper, who doesn't exactly have to be coaxed into sharing gossip.

"Doug, the UPS guy, said she sends and/or receives small, lightweight packages two or three times a week. And he says he's never seen her wearing anything other than yoga pants. Actually he said pajamas, so I'm drawing my own conclusions."

"The boxes must be related to her work," I said. "Maybe she buys and sells on eBay or makes jewelry. Did Doug have any idea what's in the boxes?"

"No, just that they're all about the same size," Di said. "A lot of them come from Florida, but she ships them all over the country."

"Florida, huh? Do you think it could be drugs?"

"Not unless she's running the most inefficient smuggling network in the world," Di said.

"I suppose you're right."

"So . . . what's the next step in our little matchmaking enterprise?" I said.

"I guess I'll try to grab a spot next to Daisy at our yoga class tomorrow night. I'll try to make conversation and mention something nice about Ted, while I'm at it."

"Which of his stellar attributes do you plan to point out?" I asked.

"He *is* tall," Di said.

"There's always that, I guess."

After Di left, I went upstairs and washed my face. I couldn't help thinking about Jasmine's arrest. I changed into a nightshirt, switched off the overhead light, and turned on the lamp on the nightstand. I had just flopped back onto the bed pillows when Larry Joe walked in.

I've never been very good at putting on a poker face, so Larry Joe could tell I was worried about something.

"What's wrong, honey?" he said. "I thought you'd be relieved now that Dave's arrested someone. Maybe things will start to settle down a bit."

"I am relieved, sort of. I'm just having a hard time believing that Jasmine actually killed Morgan."

"Would you rather believe it was one of the other members of PWAD?"

"No," I said with a sigh. "I guess not. At any rate, I've got too much on my plate right now to keep thinking about it. I've got a big engagement party this weekend and the Halloween fund-raiser the next weekend."

"Both parties will come off without a hitch," Larry Joe said as he stripped down to his boxers. "They always do, but still you worry yourself."

He kissed me good night and turned off the lamp.

I was concerned about getting everything done in time for the party and the fund-raiser, but my uneasy feeling was really because Nell and Sindhu might ramp up their Lucinda investigation now that Jasmine had been arrested. I hoped they wouldn't do anything stupid or dangerous.

I'm not sure if it was worry or my taco supper keeping me up, but it took me quite a while to fall asleep. About three AM I was suddenly wide-awake.

What if Naomi's prank phone call was somehow related to Morgan's murder?

That thought tortured my dreams for the rest of the night.

Chapter 9

On my way to the office Wednesday morning, I stopped at the hotel to see if Nell and Sindhu had backed off their surveillance of Lucinda now that Jasmine had been arrested. I didn't even have to go inside to get my answer.

They were sitting in a car in the hotel parking lot trying, I think, to be incognito. They were both wearing sunglasses on an overcast day.

I pulled up beside them, rolled down my window, and tapped on the passenger side door. Nell was riding shotgun. She rolled down her window.

"Don't you two have businesses to run?" I said.

"I don't have any appointments until this afternoon," Nell said.

Sindhu leaned around Nell. "The desk will buzz me if I am needed."

"As I'm sure you've heard by now, Dave has arrested your compadre for Morgan's murder. So why are you still keeping Lucinda under surveillance?"

"I didn't know Jasmine very well before," Nell said. "But we've spent a good bit of time together the last few days and I know for dang sure she didn't kill Morgan."

"Be that as it may, this is crazy. You know Lucinda could have you arrested for stalking, don't you?"

"You won't think it's so crazy once we tell you all the weird stuff that's been going on," Nell said.

"Well, why don't you two jump in the backseat and fill me in. I'll pull in across the street. At least maybe Lucinda and her team won't spot you so easily."

I parked a block away in a position where they could still see the front entrance and driveway, at their insistence.

"So what's going on?" I asked, turning sideways on the seat so I could see them.

They looked at each other before Nell nodded at Sindhu.

"There have been many strange things happening at the hotel since Lucinda arrived," Sindhu said.

"Like what?"

"You know how hangers in hotel closets have two pieces, with the top affixed and the bottom part that is removable? Well, a bunch of the removable parts have gone missing," she said, looking at me as if she held the smoking gun to an obvious crime.

"That means somebody stole them," I said, trying to interject a note of sanity.

"Why the heck would anybody steal a hanger that won't hang?" Nell said incredulously.

She had a point.

"Maybe some kids stole them as a prank. Maybe some teenagers thought it would be funny. I don't know," I said. "But one thing I do know is that they did not disappear into thin air."

"Okay," Sindhu said. "There have been other upsetting occurrences. One of our maids, who has never before acted strangely, now refuses to go into one of the third-floor rooms where Lucinda and her staff are staying. She insists that an unseen force growled at her viciously. She was most definitely frightened when she talked to me."

I looked to Nell, and she was nodding in agreement.

"Pets are not allowed in the hotel, right?"

"Right," Sindhu said.

"Then someone sneaked a dog in and was trying to keep it hidden. The maid heard the dog growling, but didn't see it. I'm sure that was unsettling for her, but it doesn't mean it was anything other than a dog."

They sat silent for a moment.

"If that's all you've got . . ."

"That's all we've got *so far*," Nell said. "Bryn told me that PWAD didn't pay for Lucinda to come talk to our group, and I'm certain Lucinda is not the sort to do anything out of the kindness of her heart. I'm convinced she came to Dixie to settle an old score. And I intend to find proof of it before the sheriff ends up prosecuting Jasmine, who is innocent, or arresting someone else from the retreat—like one of us."

I gave up on trying to talk any sense into them, dropped them off at the parking lot, and drove to my office. Everyone's nerves were on edge. And chances were that Nell and Sindhu knew the rumors about their husbands' involvement with Morgan, since just about everyone else in town did.

Dealing with the lunacy that Morgan's murder had stirred up, especially with Sindhu and Nell, had really sucked the wind out of my sails. Unfortunately, downtime was not a luxury I could afford at the moment. As soon as I got to the office, I decided to call in reinforcements. I phoned Holly to ask if she'd be willing to run some errands and make follow-up phone calls for me.

"Holly, if you wouldn't mind taking on some extra hours I could really use your help this week. I feel as if I'm meeting myself coming and going, trying to get ready for the engagement party and the Halloween fund-raiser and dealing with some high-maintenance friends . . ."

"It's awlright, darlin'. Of course, I'll be glad to take a few things off your plate," she said. "I do believe you've been a glutton at the buffet of good intentions. I'll drive down to the office just as soon as my pedicure dries."

As I hung up I felt my shoulders relax. Just talking to Holly was medicine for my mania. She seemed to maintain an enthusiastic yet calm demeanor, even under the heavy thumb of deadline pressure.

Holly arrived about twenty minutes after our phone call, just as I finished up to-do lists—one for her and one for me. She was decked out in a hip-skimming, belted tunic in bright orange, with off-white, wide-legged pants. Bright orange, freshly manicured toes shone from her designer sandals to complete her 1960s-inspired look. Her platinum hairstyle usually alternates between a slightly teased pageboy and a Karl Lagerfeld ponytail. Today it was Karl, pulled back with a black ribbon.

Feeling more organized and less stressed, I drove out to the country club to go over details with the chef who was catering the engagement party at the Dodds' home this weekend. The bride and her mom had decided on a buffet with a Creole flair for the riverboat gambler–themed event. Chef Felix Boudreaux, originally from New Orleans, was obviously reveling in the assignment. It's a bit of a mystery how a chef with Felix's talent and training ended up in Dixie, but he's been a godsend for my clients and me. I've heard rumors that the wealthier members of the country club pay out of their own pockets to boost his salary to a level that makes it attractive for Felix to stay.

He had already held a menu sampling with the Dodds, who had signed off on a large buffet that included fried catfish bites with Creole tartar sauce, grilled quail legs, a fried oyster salad with spinach and arugula, and spiced apples with cinnamon.

Today he was presenting samples of spice cookies iced to resemble poker chips. They looked perfect and tasted even better. His pastry chef, Mick, made the cookies and would be making the cake, the star of the desserts table. We went over the schedule for the day of the party, and he gave me a small box of cookies for Rachel and her mom to sample.

Next up, I had a meeting with Dana Cooley, the drama teacher at the high school, about the script for the murder mystery dinner, which her students would be performing at the fund-raiser.

I signed the visitors' log in the school office and waited for one of the drama students to escort me to the theater. Although I knew the way, the escort system is a protocol to prevent strangers from wandering through the school halls, and I completely support any measures that ensure student safety.

Caitlin, a chatty, giggling sophomore, was my escort du jour. She told me how excited the students were to be doing the murder mystery play and how some of the dialogue was LOL—yes, she actually said the letters *LOL*—and how the costumes were perfect for that retro thing Mrs. Cooley wanted and how she thinks she might be an actress when she grows up, or maybe a veterinarian, she's not sure yet. Caitlin was still in the middle of a run-on sentence when we arrived at the theater. I patted her on the shoulder, thanked her, and walked over to Mrs. Cooley, who was sitting in the front row.

She invited me to take a seat and watch a run-through of a scene set in the library.

The flat panel depicting the library wasn't completely painted yet, but the finished portion of a large door flanked by book-lined shelves on either side was impressive. Mrs. Cooley told me that while the theater students painted the large portions of the sets, art students were helping to fill in the details.

Mrs. Cooley called for the scene to start. Four actors were standing in front of the library flat, gathered around a small table adorned with a stack of books and a candlestick.

"I blame you for this, Professor!" said a beefy, football jersey-clad actor.

"Me? Why?" said a diminutive Professor Plum, wearing a baggy tweed suit with a purple bowtie and holding an unlit pipe.

"If you hadn't been blathering on and on at

dinner, I might have heard what that idiot butler was trying to say."

"I beg your pardon, Colonel Mustard, but I don't believe I was speaking out of turn. As I remember, you were diligently trying to impress Miss Scarlet with your medals and bragging about your prowess under fire."

"I did nothing of the sort. If you had stopped talking for just one minute, you . . ."

"Aw, cut it out, you two." I assumed the woman speaking was Mrs. Peacock, because she was wearing a crazy-looking hat with feathers protruding from it.

"For pity's sake," she continued, "we have a dead body in the kitchen. What difference does it make who said what to who at dinner?

"That's 'whom,'" Professor Plum interrupted. "Who said what to whom."

"Grammar? You're worried about grammar? There's a murderer in this house and any one of us could be his next victim!" she shot back.

"Just cool it, will ya? If we all stick together, nobody's going to get iced," said an actress I presumed to be Miss Scarlett. She had a red boa draped over her cheerleading uniform.

"Speaking of sticking together, where are the other gentlemen and Mrs. White?" Professor Plum asked.

Right on cue a young man in a green fedora, another in a butler's getup, and a tall, slender girl wearing elbow-length white gloves entered from stage left.

"Cut. Our time's about up for today," Mrs. Cooley called out. "Those of you who have costumes still out for alterations, don't forget to go by the Home Ec class tomorrow during your free period. Sophie, you and Taylor better head on out to the bus. You don't want to be late to the game. Everyone else, tidy up your area before you leave."

The cheerleader took off her boa, and she and the husky Colonel Mustard headed for the door.

"The costumes and sets look great," I told Mrs. Cooley. "Are the students going to be able to finish painting the sets, or do you need me to call in reinforcements?"

"No. We're in good shape," she said. "Most of the students are coming for a work day on Saturday—they'll get extra credit," she said with a smile. "We should finish up most everything then. Whatever odds and ends are left we can get done next week. The only costumes we still have out for alterations are Miss Scarlett, Mrs. Peacock, and Colonel Mustard. I swear he's shot up an inch and put on ten pounds since the first fitting!"

"I suppose that's a hazard when working with teenage boys," I said. "You're doing a wonderful job, Mrs. Cooley. I can't thank you enough for all the time you've put into this."

"I know you and Winette are taking a lot of hours away from your own businesses to put this together, too. We're all happy to help."

"Thanks," I said. "Can you think of anything else you need from me?"

"I will need an electrician when we install the sets and position the spotlights at the country club. I don't want any of the kids climbing up to the rafters to move lights around."

"Of course. I'm sure the country club would prefer that for liability reasons anyway," I said, scribbling in my notebook. Speaking of insurance, it reminded me I needed to double-check on the event insurance to see if we needed any additional riders. I jotted that down in my notebook, as well.

Just east of town, I pulled up the circular drive to the Dodds' large Greek revival-style home with columned upper and lower galleries. It isn't antebellum, but it's certainly a nod to the stately southern homes of the past. It was constructed with the wealth Rachel's dad had amassed from his small chain of department stores in the tri-state area—Tennessee, Mississippi, and Arkansas.

The large public rooms provided ample space for entertaining on a grand scale, and the house would provide the perfect setting for the party this weekend. Mrs. Dodd wasn't at home, so I left the box of cookies and a note with the housekeeper.

I headed back to the office to check in with Holly, who had efficiently ticked off all the boxes on her to-do list.

Since lunch had consisted of a protein bar I had scarfed down in the car between appointments, I decided supper at the McKay home this evening was going to be a bucket of fried chicken from the drive-thru and the remains of a tossed salad in the fridge.

Larry Joe had made it home ahead of me, which was unusual.

"Hey, hon," I said as I came in from the garage, toting chicken.

"*Mmm*, I can't wait to get my hands on a breast. The chicken smells good, too!" my husband said, wiggling his eyebrows à la Groucho Marx.

"You're awful sassy—and you're home early."

"I thought I'd leave the office before I killed Dad. That old man was getting on my last nerve."

"What's your dad all worked up about?"

"Oh, he was raising hell about this and that. But what it really comes down to is that Mama and I have been pushing him to cut back his hours since his heart attack. It hurts his feelings to see the business not falling apart without him there every minute, makes him feel unneeded."

"Your dad's a proud man. He's worked hard all his life, and retirement or even semi-retirement is going to take some getting used to."

"I know, I know. That's why I came home instead of taking him over my knee like the spoiled brat he's been acting lately," Larry Joe said. "Let's not talk about the old geezer anymore. It'll give me indigestion. How was your day?"

"Crazy busy. I ate a light lunch on the run and I'm starved," I said as I placed the chicken and the salad bowl on the table, along with a couple of plates.

"They held a preliminary hearing for Jasmine Green today. I suppose you saw all the hubbub around the courthouse," Larry Joe said as he helped himself to some mashed potatoes and gravy.

"No. I didn't," I said. "I was barely in the office today. I guess that means Dave has a pretty good case against her."

"I heard, thirdhand you understand, that the lab tests identified the poison used to kill Morgan. Seems it's pretty rare, not available to the average Joe. And it doesn't naturally grow in this area; you'd have to plant it. Apparently, Jasmine grows this deadly plant in her greenhouse, and she uses it in one of those herbal face potions she sells. And the poison was in the herbal tea that Jasmine personally served to Morgan."

"Wow," I said. "That sounds like pretty damning evidence. I still find it hard to think of Jasmine as a murderer. Not that it's hard to imagine someone wanting to kill Morgan. I've entertained those thoughts more than once myself. I guess they set Jasmine's bail pretty high, huh?"

"Half a million bucks, I heard," Larry Joe said.

"That's really high, isn't it?"

"It's high enough she'll be sitting in jail until the trial if a grand jury hands down an indictment," Larry Joe said.

"Can't she pay some money to one of those bail bond companies?"

"Yeah, but I think they charge something like ten percent of the bail amount. I imagine she and Dylan would be hard-pressed to come up with fifty grand."

"That's pretty rough," I said, "especially if it turns out she's innocent."

After putting the dishes in the sink, I asked Larry Joe if he wanted to join me on the patio.

"The weather's perfect this evening," I said. "Great for a light sweater and a cup of coffee."

"I'll pass, hon. I'm going to change the oil in my truck. It's way overdue, and I need to switch from straight 30 weight to 10W-30 before cold weather sets in."

I knew working on the car was Larry Joe's coping mechanism when he was stressed about his dad or work. Too bad working on remodeling the upstairs bathroom didn't have the same soothing effect on him. He disappeared into the garage, and I phoned Di to see if she wanted to imbibe with me.

"Actually," Di said, "if you're up for something a little stronger, come on over. I just whipped up a batch of margaritas in the blender."

"I'm on my way."

As I passed through the garage I smacked Larry Joe on the butt—he still has some of the cutest buns east of the Mississippi—and told him I was going over to Di's for a bit.

Di handed me a glass as I entered her trailer. She stretched out in the recliner, and I plopped down on the sofa. After a moment of silent sipping, we both said, "*Aah.*"

"You and Larry Joe finished supper kind of early tonight."

"Yeah, he came home a little early to get away from his dad. Daddy Wayne's been on a rampage because he feels like his wife and son are trying to put him out to pasture. They've been encouraging him to cut back his hours, you know, after the heart attack."

"It's *so* selfish of them to want him to live a few years longer," Di said. "If he's driving Larry Joe nuts, he's probably really driving your mother-in-law up the wall, what with his spending more time around the house now."

"I think Miss Betty handles it better. With Larry Joe there's the father and son thing, plus that whole clash of male egos."

"Did you watch any of the action around the courthouse today? I heard the news stations from Memphis were there with cameras rolling," Di said.

"No. I wasn't in the office today. Figures I'd be running all over the county the one day there's excitement outside my window. Larry Joe said they seem to have some pretty strong evidence against Jasmine, with her growing the rare poison that killed Morgan."

"Yeah," Di said. "And she's always seemed like such a harmless little peacenik."

There was a knock on the door. Di hollered, "Come on in."

Sheriff Dave stepped inside and took off his hat.

After salutations all around, I stood up and said, "Well, I was just going. . . ."

Di said, "Sit down, you're not going anywhere—you just got here. And you actually called before dropping in." The words came out of Di's mouth and hung in the air like frost, dropping the temperature in the room by several degrees.

"I won't stay. I was just stopping by for a minute," Dave said with a hangdog expression.

"You're welcome to come in and join us," Di said, sitting up and making space for him on the sofa. "There's liquor in the blender and Cokes in the fridge. Help yourself."

Dave grabbed a Coke can and sat down on the couch, leaving a safe distance between Di and himself.

I felt like an intruder, but I didn't dare move after Di's chilly words of greeting to the sheriff.

The silence was deafening. After a pregnant pause, I finally said, "So, Dave, we were just saying how it's hard to believe Jasmine could have killed Morgan, but the evidence about the poison seems pretty substantial."

Dave glanced over at Di, who was deliberately avoiding eye contact with him by picking nonexistent lint off her pants leg. He swiveled in my direction, still seemingly dumbstruck.

I continued, "I understand Jasmine had a poisonous plant growing on her property, but couldn't someone else have used the poison?"

"That's possible, of course, but not very likely," Dave said. "It's not a common poison. It's called hemlock water-dropwort and it's not even native to the U.S. It also causes that gruesome grin like Morgan had frozen on her face."

"I always thought the so-called death smile was caused by strychnine—like in all those mystery novels," I said.

"Hemlock water-dropwort apparently causes it, too. Only this poison doesn't generally cause the other more obvious symptoms of strychnine like muscle spasms and labored breathing, which Morgan didn't display, according to witnesses. And in large-enough doses, death comes pretty quickly. In fact, a botany professor at the University of Memphis said that some historians now think some of the ancient poisonings mentioned in literature previously attributed to strychnine may actually have been caused by this hemlock water-dropwort."

Di finally condescended to speak to Dave.

"So why would Jasmine even have this plant around if it's so deadly?"

"The death smile is caused by facial paralysis, a side effect of this particular poison," Dave said. "Jasmine uses it in miniscule amounts in an anti-aging cream she sells. It's akin to Botox. It relaxes the muscles, so it removes wrinkles. The professor said there's some new research into cosmetic applications for hemlock water-dropwort, but it's not widely used and hasn't been rigorously tested for safety on humans. One of the very unsettling qualities of this plant is that, unlike most poisons, it actually tastes good. It grows wild in parts of Europe, and a full-grown cow could die from eating its sweet roots. The poison can take from a few minutes to a few hours to kill someone, depending on the amount ingested."

"Has Jasmine confessed?" I asked.

"No, she maintains her innocence. But suspects rarely confess to their crimes, except on TV," Dave said.

After finishing his beverage, Dave left, and Di actually got up and walked him to the door.

The look on her face made it clear that she did not want to talk about the current state of her relationship with the sheriff, so I didn't ask. I decided to ask about Daisy instead.

"So did you get a chance to talk to Daisy at yoga class tonight?"

"She didn't even show up," Di said. "I think getting those two together is going to be like herding cats."

On the way home from Di's, I stopped by the grocery store to pick up a few items. Most of my grocery shopping lately had been grab-and-go instead of planned trips with a list.

As I was strolling down aisle five looking for Larry Joe's favorite cereal, I spotted Dave looking at protein bars. I pulled my cart up beside him.

"Seems we meet again," I said. His basket contained frozen dinners, canned ravioli, a package of bologna, and some beef jerky—a sad assortment that screamed "bachelor who doesn't cook."

"Dave, I didn't think to mention it earlier, but that phone call Naomi Mawbry received about her sister has been bothering me. It's a strange thing to happen anytime, but happening on the day of Morgan's murder seems like a pretty big coincidence. Is it possible the killer didn't want Naomi at the retreat center the night Morgan was killed?"

"Yeah, I don't like coincidences much myself," Dave said. "Morgan's dad gave us permission to look at the bank's phone records. None of the people at the retreat, including the choir folks at main lodge and those Sisters of the Full Moon, phoned the bank during that time frame."

"Wouldn't Naomi have noticed if the incoming call had a local area code instead of the hospital's Mississippi area code?"

"The bank still has an old phone system that doesn't have caller ID, so she wouldn't have been able to tell," Dave said. "The only people outside the bank that called around that time were a couple of businesses, and bank employees remember talking to them, plus one old lady who calls at least twice a week to check her account balance, and Trudy remembers talking to her.

"We also checked Naomi's alibi to make sure she was actually in Mississippi the night of the retreat. A credit card receipt from a gas station in Batesville and a nurse working at the hospital both confirm she was nowhere near the retreat center when Morgan died. Sometimes a coincidence really is just a coincidence," he said.

We said our good-nights and I rolled my cart with the squeaky wheel down the aisle, taking one last look at Dave's pitiful rations. I decided I needed to invite him over for supper sometime soon.

Larry Joe had finished changing the oil and whatever other tinkering on the car and was washing up at the kitchen sink when I came in with the groceries. I gave him a quick kiss as I stood on tiptoe to reach the cabinet beside him to put away the cereal.

"Hey, hon," he said. "How's Di?"

"I'm not sure. Dave dropped by while I was there, and things were obviously a little chilly between them. He didn't stay long. I think he was starting to feel frostbit."

"You didn't ask her why after he left?"

"No. She didn't seem receptive. In fact she's had very little to say about Dave recently," I said.

"They're both hauling around a lot of emotional baggage, what with the death of a spouse and a felon for an ex-husband," Larry Joe said. "They'll work it out in their own time."

"I hope so," I said, wrapping my arms around my husband's waist and nuzzling my face against his back. "I just want the two of them to be as happy as we are."

Larry Joe grabbed my hands, releasing the hug I had him locked in and turning around to face me.

"Aw, Liv, not everybody can bear that much happiness," he said with a smirk before kissing me on the forehead.

Chapter 10

As I was walking from my car to the office Thursday morning, I spotted Dave getting out of his truck in front of the sheriff's office. I crossed the street and caught him before he went in the building.

"I know you have evidence against Jasmine, but it's not exactly an open-and-shut case. Have you checked up on Astrid Caine from that Sisters of the Full Moon group? She sounds like a viable suspect to me."

"I haven't ruled out anyone at this point. But Miss Caine has an alibi for the time of Morgan's death. And as much as you don't want to hear it, the people at your retreat had the best opportunity to poison Morgan."

"Having the best opportunity doesn't mean they had the *only* opportunity. Some of the women at the retreat are assumed to have a motive for murder based solely on gossip about their husbands and Morgan. That's just a lot of tongues wagging. And I don't recall hearing any rumors about Dylan, so what was Jasmine's motive? Anyway, Astrid having a loud and ugly exchange with Morgan in front of witnesses is something solid," I said.

"That just puts her on the long list of folks who didn't like Morgan. To actually have killed Morgan she would have needed detailed knowledge of the retreat—who was going to be there and that there was going to be an excursion to the cemetery—in order to pull it off.

"Plus, we have the problem that the other members of her group gave statements that place the suspect dancing naked around a fire at the time Miss Annabelle wandered off—which would have been about the time of Morgan's death. And while one or two people might lie to protect someone close to them, getting seven or eight people to lie for you about something as serious as murder is extremely unlikely. It's not even like they're all dedicated pagans. Some of the women are Baptists and Presbyterians who just happened to find the back-to-nature, dancing naked, feminine bonding aspects of the event appealing."

"Whatever their spiritual beliefs, they could be lying to protect a friend," I said. "Besides, Winette said it was Astrid—and honestly, how many people named Astrid do you know?—who showed up at our lodge door to check on Miss Annabelle. According to Astrid's version of things, she got dressed, went up to the main lodge, and talked to somebody before trekking back to our lodge. And somehow she managed to do all that before you arrived about ten minutes after the body was discovered. Doesn't that seem odd?"

"Everything about her seems odd," Dave said. "But that doesn't give me a case against her."

Dave, who had received a call on the police radio, got in his car and took off. I headed to my office to do a little research on Astrid Caine. I enthusiastically embraced the idea of the murderer being someone I didn't know personally.

I put on a pot of coffee, thinking how I ought to buy one of those coffeemakers that quickly brews one cup at a time.

Through the wonders of the Internet, it didn't take long to find out that Astrid Caine, whose real first name is Brenda, owns the Cosmic Moon Cottage in Hartville. It's a gift shop that sells, among other things, crystals, candles, T-shirts, Renaissance clothing, and goddess jewelry. I wasn't sure what goddess jewelry was, but I thought it might be a perfect Christmas gift for Mama if it was a bit on the gaudy side.

I decided at the first opportunity I'd run over to Hartville to see what I could learn from Astrid. But there wasn't room in my schedule for that to happen today.

Before ten, I had already returned all the calls on my answering machine and even booked an appointment with a prospective client. I was about to refine my time line and to-do list for the Dodds' party when the phone rang. It was Mitzi, Lucinda's personal assistant.

"We have a situation here with two of the women who have been stalking Miss Grable. While I've told her she really should call the sheriff, she would very much like to resolve the issue without involving the authorities. Could you come over to the hotel right away?"

Foolishly, I said yes. I probably should have told Mitzi to go ahead and call the sheriff and just let Nell and Sindhu face the consequences of their juvenile behavior. But with Jasmine already locked up, I thought Dave might be running out of room at the jail if he brought in those two.

As I walked into the hotel lobby, Ravi Patel rushed over to me with a panicked look on his face.

"Liv, if you can convince Miss Grable not to press charges I would be very much in your debt. And please try to talk some sense into my wife. This behavior is so unlike her. I do not understand. I think it must be the influence of that kooky hairdresser."

"I'll do what I can, Ravi," I assured him. "Can you tell me exactly what Sindhu and Nell have done now?"

"Miss Grable caught them searching her room," he said in a near whisper, looking around to make sure no one was within earshot. Just then, a man I recognized as a member of Lucinda's entourage stepped out of the elevator and held the door open for me. He escorted me to Lucinda's third-floor suite, where I found Nell and Sindhu sitting in chairs facing Lucinda, looking like kids who had been summoned to the principal's office.

One of Lucinda's guys scooted an upholstered chair over to the grouping, and Mitzi, whom I had never met, but whose voice I recognized from our little phone chats, invited me to sit down.

"Thanks for coming," Lucinda said. "I think you can appreciate the awkward situation these ladies have put me in."

"I can, Lucinda. And I'm embarrassed by their behavior. You'd be well within your rights to call the sheriff. I appreciate your restraint." I looked over at Nell and Sindhu, who met my withering gaze with downcast eyes.

"I seriously considered calling the sheriff, but I heard about their friend being charged with Morgan's murder. I'm willing to give them the benefit of the doubt that they were just upset about the arrest and not thinking clearly," Lucinda said. "But this craziness really has to end here and now."

"I agree, but I'm not sure how I can help."

"I understand that people in town are suspicious of me, since I'm viewed as an outsider and my visit coincided with Morgan's tragic death. I don't want to cause any trouble. I plan to leave town after Morgan's funeral. Until then, I just want to be left alone.

"Liv." I was taken aback because it was the first time I remembered her calling me by name. "Frankly, you're the most sensible person I've had contact with since I arrived. All I ask is that you exert whatever influence you may have over your friends here and any other members of their circle to just keep clear of me for the rest of my stay."

"I'll do whatever I can," I said. "I don't think you have to worry about any more trouble from Sindhu. I believe her husband will be keeping a close eye on her after this incident. Nell, that just leaves you. Will you promise that all this silliness stops now?"

"I'll stay clear of Miss Grable, cross my heart," Nell said with the tone and expression of a petulant teenager.

"Well, then, we'll just leave it at that," Lucinda

said, making a regal gesture with her hand that I took to mean we were being dismissed.

I trailed out the door behind Sindhu, who apologized profusely to Lucinda. Nell followed us silently, and Mitzi closed the door firmly behind us.

We walked down the hall, and no words were spoken until the elevator door closed in front of us.

"I hope you two realize it's still not too late for Lucinda to change her mind and report you to the sheriff."

"As you said, you don't have to watch after me," Sindhu said, staring straight ahead at the elevator doors. "I do not think Ravi will let me out of his sight as long as Miss Grable remains at the hotel."

I looked to Nell.

"I already crossed my heart, didn't I?"

"Look, I'm not the enemy here," I said, miffed. "I came over here as a friend, because when Mitzi phoned she was threatening to call the law on you two."

"I thank you for your efforts on our behalf," Sindhu said coolly.

We stepped off the elevator, and Sindhu walked directly to the check-in counter where Ravi was waiting for her. They disappeared into the back office.

"Look, Liv," Nell said. "I'm not mad at you—I know I got my own self into trouble, and I appreciate your vouching for me. But I still believe Lucinda is involved somehow in Morgan's death. And I know in my heart of hearts that Jasmine is innocent. You don't have to worry about me trailing Lucinda anymore, because I think we've done all we can do. But I do have one favor to ask of you.

Please use whatever pull you have with Sheriff Dave to make sure he doesn't close the book on his investigation now that he's arrested Jasmine."

We exited the hotel and walked to our respective cars. I drove for a bit, taking a circuitous route back to the office. I could feel the heat of anger flushing my face.

I was mad at Nell and Sindhu for acting all peevish toward me when I was just trying to keep their butts out of jail. I was mad at Lucinda for dragging me into the middle of it. Most of all, I was mad at Nell for causing me to entertain real doubts about Jasmine's guilt. Up until now I had done a pretty good job of keeping my nose out of the whole murder business.

The last time Di and I ventured into investigating a murder, we ended up with a rifle to our heads. And I preferred not to get myself into that position again.

I drove around for a few minutes, trying to clear my head. I was too keyed up to go back to the office and actually accomplish anything. It wasn't quite eleven-thirty, but I decided to head over to the diner. I wanted to stake out a table. With any luck, I hoped a certain deputy would join me for lunch.

I was sitting alone at a table for two, waiting for my glass of iced tea and trying to decide whether to order the Greek salad with fat-free dressing or the chicken-fried steak when Deputy Ted Horton walked into the diner. It was time to tackle my assignment from Di to find out some of Ted's likes and interests as the first phase of Operation Matchmaker. Ted was glancing around the room looking for a table, so I waved and motioned for him to join me. Since the diner always fills up at lunchtime, it's not unusual for people to offer to share tables with passing acquaintances or, at times, even complete strangers.

"Take a load off, Ted," I said. "You look run off your feet."

"Thanks, Mrs. McKay," he said, even though I've told him at least a hundred times to call me Liv. He took off his hat and sat down across from me. "It's been a busy day, that's for sure."

The waitress set glasses of sweet tea in front of us. Looking to the deputy, she said, "I know you want the daily special. How 'bout you, hon?" she said, shifting her gaze to me.

"I should order a salad, but I'll have the chicken-fried steak."

"Nobody here's gonna shame you for that," she said before heading over to a table of men rattling the ice in their empty glasses—a Neanderthal signal for refills.

Ted performed the pleasantries of asking about Larry Joe and how my mama's doing. And I returned the favor by inquiring after the health of his granny.

Margie efficiently slid our plates onto the table, plopped a basket of biscuits between us, and tucked tickets under our napkin-wrapped cutlery.

Town Square Diner's chicken-fried steak is as good as any I've eaten, so it's always a hard temptation to resist. After savoring a bite or two I launched into my Q and A with the deputy.

"So, Ted, I know you eat lunch at the diner most days. It's certainly convenient to the office and beats a peanut butter sandwich. But what about at home, especially on your days off? Do you cook much, or like to cook when you have the time?"

"No, ma'am. I'm afraid I'm pretty hopeless in the kitchen. I'll throw steaks or burgers on the grill. Other than that, my fridge is generally stocked with take-out boxes and stuff from the grocery store deli.

"When I was little I was always asking my granny to let me help her in the kitchen. You know, I wanted to be on the spot when she took goodies out of the oven, especially her chocolate chip cookies. I guess she was wise to me, though. She'd shoo me out of the kitchen. But Grandpa always let me help him in the garden and in the smokehouse. I can't cook anything, but I do know how to hoe a garden and how to butcher a hog."

I started worrying that trying to fix up the deputy with a real live girl might be a hard row to hoe. Being handy in the kitchen makes a man instantly more attractive to most women. I doubt there are many women posting to online dating services looking for a man with hog-butchering experience. And that was probably just as well.

We finished up lunch, which included a slice of pecan pie for Ted, before strolling out of the diner together.

"Ted, I talked to Dave about the phone call Naomi Mawbry received about her sister. He explained how y'all checked out all the calls made to the bank around that time from the businesses and the elderly lady. What I don't understand is how Naomi could have gotten a call and there not be any record of it."

"Don't tell the sheriff I told you, but his theory is that Mrs. Mawbry made it up."

"Why on earth would she do that?"

"I wouldn't venture a guess," Ted said. "But it's really the only explanation that seems to fit with all the facts."

Ted's answer caught me off-guard. I was going to have to give this new theory about the phone call to Naomi some thought.

Chapter 11

After a quick stop by the office, I drove out to Holly's house to pick her up. We had a 2:15 appointment to meet our engagement party client, Mrs. Dodd.

Mr. Dodd had decided to wear a riverboat gambler costume to the engagement party that he and his wife were hosting for Rachel and Mark. Mr. Dodd had gone to a large costume store in Memphis and quickly decided on a circa 1880s costume, featuring a long frock coat, patterned vest, high-collar shirt with an ascot tie, and a brimmed hat. The look, which suited him perfectly, was a cross between Maverick and Mark Twain.

He had spotted a dance hall costume that he thought would be just the thing for his wife. She thought it was a bit on the tawdry side for a mother of the bride, and I tended to agree.

Mrs. Dodd, who is a little more straight-laced than her husband, had debated for weeks whether she should also wear a period costume. The guests wouldn't be wearing costumes and neither would

Rachel or Mark. I had advised Mrs. Dodd that she should wear whatever made her feel most comfortable as a hostess.

She had bought three outfits over the past month, each of which she had asked Holly and me to weigh in on. Last week, I thought she had finally settled on a tailored ivory pantsuit with a bronze silk blouse. It was elegant without being too formal, and she had found a bronze brooch with a riverboat design that perfectly complemented the ensemble.

Late yesterday afternoon, however, she had telephoned me with a note of panic in her voice. She said that she really wanted to try to find a period costume for the party. She acknowledged that it was last minute and beyond the scope of my duties as a planner, but she asked if I could please help her. The timing wasn't the most convenient, but it was obviously very important to my client, so I told her I would make some calls and get back to her in a couple of hours.

I called and explained the situation to Reesie, the owner of a vintage clothing store in Memphis who I had worked with on several occasions. I gave her my client's dress size and height. She e-mailed me photos of a few dresses she had in stock, which she thought might suit our client's needs. I forwarded the photos to Holly and discussed the situation with her over the phone. After we had a strategy in place for the fashion crisis, I called Mrs. Dodd and set up an appointment for us to meet her at Reesie's shop.

Holly and I arrived before our client and did a bit of reconnaissance shopping. We laid out a couple of dresses and left one hanging on the rack that we planned to help Mrs. Dodd "discover" on her own. After I announced I had just spotted Mrs. Dodd pulling into the parking lot, Reesie, sporting a stylish hat, put on some Dixieland music and uncorked a bottle of Chardonnay.

At first Mrs. Dodd was of the mind that she should try to find something in the same era as her husband's costume. But we didn't have much trouble talking her into fast-forwarding past the bustles and severe corsets of the late 1800s.

Reesie handed her a turn-of-the-century design. Mrs. Dodd disappeared into the dressing room with a glass of wine and stepped out wearing a white confection from 1903, very similar to a dress worn by Judy Garland in *Meet Me In St. Louis.*

She stood in front of the full-length mirror and declared, "I look like Little Bo Peep," which was an apt description.

"It's very sweet," Holly said. "A little too sweet for a gambling hall, I think."

Reesie, our resident expert, pointed out that women's fashions really began to change dramatically around 1908. So we decided to focus on dresses from the teens and twenties.

"Besides," I added, "I've done a bit of research online, and apparently riverboat travel remained fashionable well into the 1920s."

Mrs. Dodd drained the remains of her wineglass and returned to the dressing room with a circa 1916 dress. She emerged looking much more fetching. The dress had a flared skirt with ruffled layers and a faux-vest fitted bodice in a fabulous deep purple.

"That's definitely a party color," Holly said. "And I like that you're showing a bit of ankle."

Mrs. Dodd actually giggled. I discreetly gestured for Reesie to refill her wineglass.

"I agree," I said. "Getting the skirt up off the floor is a definite improvement. The dress has a little movement when you walk."

She twirled around in front of the mirror.

"I just don't know," she said. "Liv, would you and Holly try on something to give me some ideas? Pick out the sort of dress you'd choose to wear if you were me."

I chose a bold but elegant gold silk dress with a dropped waist and a V neckline. It had beadwork on the skirt and silver art deco designs on the top. Reesie handed me a matching cloche as I emerged from the dressing room.

I pulled the hat onto my head and did a few steps of the Charleston. Mrs. Dodd gave her enthusiastic approval.

Holly stepped out of the dressing room in a 1920s-style flapper dress with beadwork and fringe. She turned her head and looked over her shoulder at us, sucking in her cheeks and making fish lips. True to her usual 1960s fashion sense, she looked like a go-go dancer, except with the skirt almost to the knee.

Mrs. Dodd, Reesie, and I applauded, and we all started giggling.

Holly walked over and started casually thumbing through some dresses before pulling one off the rack for Mrs. Dodd. It was the dress we had decided would be perfect for her before she had arrived.

"I think this one has your name written all over it," Holly said, holding it out for our conservative client, who had loosened up considerably after a bit of wine and a good laugh.

We all fell silent for a moment when she stepped out of the dressing room. The dress was truly stunning on her. It was a black silk evening dress with art deco flourishes and sheer sleeves. It fit as if it were custom-made for her. Reesie slipped a long strand of faux pearls over Mrs. Dodd's head to complete the look.

"That's *it*," Holly said. "Your bob-length hairstyle works so well with it, I don't think I'd add a hat."

"I agree," I said. "That dress is elegant and perfect for a casino night in any era—from a riverboat to Monte Carlo."

Mrs. Dodd gazed into the mirror with a pleased look.

"I'll take it, Reesie," she said.

"Do you want to buy it or rent it?" Reesie asked.

After another quick look in the mirror, Mrs. Dodd said, "I'll buy it."

She was beaming as we walked out of the shop.

"I don't think I'll tell Rachel about the dress," Mrs. Dodd said. "I'll let it be a little surprise."

Holly and I climbed into my SUV and pulled out of the parking lot feeling pretty pleased with ourselves.

"Holly, you really came through for Mrs. Dodd— and me. Thank you. You know I'd pay you more if I could, don't you?"

"Aw, darlin', it's my pleasure. Besides, how many people get paid to play dress-up in the middle of the day? I am on the clock, right?" she said.

"You most certainly are," I said. "And I believe we deserve a treat. I'm thinking maybe a fabulous dessert should be in order, your pick. Where would you like to go?"

"It's been a while since I've been to Cheesecake Corner," she said.

"Ooh, that sounds like a winner."

I drove from midtown to the South Main District in downtown Memphis and snagged a parking spot in front of the eatery. We went inside and looked over the Cheesecake Corner menu, but I already knew what I was going to order. Pumpkin cheesecake is available only seasonally, so I didn't want to miss my window of opportunity. After mulling over the options for a couple of minutes, Holly ordered the caramel pecan cheesecake.

We sipped coffee until the waiter delivered our order, then dove into our sinfully rich, ridiculously huge slices of cheesecake.

"Trying on that fabulous dress makes me wish a client would book a Roaring Twenties party," Holly said. "That would be such fun."

"Yeah, it would," I said. "Why don't you throw the party? Your house was built in the 1920s. It would be the perfect setting."

"I just might," Holly said, holding her fork in midair with a faraway look in her eyes. "Would you cohost it with me?"

"You know I'd help you plan it—no charge, of

course. But you don't need a cohostess. You can definitely rock that role all by yourself."

"I've had friends over for dinner, but I haven't put on a proper party since my husband passed away," she said. "I don't know if it would be the same."

There was a sadness in Holly's voice that broke my heart.

"Holly, honey," I said. "I don't guess it would be the same, but it could be wonderful. You could invite exactly who you wanted instead of those you felt obligated to invite, which was often the case because of your husband's position, right?"

Holly's late husband had been an army general and they had frequently entertained military brass and government officials, as well as hosting charity events.

"You're right," she said assertively. "I could make up my dream guest list for once."

"Who'd be on that list?"

"Well, Tom Selleck, if he's available," she said with a sly smile. "And of course, you and Larry Joe, and your Mama and Earl . . ."

"My mama. You're hankering for drama, huh?"

We both laughed.

"I'm going to give this party idea some thought," she said. "We're too busy from now until New Year's, but after that . . ."

Holly and I finished our cheesecake and waddled back to the car. We had fun on the drive back to Dixie as we continued tossing around ideas about a hypothetical Roaring Twenties party.

"Why don't you and Larry Joe ever throw a big bash?" Holly said.

"In our house, a big bash might turn into a big crash," I said. "You know our decrepit house is actually more of a construction zone. It's too unsafe and unsightly for guests. I guess I'm a little like that old saying about the cobbler's kids not having any shoes. I'm a party planner who never has parties of her own."

By the time I dropped off Holly and made it home, I was feeling a little bummed out about the lack of progress on the house. I gave Larry Joe kind of a hard time about it over dinner. With a sheepish expression he promised to ramp up his efforts. He headed dutifully upstairs to work on the never-ending bathroom remodel—and no doubt to escape from his nagging wife.

I called Di to see if she was up to my dropping by. I wanted to fill her in on what I had learned about Ted over lunch.

I took a seat on Di's sofa and told her the gist of my conversation with the deputy.

"So you didn't find out anything about Ted, besides the fact he knows how to make bacon?" Di asked.

"Sure, lots," I said defensively. "Just nothing helpful. He can't cook. He likes to fish. He hates to shop. His house is still furnished mostly with cast-offs from his parents' home. He doesn't even own a suit. Oh, and his favorite movie is *Scarface*."

"I'll grant you he doesn't look good on paper," she said.

"On paper? He couldn't place at the county fair if we put lipstick on him."

Di nodded and heaved a heavy sigh. "Actually, Ted may look like more of a catch than you think after you hear what I learned about Daisy."

"I find that hard to believe—unless she has hooves."

"Mrs. Roper followed me down the street today, telling me how Daisy gives her the creeps," Di said. "She claims she's spied Daisy on more than one occasion in the backyard picking up insects with her bare hands and putting them in a jar."

"What's really creepy is the way Mrs. Roper spies on her neighbors," I said. "But I'll admit that does sound a little odd," I said. "Maybe she has a hamster that eats insects."

"I'm pretty sure hamsters are vegetarians. Maybe it has something to do with her work," Di mused.

"Yeah. Hey, maybe she arranges little insect collections on boards, you know, like they did in Victorian times."

"I suppose that makes as much sense as anything else."

"Okay, look," I said. "Maybe Ted isn't exactly smooth, but we know him well enough to know he's a good guy, really solid. Maybe we should try to find out a little more about Daisy before we throw her into Ted's arms."

"It's not like I haven't been trying," Di said. "I've tried to talk to her after yoga class, but she always rushes out. Last night she didn't even show up.

"So what now?"

"Next week while she's at yoga class I'm going to do a bit of investigating," Di said. "I'm not saying

I'll actually break into Daisy's house, but I'm at least going to take a peek through the windows to see what I can find out about our strange little wallflower."

"You'll need an accomplice to keep a lookout," I offered.

"I was hoping you'd say that," she said. "We'll leave my place next Wednesday about ten til six—and wear dark clothes."

Chapter 12

I drove home from Di's place and went upstairs to rummage through my closet. I needed to choose an appropriate outfit for breaking and entering, or at least something closely akin to it. I settled on black jeans and a black cotton turtleneck.

I don't know if it was the excitement of planning a spying foray at Daisy's house, the romance of trying to bring two lonely hearts together, or the fact that I'd given Larry Joe such a rough time earlier, but I was feeling kind of amorous. I found Larry Joe stretched out on the sofa in the den. I guess we must have worked up an appetite. After our frisky bit of exercise, we ended up in the kitchen drinking hot chocolate and sharing a slice of pumpkin pie from the diner. Larry Joe and I decided to call it an early night and headed upstairs to bed.

About two AM, the Newsoms' car alarm started blaring—a much too common occurrence on our street. I got up and peeked through the curtains to see Mrs. Cleats, our neighborhood snoop and all-around pain in the patootie, padding out onto her front porch in slippers and a bathrobe. She started yelling for the Newsoms to turn off that "ding dang" racket before she called the sheriff. As if they could have somehow missed the earsplitting screech.

I fell back into bed and clasped my hands over my ears.

Mrs. Roper doesn't know how good she has it, I thought. I could only wish my biggest problem was a neighbor who kept to herself and quietly picked up bugs in the backyard.

After the alarm fell silent, Larry Joe rolled over and was out like a light. I went back to sleep almost as quickly. I woke up a little earlier than usual and even whipped up a batch of pancakes while Larry Joe was in the shower.

My smiling, hungry husband ploughed through a stack drenched in sorghum molasses and hurried off to work. I took my time getting ready and still made it to the office by eight-thirty.

That Friday morning, there were plenty of odds and ends at the office that I needed to catch up on. But I was in reasonably good shape for the engagement party this weekend. It occurred to me that the best way to throw Nell and Sindhu off Lucinda's scent would be to give them another suspect. After the snippets of gossip I'd heard about Astrid, I couldn't help but wonder if Dave was paying as much attention to her as a suspect as he should. Maybe this was one thread I could help him unravel.

I drove over to Hartville to check out Astrid's

shop. I pulled into the parking lot of the strip mall that houses the Cosmic Moon Cottage, sandwiched between a Chinese restaurant and a shoe store that specializes in orthopedics.

A cloud of incense and tinkling bells greeted me as I entered. A woman dressed in a black print blouse and black broomstick skirt greeted me.

"Peace. My name is Astrid. Can I help you find anything?"

"I'm always looking for unique jewelry."

She led me to a case with a sign above it that said GODDESS JEWELRY. Several pieces looked like primitive fertility symbols, but others were pretty and featured female figures with an art deco vibe about them.

We made small talk, as Southerners are wont to do, and Astrid explained the symbolism behind some of the jewelry. I couldn't think of any way to ease into a conversation about Morgan, so I just took a shot.

"Weren't you with the group at St. Julian's last week?"

"Yes, I'm a member of the Sisters of the Full Moon. We held a gathering there recently. Were you there with the church group?"

Since I didn't have the requisite holy hairdo, I had a feeling she was just trying to be cute.

"No, I was there with the businesswomen's retreat. I believe you were the woman who came by to check on Miss Annabelle, the elderly lady who wandered off into the woods."

"Oh, yes. We were all pretty concerned about her after it became clear she was a little confused. I just wanted to make sure she was safe. Is she okay?"

"Yes, thank God. She really had us worried for a while." I paused for a beat before continuing. "Not that our relief lasted for long. I'm sure you heard about the death of Morgan Robison."

"Of course," she said. "The sheriff questioned all of us who were staying at Sparrow Lodge. But then I'm sure you already knew that," she said, her tone suddenly turning chilly.

"Yes, I had heard," I said. "I also heard that you recently had a very loud and very public altercation with Morgan."

If eyes were daggers, I would have dropped dead on the spot.

"I don't see how that's any of your business."

"Look, you can't honestly be surprised that under the circumstances people are gossiping about your run-in with Morgan. I knew Morgan well enough to know she wasn't the easiest person to get along with. I'd be interested to hear your version of the argument, that's all. I've heard the version that Morgan's coworkers are putting out there."

"Fine. I have nothing to hide—and for the record I've already talked to the sheriff, who doesn't seem to consider me a suspect," she said. "Unlike you and the other Dixie businesswomen, I didn't know Morgan personally. My dealings with her were purely business, and she acted in a completely un-professional manner. Abusive, in fact, telling me that nobody around here was interested in my little 'heathen baubles,' as she put it.

"I had signed a five-year lease on this place with Morgan's uncle, Ward Robison. After his death ear-lier this year, Morgan came up with some kind of loophole and tried to oust me and the other tenants from this shopping center. She said she and her dad had plans to develop something else here—she didn't share the details with me. But apparently she had pressured the restaurant and the shoe store owners into ending their leases early. Mr. Ling struggles with English and Mr. Brown is about ready to retire anyway. But this is my livelihood and I wasn't willing to play along just because Morgan's a spoiled brat who's used to getting her way.

"I was foolish enough to let her goad me into a shouting match at the bank. After that little episode I talked to Morgan's dad—which is what I should have done in the first place. He assured me he would honor my lease, which has nearly two years left on it. He explained that they had discussed a possible development plan for this property, but it would be at least two years before anything happened with it. He apologized for Morgan, saying she was just 'a little high strung.' Since he was her daddy, I bit my tongue and didn't tell him what she really is, or was.

"That's the truth. Everything was settled with Mr. Robison before Morgan's death, so I had no motive to kill her," she said. "Although I'm sure the inbred hicks over in Dixie would prefer to believe that someone from Hartville killed her."

She gave me a smug little smile, and I bared my teeth at her. I had considered buying a pair of goddess earrings I thought Mama might like, but after Astrid's snippy little inbreeding remark I just turned and walked out.

As I drove back to Dixie I wondered if everything

really was settled with Mr. Robison before Morgan's death, or if that conversation had happened afterward. I also wondered about those Baptists and Presbyterians who were among the participants at the Sisters of the Full Moon ritual. Maybe they weren't lying to protect Astrid. Maybe they were lying to protect themselves. I strongly suspected that some of them would prefer that their church friends didn't know about their extracurricular pagan activities.

Against my better judgment I phoned Dave and shared my doubts about Astrid. Predictably, he told me to butt out. Although he did say he had confirmed with Mr. Robison what Astrid had said about the lease.

I called Nell to encourage her to snoop on Astrid instead of Lucinda. Not that I really had a bone she could chew on, but I hoped Astrid's derogatory remark about Dixie would be enough to stir up Nell's ire.

I did my best to make Astrid sound like a worthy suspect, but Nell wasn't buying it.

"Oh, please," she said. "I shop at the Cosmic Moon Cottage all the time, and I can tell you Astrid's just as harmless as Jasmine. She was just being snarky to you because you were getting all up in her business. Hon, you don't have to worry about me chasing after Lucinda anymore. But mark my words, that woman's a cold-blooded killer."

She hung up, and I decided maybe she was right. There was just as much evidence against Lucinda as there was Astrid, which was zero.

On the way back to the office I stopped by the

supermarket deli and picked up a chef's salad to go. I ate lunch at my desk as I checked and double-checked with vendors for the Dodds' engagement party.

I phoned and confirmed times with the caterer for the food and the waitstaff. I confirmed delivery of the various game tables and for the specialty decorations and extra chairs. Everything was going smooth as silk until I hit a snag with the limousine service.

"Let me see here, Mrs. McKay," the vendor said over the phone. "Yep, it looks like we're all squared away. That's one limo picking up guests at the hotel in Dixie at 6:40 PM, two limos picking up guests at the Peabody in Memphis at 5:45 PM, and three limos picking up guests from the casino hotel in Tunica at 4:45 PM tonight."

I was nodding and playfully twirling a pen in my hand until he said the word *tonight*. Then my eyes flew open wide and I sat up ramrod straight.

"Tonight?" I said. "You mean tomorrow night."

"No, ma'am," he said. "Your drivers are on the schedule for tonight."

"But that's not possible," I said, trying to breathe steadily. "The party is tomorrow. Double-check the date. You must be on the wrong page."

He argued with me until I demanded to speak to his supervisor. The supervisor put me on hold while he looked up the original files from when the party was first booked. After a tense few minutes, he returned to the phone and explained that they had limos booked for a party named "Dodge," as well as for my party under the name "Dodd." Somehow the scheduler for the limo service had transposed the two when he wrote them onto the drivers' dispatch roster.

"I'm really sorry about the mix-up, Mrs. McKay. But I'm awful glad you called and we discovered this snafu before our drivers showed up at the wrong addresses tonight for the Dodge party."

I went over the details with him one last time, just for my own peace of mind, and thanked him for his personal attention to the matter.

My tense shoulders finally relaxed, coming down from my earlobes. This is why it's always a good idea to check and recheck every detail of an event. Mix-ups happen.

Holly and I were due at the Dodd's house at three this afternoon to supervise a work crew.

I drove to our clients' home and spotted Holly's car turning into the driveway just ahead of me. Over the next few hours, the movers hauled dozens of pieces of furniture into rooms that would be closed off during the party and rearranged tables and seating areas. With the heavy lifting taken care of, I could return with the party crew in the morning to oversee the unloading and placement of the game tables and furniture and do the final setup and decorations.

When I arrived a bit after nine Saturday morning, Harold, my go-to electrician, and Kenny, my go-to jack-of-all-trades, were already draping lights on the huge oak tree in front of the Dodds' house. White lights dripping like luminescent moss would be the first sight to greet tonight's guests.

Harold and Kenny look like the odd couple. Harold: sixtyish, hefty, short, white and bald. Kenny: early twenties, slender, tall, and black, with a mop of short dreadlocks. But together they are an impressively capable and efficient team.

The two men had already placed posts strung together with heavy rope flanking the porch steps to give the impression of a gangplank. We would also be placing a large ship's wheel and steamer trunks on either side of the front door to establish the riverboat theme. The gambling aspect of the party would come to life as soon as guests walked through the front door. The cake table was positioned in the center of the circular stairway in the expansive entry hall. Holly and I got to work right away hanging two large posters from the banister above the cake table—oversized king and queen of hearts cards.

Away from the rest of the work crew downstairs, Holly asked me in a hushed voice, "Do you think that woman who makes the herbal products, the one Sheriff Davidson arrested, really killed Morgan? I'm not sure I've ever spoken to her. I've seen her around town, of course."

"I don't know," I admitted. "She's a pleasant, kind-spoken person. It's hard for me to imagine her actually killing somebody. But then that's the kind of thing neighbors usually say about serial killers after they've been arrested."

"That's true," Holly said. "One of my father's best friends was the nicest man you'd ever want to meet, a real Southern gentleman. I later learned that people believed he had murdered his first wife. She had drowned, but no charges were ever brought against him. I always did think it was odd that she had drowned in the kitchen sink," Holly said as we finally got the king of hearts poster positioned exactly the way we wanted.

The first floor of the Dodds' 8,000-square-foot home was perfectly designed for entertaining on a grand scale, which was fortunate because seventy-five people were expected for the engagement party. To the right of the entry were the front and rear parlors, and just beyond the formal parlors were the dining room and kitchen. From the side porch off the dining room, it was just a few steps to Mr. Dodd's office. To the other side of the entry hall were the library and family room, and just beyond those rooms on the left was a large guest bedroom.

For the evening, the main floor would be transformed into a casino, except for the front parlor, where the buffet table would be set up, and the entry, which would showcase the desserts.

After decorating the upstairs railing, Holly and I got to work on the buffet table. We overlaid white tablecloths with fishing net and attached buoys to the net across the front of the table.

The party rental company truck arrived, and the crew began setting up the game tables. Two roulette tables were placed in the rear parlor and four felt-lined poker tables were set up in the dining room. The entrance to the butler's pantry between the rear parlor and the kitchen was blocked off with a whiskey barrel, across which Holly had stenciled the word SALOON in a vintage script. This point would serve as the walk-up bar, while servers would circulate through the rooms with trays of drinks.

The library was outfitted with two blackjack

tables, and the large guest bedroom had been set up for bingo.

Finally, Mr. Dodd's office was transformed into a whiskey and cigar lounge. The office was already furnished with a leather sofa and two leather club chairs. Four additional leather wingback chairs were moved into his office from the library. An antique sextant and sea captain's hat adorned the desk, and a large steamship model was placed in the center of the handsome bookcase behind the desk.

Loveseats, sofas, and rented upholstered folding chairs were arranged along one or two walls of each game room to accommodate guests who preferred just to watch the action.

Holly and I placed a few decorations on the mantles and in one corner of each room to continue the theme without intruding into the space so guests could freely move about. A framed poster of the Delta Queen replaced a family portrait over the mantle in the library, and wooden crates and fishnets in the corner of the dining room and a steamer trunk overflowing with circa 1900 clothing and travel souvenirs in the family room were among the decorative props.

Holly and I furnished the bingo bedroom with rockers and wicker chairs from the screened porch. We placed a dressmaker's form in the corner. Holly outfitted the form with a vintage nautical-inspired dress, while I arranged Victorian-era gloves and parasols on the mantle. The bingo room was set up with the more senior guests in mind, with comfortable seating and an adjoining bathroom.

A little after one o'clock, Holly and I took a

break to eat turkey wraps and potato chips. I had picked up box lunches for the whole Liv 4 Fun crew.

Holly and I walked outside and sat down on the front porch steps to eat our sandwiches, watching as Harold tested the tree lights. They looked gorgeous.

"Liv, I can't stop thinking about the recent tragedy," Holly said, turning toward me. "I was at school with Morgan's father. My heart just breaks for him and her poor mother. I read a newspaper article listing the PWAD members at the retreat, and I didn't know Jasmine or the lady who owns the hotel. But of the members I know, the only one I could possibly imagine committing violence is Nell Tucker. I'm not saying she's a murderer, mind you. I'm just saying she's well known to be a bit of a hothead."

"That's what my mama said," I noted. "She once saw Nell lob a hot curling iron at another hairdresser. I know Nell often speaks, and acts, without thinking. But I don't really see Nell as a killer myself. I can tell you that Nell and Sindhu insist Jasmine is innocent. They think Lucinda Grable killed Morgan."

"I was acquainted with Lucinda's parents, but I was married and had moved away by the time Lucinda came along," Holly said. "It was tragic the way she lost her parents at such a young age. And with her being in the backseat when they had the car accident that killed them . . . who knows what that kind of trauma can do to a child."

"I knew her parents died in a car crash, but I'd never heard that Lucinda was in the car, too."

"Yes," Holly said, shaking her head. "She was barely more than a baby, so I don't know how much of it she remembers."

Satisfied with the way the tree looked, Kenny and Harold took a break for lunch before they set about hanging red, white, and blue bunting from the upper gallery railing.

About three-thirty, the catering staff from the country club arrived, except for Chef Felix. It took three guys to carefully carry the cake up the porch steps and place it on the table in the entry hall. The large cake, masterfully sculpted in the shape of a riverboat, certainly deserved its prominent display space. A smaller table in the entry would hold other desserts, including the iced "poker chip" cookies.

About five o'clock, Chef Felix arrived to oversee the final preparations. The photographer arrived about the same time. He would be strolling through the rooms during the party, taking candid shots. Mark and Rachel planned to have the photos on display at their wedding reception for the family to enjoy. At 5:45, five servers and three bartenders arrived dressed in the costumes Holly had dropped off at the country club that morning. I got on the phone to find out why the sixth server had not yet arrived. He said he was on his way. A few minutes later the dealers for the blackjack and roulette tables arrived, along with the bingo caller—all moonlighting professionals from one of the Tunica casinos.

The servers and bartenders—both male and female—were wearing black pants, red-and-white-striped shirts and straw boater hats with red bands.

The dealers were outfitted in black pants and black shirts, sporting a red garter on their right sleeve.

Holly and I quickly changed into the black pants and white tuxedo shirts we often wear for parties.

At 6:20, Mrs. Dodd came downstairs, looking fabulous in her vintage evening dress.

"I'm not sure it's proper for you to look as beautiful as the bride at her engagement party," Mr. Dodd said adoringly as he watched his wife make her entrance.

We did a walk-through with Mrs. Dodd so she could take it all in.

"Oh, Liv, this is perfect—even better than I had envisioned from the plans you showed us," she said. "Now if all the guests will just behave, especially Uncle Ira, we'll be golden. I suppose if Mark still wants to marry Rachel after meeting the whole family, we'll know he's a keeper."

"Don't worry. We have several different game areas, so if a guest seems to be causing difficulties in one room, we'll encourage him to try his luck with a different game," I said.

Rachel was set to arrive with Mark. She wanted to see his expression when he got his first look at the riverboat gambler theme.

About ten minutes to seven, the first of the six stretch limos arrived with a carload of guests. Some guests would be driving their own vehicles, but the majority, most of whom had traveled from out of town for the party, were being transported to and from hotels in Dixie, Memphis, and Tunica.

Rachel and Mark emerged from one of the limousines, along with Mark's parents, grandparents, brother, and uncle. Mrs. Dodd welcomed them while I went in search of Mr. Dodd to let him know the guests were beginning to arrive. I found him in his office, steeling his nerves with a shot glass of whiskey. I resisted the temptation to pour one for myself.

Mark, Rachel, and both sets of parents stationed themselves in the entry to welcome guests as they arrived. Holly and I invited guests into the other rooms to survey the various games available, and the bartenders started taking drink orders.

After the last of the limos had arrived, all the guests were invited to the entry and adjoining doorways. Glasses of champagne, and sparkling grape juice for the nondrinkers, were distributed as the father of the bride and the father of the groom each made a toast to the happy couple and extended kind words of welcome to the future in-laws.

After the toasts, Mr. Dodd, who was supposed to explain how the games and the chips would work, instead called me up to explain.

"Welcome, everyone," I said. "I know you're going to have a lot of fun getting to know each other—and gambling for a worthy cause.

"Each guest who would like to play will be issued one hundred dollars in chips, courtesy of the Dodd family. The seventy-five-hundred dollars represented by these chips will be donated to St. Jude Children's Research Hospital, the charity chosen by Rachel and Mark."

There was a round of approving applause.

"Additional chips may be procured in twenty-five-dollar stacks. All of that money will also be donated to St. Jude. So no one really loses tonight, you simply give more to charity. And winners claim bragging rights.

"The chips will be used in the usual manner for placing bets at the poker, roulette, and blackjack tables. Those choosing to play bingo will be issued four cards. You may purchase additional bingo cards to play for twenty-five dollars per pair of cards.

"The biggest donor of the evening will be awarded a lovely gift basket from our newly engaged couple.

"Please help yourself to the buffet or check out the gambling options. Waiters will be coming around with trays of drinks and snacks, if you'd prefer to head straight to the tables. There's extra seating in each area for those who would like to watch the gamblers in action and get a feel for the games, as well as chat.

"The dealer or caller for each game will issue chips and be able to answer any questions you may have."

I turned to Mr. Dodd, who added, "Let the games begin!"

Before I'd moved three steps, I noticed one elderly lady at the desserts table stuffing cookies into her pockets. I wasn't sure if she was just hungry or mistakenly thought the iced poker chip cookies could be used for placing bets. Either way, I decided we'd better keep an eye on her and discreetly pointed her out to Holly. I also scoped out Uncle Ira, just in case. He was drinking pretty freely. Luckily, the only misbehavior I witnessed all night was when Ira pinched some woman's bottom. If she minded, she didn't show it.

We had originally proposed having a roving barbershop quartet or banjo player at the party, or simply playing light jazz through the whole-house stereo speakers. Rachel had feared that music, plus all the noise from the game tables, might impede conversation. After much discussion, she and her mother had decided against having music playing during the evening. I think they made a wise choice. The echo of loud chatter and laughter filled the rooms almost immediately. We had some CDs Rachel had selected set up and ready to play if a pall of silence should fall at some point.

Mark and Rachel strolled from room to room and played a couple of rounds at some of the tables, as well as chatted with the onlookers. When they got trapped by some overly chatty soul, Holly or I would intervene and say someone was asking for them in another room.

I sat in the bingo room for a couple of rounds to help a lady with failing eyesight play her card. The only room I didn't venture into all night was the cigar lounge. I did step out onto the side porch to see if I could hear any altercations emanating from Mr. Dodd's office, but all was quiet on the Western Front.

The catering staff and dealers were all pros, so things went pretty smoothly. Chef Felix was called out of the kitchen by Mrs. Dodd to accept accolades for the delicious buffet, which he created, as well as for the stunning cake, which he did not—but he didn't let that stop him from accepting the credit. He departed shortly thereafter and left his competent crew to handle refills and cleanup.

About ten, things began to quiet down, so Holly popped in a CD with a mix of Dixieland, light jazz, and big band music. Mark swept Rachel into his arms and danced from the roulette room through the entry and into the blackjack room. A few other couples followed suit, dancing into the entry hall. It was one of those beautiful, spontaneous moments you try to set the stage for and always hope will happen at your parties, but can't be orchestrated. Fortunately, it looked as if the photographer captured a few shots for posterity.

Around eleven-fifteen, I noticed Rachel and Mark were looking a little tired, with pasted-on smiles and drooped shoulders. They deserved a break. As soon as I was able, I whispered that they should sneak up to the second-floor sitting room via the back stairs and I would bring them some refreshments.

I delivered some sweets and champagne on a tray and found them plopped on a settee, Rachel's head resting on Mark's shoulder. I sat the tray down on a table beside them, pulled back the curtains, and opened one of the French doors. This gave them a bit of fresh air and a clear view of the oak tree, its strings of lights twinkling against a velvet sky. Then I quietly slipped away to let them enjoy a bit of alone time before they were discovered missing.

A little before midnight, the first of the guests began to depart. Soon most of the other guests started piling into limousines. A couple of guests had to be prodded into leaving by their carpool buddies. Mark and Rachel departed in her dad's car, rather than riding back to Tunica with his family. Mr. and Mrs. Dodd thanked me and the catering crew and said their good nights.

I checked with the kitchen and found that all the plates and glasses had been washed and either packed or returned to the owners' cupboards.

Mrs. Dodd had opted to use her own china to serve the cake.

The party wasn't over for my team and me just yet. Sunday morning, Holly would return to pack up decorations and oversee pickup by the party rental crew. In the afternoon, I'd return to supervise the movers as they put all the furniture and accessories back in their original spaces.

But for now, we were both ready to go home and fall into our respective beds.

Chapter 13

I'd been up less than half an hour Sunday when Nell phoned and asked if I would drop by the beauty salon later that morning. She said she had something to give me, but she wouldn't say what.

Larry Joe had taken off for the golf course before I woke up. I dressed, poured some coffee into a travel mug, and drove to the salon.

When I walked through the front door, Nell was the only stylist in the shop, tending to a lone customer. She motioned for me to come through to the back office/supply room.

"I didn't know you were even open on Sundays," I said.

"Officially, we're not. I have some customers who prefer their privacy. So one Sunday a month I schedule a couple of appointments."

She pushed the door shut and pressed a sheet of notepaper into my hand.

"What's this?"

"That's the one piece of evidence Sindhu and I

were able to turn up in Lucinda's room before her assistant walked in on us."

Curious, I took a look at the crumpled paper. A pencil had been brushed across the sheet to reveal indentations. It read, "P.D.—1:30 p.m. Sun. @ Red's."

My face must have signaled my confusion.

"That heifer Mitzi had the nerve to make us empty our pockets after she discovered us. Fortunately, I had tucked this into my bra."

I eyed the paper, not sure how I felt about handling something that had been nestled in Nell's cleavage.

"What does it mean?" I asked.

"It means Lucinda is meeting somebody at one-thirty today at Red's Steakhouse in Hartville."

"Who's P.D.?"

"It could stand for private detective," Nell offered. "Or it could be someone's initials. I don't know. I promised to stay clear of Lucinda. I've got a one o'clock appointment, so I can't get away anyhow. Ravi will hardly let Sindhu out of his sight, and the sheriff apparently isn't interested in looking for another suspect since he locked up Jasmine—despite what you said about Astrid after confronting her at her shop. Liv, I really hope you'll check this out and at least see who Lucinda is meeting. But I've passed the information on to you, so my conscience is clear. That's all I can do at this point."

She didn't ask for promises and I didn't make any. A timer dinged in the front of the salon, and Lucinda hurried off to check on her client's perm.

I walked from the salon to my office down the street and put on a fresh pot of coffee, checked my messages, and stared for a really long time at the piece of paper Nell had given me.

I called Holly to see if she could stick around for a while this afternoon to supervise the movers. I told her if she didn't feel up to it I'd call Kenny to see if he could come out and keep an eye on things. She said she didn't have plans and would be glad to stay.

Then I called Di to see if she wanted to ride over to Hartville with me for a stakeout at the steak house.

To my surprise, instead of trying to dissuade me Di seemed almost enthusiastic about the idea of tailing Lucinda.

Since I was at the office I decided to catch up on some paperwork.

At 12:35 PM, I picked up Di. We hit the Wendy's drive-through and picked up a couple of burgers to sustain us during our lunch hour surveillance job.

"Di, I kinda figured you'd try to talk me out of spying on Lucinda, tell me to keep my nose out of it. You surprise me."

"I surprise myself," she said. "I guess I'm beginning to have my own doubts about Jasmine's guilt. It all seems a little too pat, you know."

Red's Steakhouse is located on a busy commercial strip of highway going into Hartville. We parked in a retail shopping center directly across the street from Red's, with a clear view of the restaurant's parking lot and front entrance.

The small shopping center was busy, with cars coming and going all the time. Lucinda wasn't likely to notice us, especially since I hadn't been following her and she had never ridden in my SUV, or even seen it as far as I knew.

It was easy enough to spot Lucinda, still driving the Bentley. She parked along the side of the building. In a couple of minutes, a Mercedes convertible pulled in next to her.

Pierce Davenport emerged from the car, and he and Lucinda slipped into the restaurant through a side door, avoiding the main entrance.

I've arranged enough parties at Red's to know that the restaurant has a main dining room, divided into two areas, and three private dining rooms—one large, one an average size, and one intimate dining room designed for parties of four to eight.

Knowing that Lucinda, and Red's staff, would recognize me, Di volunteered to go in and check things out. I was supposed to text her if our quarry exited the building.

Di waited about five minutes, giving Lucinda and Pierce time to get settled, before getting out of the car and crossing the highway to the restaurant to take a look around. In a bit Di rejoined me in the car. She recounted that she had asked for a menu and information about private parties while surveying the main room to see if by chance Pierce and Lucinda were seated out front. As expected, they weren't.

A waitress offered to show Di the private dining rooms that were not currently in use. She had pretended to be interested in the big and medium rooms while sneaking a peek at the small dining room. Through the glass-panel door she could see Lucinda and Pierce, but couldn't hear what they were saying.

About forty-five minutes after Di returned to the car, Lucinda and Pierce exited through the same side door. They shared a very friendly hug before leaving in their separate cars.

"They seem pretty chummy," I noted.

"They looked pretty cozy in the restaurant, too," Di said. "Still, it was a hug, not a kiss. And that little dining room is private enough for discreet chats, but the glass door nixes any take-off-your-clothes kind of privacy."

"You think there's any point to following either one of them?"

"Naw," Di said. "If they were going to get physically intimate, they would have just met at a hotel or apartment to begin with."

"Pierce is an attorney," I said. "I suppose there's a chance she's talking to him about a legal matter."

"There's a better chance pigs can fly. I'm sure Lucinda has some big celebrity attorney in L.A.," Di said. "Besides, if it was strictly business, I don't think they'd bother with the whole cloak-and-dagger kind of meeting."

"Well, we're pretty sure Morgan and Pierce were having or previously had an affair. And Pierce, Morgan, and Lucinda all went to college at Ole Miss. Morgan and Lucinda were a little younger than Pierce. I'll try to find out if their time at Ole Miss overlapped—maybe they're simply old school chums."

"I'd like to know just how chummy," Di said.

Chapter 14

I dropped Di off at her place and drove out to the Dodds' house to check on things. The movers were just about finished. Holly said the day had been pretty uneventful—nothing broken, fortunately. I told her I'd stay so she could still salvage a bit of her Sunday.

Mrs. Dodd had asked us to leave the lights hanging from the oak tree. She thought they'd make a nice addition to their holiday decorations. For Halloween, I suggested they could aim a spotlight covered with an orange filter upward from the base of the tree.

I hurried over to the Dixie Public library, which closes at five on Sundays. Miss Hicks, the librarian, cast a look of displeasure in my direction when I walked through the door at five minutes to five o'clock. But I had just enough time to check the Dixie High School yearbooks.

I quickly calculated Morgan's year of graduation based on the age listed in her newspaper obituary. I thumbed along the shelf and picked the book from two years before her senior year. It only took moments to flip through the class pictures. Pierce Davenport was a senior when Morgan and Lucinda were sophomores, so their time at Ole Miss could have overlapped with Pierce's by two or even three years, depending on his course load. I strolled leisurely past Miss Hicks and out the door before the clock ticked to the hour mark.

I got in my car and phoned Di to let her know that Pierce, Lucinda, and Morgan were all at Ole Miss at the same time.

"So he could be an old flame who's burning brightly again," Di said.

"Could be," I acknowledged. "Di, I can't remember if I told you, but when I had lunch with Ted I asked him about that phone call to Naomi. He said, off the record, that Dave thinks Naomi didn't really get a phone call—that she just made it up. I'm having a hard time believing that."

"Yeah, me too," Di said. "I chatted for a minute with Trudy while she was home for lunch on Friday, and she said she'd never seen Naomi as upset as she was after she got the phone call about her sister's death."

"Is Dave sure nobody else called the bank besides those two businesses and the old lady?"

"When I'm back on speaking terms with Dave, I'll ask," Di said.

I drove home and rushed inside the house to change clothes. We were supposed to be at my in-laws' house for dinner at six. It was Daddy Wayne's birthday. I had offered to plan a party at a local restaurant to celebrate since we had almost lost Larry Joe's dad a couple of months ago when he had a major heart attack. But my father-in-law flatly refused to let us make a fuss over his birthday. His exact words were, "Sixty-three is not any kind of milestone. Y'all are trying to trick me by throwing a retirement party and inviting witnesses."

We were doing no such thing, of course. We were genuinely thankful to still have the old curmudgeon around after his close call with the grim reaper. Still, we didn't want to raise his blood pressure, so we settled on a private family dinner with my in-laws, Larry Joe and me, and my mom and Earl.

Mama always feels the need to point out that Earl isn't family, just a good friend. I don't know if she's trying to convince me or herself.

I arrived home and called out to Larry Joe as I ran up the stairs. "Honey, are you about ready to go to your folks' house?"

He stepped out of the upstairs bathroom with uncombed hair, wearing a stained T-shirt.

"We don't have to be there for another forty-five minutes," he said.

I kissed him on the cheek, looked him up and down, and said, "That should give you just enough time to shower and change."

He groaned. "It's not exactly a dress-up affair, you know."

"I think hygiene is in order whether it's a dressy affair or not. Besides, you know Mama will dress nice and she'll probably make Earl wear a tie."

"I'm not wearing a tie."

"I think a shirt with buttons will be just fine."

Larry Joe dropped his wrench into the toolbox and shuffled down the hall with a schoolboy pout.

"I bet Daddy will be wearing a sweatshirt," he groused.

"He's the birthday boy. He can wear what he wants."

"Does that mean I can wear a sweatshirt for my next birthday party?"

"Sure," I said. Since his birthday is at the end of June it was a pretty hollow threat.

I changed into brown dress slacks and a blouse with an autumn leaves design and then called to see if Miss Betty needed us to pick up any last-minute items from the store.

"No, hon. I think I have everything."

"I have a full pitcher of sweet tea in the fridge. Do you want us to bring it along?"

"No thanks. I made up two big pitchers myself— one with real sugar and one with Splenda."

"Sounds good. We'll see you in a few minutes."

"Oh, Liv, " she said just as I was about to hang up, "could you ask Larry Joe not to bring up politics? With the November elections coming up soon, Wayne's been reading the papers and fussing and cussing about politics and taxes and everything else."

"I'll remind Larry Joe to keep the conversation upbeat. I think that you, Mama, and I can keep the conversation under control if we pull together."

I called out to Larry Joe that we needed to get going and then gave my mom a quick call.

"Mama, Miss Betty asked me to tell Larry Joe to

avoid talking politics tonight. She's afraid Daddy Wayne will get all riled up. Could you ask Earl to steer clear of election talk, too?"

"Sure, Liv. Talking football and golf should be enough to keep them busy. What are you wearing?"

I told her what I had on.

"I hope I'm not overdressed. I've got on my red silk pantsuit."

"That sounds good to me. Daddy Wayne probably won't dress up, but I'm sure Miss Betty will wear something spiffy."

"You're probably right. I tried to get Earl to wear a tie, but he made a big stink about it. I finally told him to wear whatever he dang well pleased, as long as his shirt had buttons up the front. I'll see you in a bit."

Click.

Realizing I had said pretty much the same thing to Larry Joe about what he should wear made me worry I was turning into my mother. I felt a little better when I saw Larry Joe bounding down the stairs wearing a light blue button-down with jeans. Earl might rebel about wearing a tie, but he wouldn't dare wear denim, especially when Mama was wearing her red silk pantsuit.

Earl was helping Mama out of the passenger seat of her Cadillac when we pulled up in front of my in-laws' house. He was wearing khakis, as I'd expected, with a green-and-tan checked button-up shirt.

Earl retrieved a wrapped package with a big bow

from the trunk and handed it to Mama. I walked over to her, carrying a gift bag. Miss Betty was holding the front door open for us as we approached the house.

"Y'all come on inside," Miss Betty said. "It's starting to get chilly out."

We entered the living room and set the birthday gifts on the coffee table before sharing hugs all around.

"That's a big box, Virginia," Miss Betty said. "I'm not sure Wayne's been that good."

"I know he hasn't, but I'm too old to give him the birthday whupping he deserves," Mama said.

"Age hasn't slowed Betty down any," Daddy Wayne said. "She's been on my back nonstop since I got out of the hospital."

"Well, good for her, you old goat," Mama said.

This kind of talk was the way my mama and Daddy Wayne showed their affection for one another.

"Something sure smells good," Earl said.

"Sure does. What's for supper, Mama?" Larry Joe said.

"Chicken and dressing," she replied.

"I hope y'all are hungry, son," my father-in-law said. "Your mother made enough to feed an army."

"Oh, Wayne," my mother-in-law said. "It's not like you can make just a little bit of chicken and dressing. If everybody's ready to eat, why don't you go ahead and say grace, honey."

My father-in-law thanked God for family and friends, good food, and the hands that prepared it. We all punctuated his prayer with an "Amen."

We gathered around the table with Daddy Wayne

at one end and Earl at the other. Mama sat next to me, and Larry Joe took a seat next to his mom.

We passed around serving dishes. Green beans, glazed carrots, deviled eggs, and buttered biscuits accompanied the chicken and dressing.

"I'm getting to eat real food because we have company," Daddy Wayne said. "Most days she only lets me have lettuce and cottage cheese."

"Oh, Wayne McKay, just shut up and eat your supper," Mama said. "It's a mystery why Betty puts up with you at all."

"I could say the same about Earl with you," he said.

Mama narrowed her eyes and gave him a mean squint.

"But I won't," Daddy Wayne added, wisely deciding not to go there.

"So Virginia, when's Emma going to have that baby?" Miss Betty said.

"In about three weeks, we expect."

"How exciting. Does she know if it's a boy or a girl?" Miss Betty said.

"No," I chimed in. "She and Hobie wanted to be surprised.

"Surprised," Mama said. "Isn't that the most ridiculous thing you've ever heard? I wish we could've found out back in my day. It sure would've helped with buying clothes and decorating the nursery."

"Oh, Mama, it's easy enough to buy baby clothes that will work for either a boy or a girl."

"I bet Hobie's hoping for a boy this time since he's already got a little princess," Daddy Wayne said.

"I don't know if she's a princess," I said. "She's a mess."

I shared the story Emma had told me about Lulu refusing to share her drawer space with the new baby.

"I've never known a woman yet who thought she had enough drawer or closet space," Larry Joe said.

"Lulu's got your eyes, Virginia," Miss Betty said.

"Sounds like she's got Virginia's mouth on her, too," Daddy Wayne said.

"Have they picked out baby names?" my mother-in-law quickly interjected.

"I don't know if they've settled on a girl's name, but if it's a boy they're naming him the third, after Hobie and his dad," I said. "They'll probably call him 'Trey.'"

We had made it through most of our supper peacefully enough. Then Earl said, "So, Wayne, how's business?"

This may have seemed like an innocuous question to an outsider, but it turned out to be the incendiary that lit my father-in-law's fuse.

"Damned if I know, Earl," he said. "Nobody tells me a blessed thing. Even our new shop manager goes around me to talk to Larry Joe. Betty's insisted I cut my hours, and she and my son are conspiring behind my back to shut me completely out of the business I helped my daddy build."

"Now, Wayne, you know that's just not true," my mother-in-law said.

"It's a crying shame the way they're trying to keep you from killing yourself, you old goat," Mama said.

"This old goat would be doing a whole lot better if they weren't hiding things from me. I can handle problems at work. Been doing it for more than forty years. What I can't handle is not knowing what the hell's going on in my own company and having my family trying to make decisions for me. I'm not a child," he said, getting up from the table and storming out of the room.

"I'm so sorry for Wayne's behavior," Miss Betty said.

"You don't have to sorry about anything, Mama," Larry Joe said. He excused himself from the table and went after his dad.

"Larry Joe's right, Betty. Don't you worry about us," Mama said. "We're family. And if Wayne's going to blow off some steam, it's better for him to do it at home."

Miss Betty, Mama, and I started clearing away dishes. Earl hovered awkwardly in the corner of the dining room, not sure if he should venture into the other room where Larry Joe was trying to calm his dad.

"Earl, go on in the den with Wayne and Larry Joe," Mama finally said. "Maybe you can serve as a buffer. Try to get Wayne talking about football or something."

My mother-in-law was close to tears.

"It's been less than two months since Wayne had his heart attack and had those stents put in," Miss Betty said. "We've just been trying to get him to do what the doctor said."

"We know that," Mama said. "And Wayne knows that, too. He's just stubborn and too proud for his own good. He doesn't understand the stress he's putting on you. Betty, you'd better take care of yourself, too. If you need to talk, day or night, or if you need me to come over and kick Wayne McKay in the seat of his sassy pants, you call me, you hear?"

My mother-in-law smiled, and I heard the men tossing around names I recognized as football players. We lit the candles on the cake and I carried the cake in, followed by my mother-in-law carrying plates and Mama carrying forks and napkins.

I set the cake plate on the buffet and we all joined in as Mama started singing "Happy Birthday." While the rest of us sang "Dad," "Daddy Wayne," or "Wayne," Mama warbled "You old goat."

My father-in-law opened his gift from us, some kind of attachment for the drill press in his workshop that Larry Joe had ordered. He seemed pleased when he opened the oversized box from Mama and Earl that contained a ball cap with the logo of his favorite football team; one of those big, foam hands signifying his team is Number One; and a whistle he can blow whenever he disagrees with the referees. That one will probably wear on Miss Betty's nerves after a while.

After Daddy Wayne had opened his gifts, he thanked everyone with a sheepish look and my mother-in-law started serving the birthday cake.

We talked about the upcoming Halloween fundraiser and how Christmas would be here before you know it as we savored Miss Betty's double fudge chocolate cake.

Suddenly, Daddy Wayne went all quiet, set his plate down, sat up ramrod straight in his chair, and slapped his hand to the middle of his chest. We all froze as we watched him with concern. Larry Joe leaned over and put his hand on his dad's shoulder.

"Daddy, are you okay?"

Just then my father-in-law let loose a roaring belch that practically rattled the windows, followed by a look of relief.

"Ah, I feel better now," he said.

"Wayne McKay, don't you dare scare me like that again," Miss Betty said.

We all relaxed and started laughing. In a bit, we finished up our cake and said our good nights.

On the way home I noticed a number of houses had put up Halloween decorations since I last drove past. Some were as simple as a lighted jack-o'-lantern by the door or a strand of orange lights strung along the porch railing. One house, though, had gone all out this year. A giant spider web adorned the front door, and a life-size inflatable witch stood beside a large cauldron on the front porch. Orange light strands framed the door and wrapped the porch columns. Plastic bats and ghosts hung from a tree, and the front yard was filled with plastic tombstones.

"I don't remember that house ever being decorated for Halloween before," I said.

"New people live there," Larry Joe said. "I remember seeing a moving van there a few weeks back.

As we pulled into our driveway, I couldn't help but note that our house was devoid of any seasonal decorations, although our slightly dilapidated Victorian had a certain scary gothic vibe that was perfectly suited to Halloween even without decorations.

After we'd gone inside, Larry Joe switched on the TV in the den to watch the news. I headed upstairs, dressed for bed, and gave Di a quick call.

I filled her in on the birthday dinner and our little family drama.

"Hopefully your father-in-law will start coming to terms with his need to take things a little easier," she said.

"I hope so. I know when he blows up like that, Miss Betty worries he'll have another heart attack," I said. "I tell her he's probably more likely to have a heart attack if he holds it all in."

"That's true," Di said. "It's exciting to think you'll have a new little niece or nephew in a couple of weeks. Have Emma and Hobie picked out names?"

"Not sure for a girl, but if it's a boy they're going to name him Winfield Hobart Phillips the Third," I said.

"Does the world really need three of them?"

"I don't know," I admitted. "They plan to call him 'Trey.'"

"That's a cute name, anyway," she said. In a moment she added, "Liv, I've been thinking about Lucinda. Nell and Sindhu may be crazy, but I think they may also be onto something."

"Like what?"

"Like Lucinda and Pierce's little lunch meeting. They may have been at Ole Miss at the same time, but there's got to be more to it than two old college chums reminiscing. And their most obvious connection is Morgan. Pierce was sleeping with her, and Lucinda accepted Morgan's invitation to speak at the retreat, seemingly out of the blue. Something about the whole setup stinks."

"I agree," I said. "But I have no idea how to discover Lucinda's true motivations. We might turn up something if we searched her room, but I'm not inclined to try that, since Nell and Sindhu already got caught and since I agreed with Lucinda about how that was inappropriate behavior."

"I was actually thinking about a more direct approach," Di said. "Let's tell Lucinda we happened to see her meeting Pierce and find out what she has to say."

"Why would Lucinda even talk to us?"

"Seems to me she kind of owes you after dragging you into the whole Nell and Sindhu drama."

"*I* think she owes me. But I'm not sure if Lucinda or her obnoxious assistant will see it that way."

"Oh, by the way, I asked Dave about the phone call to Naomi," Di said. "Besides the two businessmen and the old lady who obsessively checks her bank account, all of whom other bank employees confirmed talking to, the only person who called around that time was Morgan. And she calls the bank regularly to check in—and to talk to Daddy."

"Did Dave confirm who Morgan talked to?"

"He didn't say," Di said. "But we know Morgan didn't kill herself."

"No, but if Morgan is the only person who could have made the prank call—and Naomi didn't just make it up, which neither of us believes she did—it must mean Morgan didn't want Naomi at the retreat for some reason. And that reason could be connected to why Morgan was murdered."

Chapter 15

Monday morning Larry Joe left for work, leaving me alone with my coffee and my thoughts. No matter how hard I tried to occupy my mind with other matters, the idea that Morgan must have made that cruel prank call to Naomi kept insinuating itself into my thoughts.

Finally, another idea occurred to me. It was Monday, which meant the bank was closed and Naomi would be at home. As a small-town, family-owned bank, Dixie Savings and Loan still kept bankers hours, or at least a twenty-first-century version of them. It's open nine AM to six PM during the week, plus a half day on Saturday and extended hours on Wednesday evenings. But it's still closed on Mondays, as well as Sundays, except for the drive-through ATM. I seem to remember when I was a kid the bank actually closed at three o'clock in the afternoon on weekdays.

Dave might not be curious, but I certainly was. I decided to seize the opportunity to talk to Naomi privately. I'd drop by her house to see if I could find out what reason Morgan might have had to want her out of the way for the retreat. I thought it would look less suspicious if I didn't come empty-handed, so I set about making some banana pudding to take with me. Using boxed vanilla pudding and overripe bananas, I whipped together the banana pudding in less than thirty minutes. I put it in the freezer to quickly chill while I showered and got dressed. I decided I'd use the pretext that PWAD needed to elect a new president and ask Naomi if she had any opinions on the matter. Since Naomi is never at a loss for words, it was a safe bet she'd have something to say about it.

With freshly made banana pudding in hand, I rang the doorbell. Naomi answered the door.

"Well, this is a surprise," she said. "Please, come in."

I stepped onto the white carpet in Naomi's living room, which had shelves lined with Hummel figurines.

"I've been meaning to bring something by for you since you had that awful scare about your sister. And I also wanted to ask you about the appropriate time and procedure to replace Morgan as president of PWAD."

"I thank you," Naomi said. "That's very kind of you. Come on through to the kitchen. I appreciate the dessert—and banana pudding is a favorite of mine."

She offered and I accepted a cup of coffee. I could see there was still half a pot's worth. I declined her offer of banana pudding, but she dished up a generous helping for herself.

"*Mmm*, this is wonderful," she said.

"I'm glad you like it."

I decided to ask Naomi about a new replacement for the PWAD president position—about which, as I'd suspected, she had plenty to say—before broaching the more delicate matter of the bogus phone call.

After we'd chatted for a bit and she seemed to be enjoying a sugar rush from the banana pudding, it was as good a time as any to delve into the Morgan question.

"Naomi, did you talk to Morgan at all the day she died?"

"I don't think so," she said.

"You didn't have any contact with her?"

"No," Naomi said. "Why do you ask?"

"I don't know if I should even tell you this, but . . ."

"What is it, Liv?"

"Well, I overheard Dave and Ted talking," I lied. "And they checked all the phone records and confirmed who phoned the bank and who talked to whom around the time you received the prank call, and . . ."

"And?"

"Morgan is the one who made the call."

"That's not possible," Naomi said, looking truly surprised. "I know there are plenty of people who had problems with Morgan, but I've never had anything but a good relationship with her. Known her virtually all her life."

"I'm sorry, Naomi."

"They really know this for certain?" Naomi said, misty-eyed.

"I'm afraid so," I said. "There were only a handful of phone calls to the bank during that time."

"I can't even imagine why Morgan would want to do something so hurtful," she said. "I've never given her any cause."

"Naomi, what Morgan did to you was certainly hurtful," I said. "But maybe that wasn't *why* she did it. Maybe that was merely an unavoidable consequence."

"What do you mean?"

"What if for some reason she wanted to keep you away from the retreat?" I said. "Because, other than hurting you, that would seem to be the most likely reason for her to make such a phone call. Your missing the retreat was certainly the outcome."

Naomi looked puzzled.

"Is there anything you knew or heard or noticed recently about Morgan or bank business or one of Morgan's boyfriends? Did you overhear Morgan making an appointment or having an angry conversation? Anything like that?"

Naomi sat silent for a long moment with a faraway look.

"Try to think, Naomi. If there is anything along those lines, anything at all, it could have something to do with Morgan's murder."

"I didn't talk to Morgan on Friday," Naomi said. "I guess the last words I heard her speak were on Friday, or maybe it was Thursday, I don't know. Anyway, I was walking past her office and dropped some files. I bent down to pick them up and overheard Morgan talking on the phone. She said something about patents pending and they should be able to start manufacturing early next year. I have no idea what it was about. I assumed it was concerning some bank investment or personal investment of Morgan's. But when she noticed me she walked over and closed the door."

The mention of patents and manufacturing sounded a lot like what Nell had mentioned about Morgan's proposal for Jasmine's anti-aging cream. But since Jasmine wasn't interested in Morgan's plans, maybe Morgan was scheming to somehow circumvent her and sell or patent the formula without Jasmine's consent. If that was true, it would have given Jasmine a strong motive for murder.

I knew I really needed to share this information with Dave, even though it would seem to secure the noose around Jasmine's neck. Nell and Sindhu would never forgive me.

I went to the office and tried to lose myself in work. After a phone call to straighten out a vendor who had sent me a bill for more than we'd originally agreed upon, I remembered I was supposed to try to set up a meeting with Lucinda about her rendezvous with Pierce Davenport. I wasn't looking forward to talking to Mitzi, but I finally worked up the courage to call the hotel.

Naturally, my pal Mitzi answered the phone. She wasn't eager to surrender her position as gatekeeper or set up a meeting with Lucinda without knowing all the particulars. But she eventually acquiesced when I strongly implied it would be to Lucinda's advantage to do so.

Mitzi hung up in a huff. She called back a short time later to tell me Lucinda would give me a few minutes of her valuable time tomorrow afternoon. I was instructed to arrive at Lucinda's suite promptly at four PM.

I texted Di to let her know the time.

I'd just about tied up the loose ends from the Dodds' party and had prepared my final bill for them when I got a call from Dave. My first thought was that he'd heard about my visit to Naomi. But I was wrong.

"Liv, I'd like you to do me a favor," he said.

"I always do my best to cooperate with the authorities."

"Nell and Sindhu finally wore me down. I told them they could come visit Jasmine at the jail this afternoon about three-thirty," he said. "The D.A. said he didn't think it would do any harm. Anyway, I'd appreciate it if you tagged along for their visit."

"I suppose I can sit in. Although I'm not sure why you need me there. I kinda doubt she's going to make a confession about killing Morgan."

"It's not so much Jasmine I'm worried about," he said. "I don't want Nell and Sindhu hatching some crazy scheme."

Why does everyone in town seem to think it's my responsibility to keep an eye on Nell and Sindhu? I thought. Fortunately, I stopped myself from saying it out loud, since I didn't really want to have to explain their stalking and room-searching activities to Dave.

I guess I was caught up in my thoughts for a bit, because Dave asked, "Are you still there?"

"Yeah, I'm here. How do you want to play this? Should I just show up or should I call Nell?"

"I think it would look better if you called Nell and told her you heard about the visit and would like to go with them," he said.

"Right. I'll see you later," I said before hanging up the phone.

Nell was agreeable to my coming along to visit Jasmine. She seems to think I have some magic powers of persuasion with the sheriff. As if.

I met Sindhu and Nell just outside the sheriff's office. Nell was carrying a paper bag, and Sindhu held a covered plate.

"It seems I'm the only one who showed up empty-handed," I said.

"I've just got some clean clothes that Dylan asked me to deliver," Nell said.

"These are some chocolate chip cookies Darsha helped me to make for Jasmine," Sindhu chimed in.

"Sheriff Dave said it would be okay to bring some sweet treats," Nell said. "We figured cookies would be a safe bet. If we brought a cake, he'd probably search it to see if we'd hidden a file or a knife in it."

Dave met us in the lobby and showed us to the interrogation room. We took a seat, and a moment later he brought in Jasmine. After hugs all around, we settled into chairs at the table in the center of the room. I didn't know if Dave was listening in or watching through the two-way mirror, but I knew he could if he wanted to.

Nell was obviously aware of this fact, too. She apologized to Jasmine for not having visited sooner.

"It's not that we didn't want to come, hon," she said. "The powers that be wouldn't let us in until now," she said, glaring at the two-way mirror for a moment.

"I know," Jasmine said. "Dylan told me you two had been asking about me and bringing by casseroles and desserts for him. I really appreciate your looking after my guy—and worrying about me."

"What's going on with your case, Jasmine? Do you know what happens next?" I asked.

"At my preliminary hearing the case was bound over to the grand jury. If they return an indictment, I'll have to go to court for the arraignment and enter a plea. After that, I'd go on trial for murder. I can't believe I'm actually saying those words. It still seems so unreal," she said.

"We have to hope it doesn't come to that," I said, trying to sound reassuring.

"It's completely ridiculous that you got arrested to begin with," Nell said.

"It must be very difficult being kept behind bars like this," Sindhu said.

"I'd rather be at home, of course," Jasmine said. "But everyone here has been really nice."

"I can't believe they're keeping you locked up here without a snowball's chance of making bail," Nell said indignantly, casting an angry look toward the mirror again. "You haven't been convicted of anything."

"I'm sure if the sheriff continues his investigations, he will discover evidence that proves you are innocent," Sindhu said in a confident voice.

Jasmine gave her a doubtful smile. Looking at Jasmine, I couldn't help thinking that here was one of the most optimistic and upbeat women I'd ever met. But spending a week in jail, and facing the specter of a much longer prison term, had taken the shine off her sunny optimism.

"Jasmine," I said. "The police know the poison that killed Morgan is from that plant, what's it called?"

"Hemlock water-dropwort," she said.

"Yeah, that," I said. "But you use some of that in your anti-aging cream, and that cream is really popular. Women all over town use it. Could someone have put a little of that cream into Morgan's tea to poison her?"

"No," Jasmine said. "I'm afraid not."

She explained that the cream contains only a tiny amount of the hemlock water-dropwort. Apparently, even if someone consumed a whole jar of the stuff it wouldn't be deadly.

"Besides," she added, "hemlock water drop-wort is naturally sweet-tasting, as are the other ingredients in the cream, so I add a bit of motherwort—a really bitter herb. It's harmless, but it tastes so bad that if a child or a pet accidently ate some of it, they wouldn't eat more than a bite. So Morgan couldn't have eaten or drunk something with the cream in it without tasting it."

"You hear that, Sheriff?" Nell stood and talked to

the mirror once again. "Jasmine goes to great pains just to make sure nobody accidently gets a little sick. That really sounds like a cold-blooded killer, doesn't it?"

"Nell, please calm yourself," Sindhu said. "The sheriff might cut short our visit if you agitate him."

Nell sat down, but continued to fume silently.

"Jasmine, tell me about this proposal Morgan made to you to have your face cream manufactured," I said.

She told me what I'd basically already heard. Morgan wanted to finance the manufacture of the anti-aging cream in exchange for a fat cut, but Jasmine wasn't interested. Jasmine's idea of expansion was to extend her distribution network through a few other herbalists she knows personally.

"If that poison didn't come from your cream and you didn't make it from the plant at your place—which we know you didn't," Nell said, "it had to come from someone who could get hold of some of that poison. We know it's not easy to come by here in the states, but it grows wild in parts of Europe, right?"

"That's true," Jasmine said. "In fact, I've read that some cattle have died from eating the roots of it growing along streams in Britain."

"Well, what little globe-trotter do we know who's recently filmed episodes of her show in England?" Nell said with a cat-that-ate-the-canary look on her face.

"Yes!" Sindhu said. "Lucinda could have obtained the poison plant on her travels."

"I hate to place a damper on your enthusiasm," I said. "But for Lucinda to choose this particular plant in order to frame Jasmine, she'd have to have known Jasmine had the plant. If Lucinda didn't know and she chose this poison at random to kill Morgan, that would be an awfully big coincidence."

Jasmine looked forlorn when we said our good-byes. Later that night, while I was lying under the covers in my comfy bed next to my snoring husband, I couldn't stop thinking about Jasmine sleeping alone in a jail cell.

Chapter 16

Larry Joe took some time away from the office Tuesday morning to help me with a special project. We drove his truck to a metal fabrication shop just a few miles outside Dixie.

Mr. Goddard, the owner of the company, also happened to be an elder at Winette's church. Nathan Sweet, my landlord and Winette's boss; Winette's son, Marcus; and I had cooked up a surprise for Winette. I was so excited, I could hardly wait to see it.

We parked in front of a metal building with two large bays connected to a windowed office area. Mr. Goddard waved us over to the first of the bays, open to the outside with its huge garage door raised.

"Howdy," Mr. Goddard said, peeling the glove off his right hand before shaking hands with Larry Joe and me. "Come on back and take a look. I think y'all are going to be pleased. I'm pretty happy with it."

We followed him into a small, carpeted room. He picked up a cloth-wrapped sign that was leaning against a wall and set it up on a long table. I felt butterflies in my stomach as he unwrapped it.

"Oh, Mr. Goddard," I said, tears welling up in my eyes. "It's just beautiful."

Larry Joe wrapped his arm around my shoulders and gave me a squeeze.

"That's mighty fine work, Mr. Goddard," Larry Joe said.

"Thank you, kindly," he said. "I admit I'm right proud of how it turned out."

We stood for a moment admiring the custom-made sign, featuring the Residential Rehab logo in mirror-finish stainless steel lettering against a brushed steel background. Marcus, who's an architecture major in his sophomore year at college, had designed the handsome logo, which is on all the stationery and promotional materials for RR. At my suggestion he designed the plans and consulted with Mr. Goddard on fabricating the sign. Mr. Goddard donated his time and equipment to make the sign, and Mr. Sweet paid for the materials.

The craftsman rewrapped the sign in a large chamois cloth, and Larry Joe carried it out and loaded it into the bed of his truck.

I couldn't wait to see Winette's face when she saw it. Since Winette, as the chairman of Residential Rehab, often holds meetings with volunteers and benefactors in the conference area at Sweet Deal Realty, Mr. Sweet had agreed it would be appropriate to hang a sign with the RR logo in the office. The sign could also be transported to special events, and even outdoor gatherings since it's made of stainless steel. I had already arranged a spot for the sign to be displayed at the entrance to the murder mystery dinner at the country club on Halloween night.

Larry Joe carried the somewhat unwieldy sign into the office at Sweet Deal Realty. Mr. Sweet had already placed one of the hangers on the wall but had waited to make sure it was perfectly positioned before attaching the final hardware. Larry Joe helped him, and the two of them lifted and hung the 44" × 38" sign on the back wall behind the conference table.

The previous afternoon I had casually inquired to Winette about her schedule to make sure we could surprise her.

Larry Joe and I loosely draped the sign with the cloth so that Mr. Sweet and I could do a dramatic unveiling for Winette when she arrived. Then my husband gave me a kiss and headed off to work.

"I sent Winette a text telling her to let me know when she was heading this way," Mr. Sweet said in his usual deadpan manner.

"Won't that make her suspicious?"

"Naw. I'm always asking her to stop by the bank or the title company to pick up or check on something. I figure she should be finished with her meeting any time now."

I poured myself a cup of coffee and sat down behind Winette's desk. Mr. Sweet regaled me with the details of his latest retail development project.

In a few minutes the phone on his desk rang.

"Oh, hi, Winette," he said. "Yeah, I thought I needed you to run by the title company, but I talked to them just a few minutes ago and we're good to go. So you can just come on to the office unless you've got other business. All right, good."

He hung up the phone and turned to me. "She'll be here in about five minutes."

I felt a rush of excitement. Mr. Sweet and I both leapt up from our chairs as Winette came through the front door.

"What are you two up to?" she asked in a wary tone.

"Liv here has a little surprise for you," Mr. Sweet said.

"Winette, come this way, please," I said, walking over to the sign. Mr. Sweet ambled over to the conference area, but kept a distance from Winette and me.

I lifted the cloth off the sign and quickly looked over to Winette for her reaction. She clasped both hands to her face, covering her mouth and nose and shaking her head.

"I don't know what to say," Winette said. "It's beautiful."

"It's portable, too," I pointed out. "You can take it to events, and I already have a spot reserved for it at the fund-raiser this weekend."

She stepped over and hugged me as tears streamed down both our faces.

"I should be mad at your for messing up my makeup like this," she said, grabbing a tissue from the box on the conference table and dabbing mascara streaks from under her eyes.

Then she said in that down-to-business voice of hers, "As much as I love it, I hope you didn't dip too much into our fund-raiser money for it."

"I didn't dip into our fund-raiser money at all. Marcus worked out the design with Mr. Goddard, who donated his labor and expertise to fabricate the sign, and Mr. Sweet paid for materials," I said, looking over to see that Mr. Sweet had disappeared into his back office.

"That old coot. He's really just an old softie under that gruff exterior," Winette said with affection. Then she raised her voice a bit, and added, "You're not fooling anybody with your tough-guy act. I know you can hear me in there."

"Don't you two have work to do?" he asked before closing the door.

When I left to go upstairs to my office, Winette was still admiring the handsome sign.

Di had packed a change of clothes and drove directly to my house after she got off work at three-thirty. She slipped into her civilian clothes, and we set off to the hotel.

Lucinda's beefy bodyguard met us in the lobby. At first he wasn't agreeable to allowing Di to go up with us in the elevator, since he had been informed that only I was meeting with Lucinda. But I convinced him that I had some information of interest to Lucinda and the lady with me was the source of that information.

We walked down the hall and entered the sitting room of Lucinda's suite. She invited Di and me to sit on the love seat while she sat down across from us in a plump club chair. Mitzi was loitering in an interior doorway until Lucinda shooed her away.

"I don't have a lot of time, Liv. But since you've been helpful during my visit I agreed to see you," Lucinda said. "What's this all about?"

"This is my friend, Di Souther," I said. "I'll come

right to the point. She shared with me that she saw you having lunch with Pierce Davenport in a private dining room at Red's on Sunday."

I paused, hoping for a response, a confession, some juicy details.

Lucinda simply said, "And . . ."

"And," Di picked up the conversation, "since I knew Liv was somewhat acquainted with you, I asked her advice about what I should do with this information, as it might be relevant to an ongoing murder investigation."

Lucinda shifted her gaze from Di to me. "Liv, am I to understand that I'm still being followed? First by that hairdresser and hotel clerk, and now by this friend of yours?"

"In the first place, Sindhu is not a clerk; she and her husband own this hotel. Second, Di was not following you," I lied. "She simply happened to be in the little shopping center across the street from Red's when she saw you and Pierce arrive. She thought it was you, but went inside the restaurant to get a closer look. Face it, Lucinda, you're a celebrity. It's hard for you to go anywhere unnoticed. And around these parts, someone driving a Bentley doesn't exactly blend in with the scenery."

"I guess not," Lucinda said. "It's not that mysterious. Pierce and I went to college together, along with Morgan, of course," she said, dismissively.

"You can see how this little college reunion might not seem so innocent in light of the not-so-well-kept secret of Morgan's ongoing relationship with Pierce," I said. "I just wanted to hear you out before I decide what, if anything, I should tell the sheriff— or Pierce's wife."

"I don't care what you tell Pierce's wife, and I doubt he does, either," Lucinda said. "As for Sheriff Davidson, I think he and I have a pretty good rapport," she said, cocking her head to one side and twirling a lock of blond hair around her finger.

"I doubt your rapport with the sheriff is quite as cozy as Di's," I said, punctuating the word *rapport* with air quotes. I looked over at Di, who put on a perfect little Mona Lisa smile right on cue.

"I see," Lucinda said, exhaling a heavy sigh of resignation. "I don't appreciate being quizzed on personal matters, but I would like to avoid publicity if possible. What exactly is it you'd like to know?"

"Just the truth," I said. "You could start with why you really agreed to speak at the PWAD retreat. And don't give me that line about you and Morgan being old college roommates."

"You can believe it or not," Lucinda said, "but that's basically what it came down to. It's true that Morgan and I haven't been close in the past few years, but we were close while we were in college together. This probably doesn't speak well for me, but Morgan and I were actually a lot alike back then. We thought it was great sport to steal boyfriends from our sorority sisters, including from each other.

"So when Morgan started dating Pierce, who was pretty much big man on campus, I immediately set my sights on breaking them up. And I did.

"Only that time instead of laughing about it, Morgan was really and truly hurt. She was actually in love with Pierce and believed the feeling was mutual."

Lucinda went on to explain that after Pierce, who was a couple of years ahead of them, graduated and moved away, Morgan tried to pretend it was no big deal. The two of them went back to stealing boyfriends for fun, but things were never quite the same between them.

"I remember later, when a mutual friend told us Pierce had gotten married, Morgan put up a brave front. But later I heard her sobbing in the dorm bathroom," she said. "I wasn't at all surprised to hear that Pierce had married a U.S. senator's daughter. He'd been president of the Associated Student Body and had political ambitions even in college."

Lucinda told us that a couple of months ago Morgan had sent some fabric swatches in the mail and asked her which she'd prefer for a bridesmaid's dress.

"I took the bait," Lucinda said. "I called her up and asked her who the lucky guy was. She said it was Pierce.

"I said I thought Pierce was already married, and she told me that he wouldn't be for much longer. Then she launched into telling me about all the plans they were making for the future, including Pierce having his sights set on moving into the governor's mansion someday.

"She was absolutely giddy. She told me it had always been Pierce and she knew they'd eventually end up together. She asked me if I could come for the retreat so the two of us could start planning the wedding. I knew Morgan well enough to know she didn't have many female friends, which explained why she was asking a college roommate she hadn't talked to in at least two years to be her maid of honor.

"I'd always felt badly about breaking up Morgan and Pierce. If I'd realized at the time she actually had feelings for the guy, I never would have gone after him. I figured being in her wedding was the least I could do to make it up to her," Lucinda said, finally relaxing and slumping down in her chair.

"That still doesn't really explain why you met with Pierce," I said. "What did you two talk about?" I almost added "for over an hour," but caught myself. I didn't want to admit we really were spying on them.

"I guess I wanted to apologize for how I acted in college, coming between him and Morgan," she said. "Mostly, we just reminisced about our college days and shared some memories of Morgan. She really could be a lot of fun.

"We talked about parties and a wild spring break trip a bunch of us took to Pensacola. Pierce remembered the dress Morgan wore to his fraternity formal, which was ridiculously revealing even by frat standards. We talked about how Morgan always drank those health shakes and went jogging every morning, even after a late night out. She was a health freak even back then. Pierce said he couldn't help thinking about that when he first heard about Morgan's death. It struck him as ironic for such a health nut to die from drinking herbal tea.

"And, of course, he went on and on about his exploits on the football field. Pierce always had a big ego. Silly college girls, like Morgan and me, chasing after him probably didn't help matters."

"Did he seem broken up over Morgan's death?" I asked.

"Not really," she said. "But then Pierce isn't really the kind of man to display his emotions—you know, tough guy, ex-jock."

"What did he say about his wedding plans with Morgan?" Di asked.

"He said it was all complete fiction, that he and I both knew Morgan had a penchant for making things up—which is true. He said he and Morgan had always enjoyed each other in a romantic sense, but they had never talked seriously about marriage—in college or since. He seemed to think Morgan was just playing me, making up the whole wedding thing to get me to do her bidding, and making herself look like a big shot by roping her celebrity pal into speaking at her little nothing businesswomen's retreat.

"That's the truth. Tell the sheriff whatever you like," she added.

Lucinda showed us the door, and I left feeling more confused than ever. Di and I walked silently to my SUV.

"I tend to believe Lucinda's telling the truth," I said, as we pulled away from the hotel.

"Me too," Di said. "Then again, she does make a living putting on a phony psychic act and trying to convince people that ghosts are real. Do you think I should tell Dave what she said—on the off chance he'd actually listen?"

"Not yet," I said. "Wait until after I have a chance to talk to Bryn. I'll try to talk to her tomorrow."

"Are you going to tell her about Pierce's meeting with Lucinda?"

"I have a feeling she already knows," I said. "She had to have known about Pierce and Morgan, since everybody else in town did. She'd have to be a fool not to know—and Bryn doesn't strike me as a fool.

Chapter 17

I phoned Bryn first thing Wednesday morning and asked if there was a convenient time I could drop by to talk to her for a few minutes. She said to come by about eleven-thirty, that she had some open time in her schedule before lunch. At 11:20, I locked up and walked over to the chamber of commerce office, located on the back side of town square. It's adjacent to a parking lot shared by the chamber and other offices, as well as the restaurants and businesses that face the courthouse.

I walked into the entry. Bryn's office door was ajar. She stood up and walked around her desk to peek through the door, then motioned for me to come through.

"Hello, Liv," she said. "Have a seat. What can I do for you today?"

I can't say Bryn and I were close, but we had served together on various community projects and committees and I considered her a friend. I felt badly about what I was about to say.

"This isn't exactly a social call, Bryn, so I won't

beat around the bush," I said. "Lucinda Grable claims that Morgan told her Pierce was getting a divorce and that Morgan and Pierce planned to be married. She says Morgan even asked her to be her maid of honor. We also know that Lucinda and Pierce met Sunday afternoon in a private dining room at Red's. Normally, I'd consider this none of my business. But this information could have a bearing on a murder investigation, so I feel obligated to tell the sheriff. Since you and I are friends, I wanted to speak with you first."

"I see," Bryn said. "Well, I have no problem believing Morgan would tell such a tale to Lucinda or anyone else. But if Lucinda did meet with Pierce, which I don't doubt, he would have told her that Morgan's story about getting married was a bunch of nonsense."

"So you knew that Pierce and Morgan were having an affair?"

"Of course I knew," Bryn said. "I'm not a fool. And I even told the sheriff when he interviewed me at the retreat center that I knew about Morgan and Pierce, which I assumed made me a suspect. But while Morgan was obsessed with Pierce, she didn't exactly reserve herself for him alone, so there are plenty of other suspects on that score. And Pierce wasn't faithful to Morgan any more than he is to me."

"Did you know Pierce had also been involved with Lucinda, at least when they were in college?" I asked.

"Oh, sure," she said. "Pierce liked to brag about that once she became a celebrity. Not to me, of course, but I always hear about these things. Some people think it's their Christian duty to inform me of all my husband's misbehavior."

"I'm truly sorry to be one of those people, Bryn," I said sincerely. "But I felt it was only fair to talk to you before going to the sheriff."

"I understand that, Liv," she said. "I don't enjoy talking about this, but I do understand that someone has been arrested for Morgan's murder and some people in town have serious doubts about her guilt. The sheriff has to look at every possibility to make sure an innocent person doesn't go to prison. I frankly have some doubts about Jasmine's guilt myself."

"Why is that?"

"Morgan was really and truly unstable," she said. "She periodically made crazy and even threatening phone calls to me—usually after Pierce had broken things off with her, which he had done again recently.

"The Monday after the retreat there was one of those crazy phone calls on the answering machine here at the office. Here, I'll play it for you. I saved it, just in case," she said before pressing PLAY on the answering machine.

Ghosts are real and you may join them, unless you accept the truth.

Click.

The voice sounded weird and otherworldly. The caller was obviously trying to disguise her voice.

"At first I assumed it was another call from Morgan, but when I looked at the time stamp, I realized the call must have been made after Morgan's death," she said.

"Did you tell the sheriff about this?"

"No. I thought about it, but I figured it was just a prank call. As I said, I've had calls like this before. But I have wondered since then if it could be Lucinda."

"It does sound kind of like that recording of the ghost voice they played for us out in the cemetery at St. Julian's," I said. "I think you should play it for the sheriff."

"Maybe you're right," Bryn said. "I guess I've been trying to avoid thinking about Morgan or the call or the whole murder business. But if there's even a chance it has something to do with Morgan's death, I have an obligation to share it with the sheriff."

Just then, I noticed an odd mist seeping into the room. It grew suddenly thick and surrounded us like a fog around our ankles. It didn't smell like smoke, but we weren't taking any chances. The two of us sprang from our chairs and hurried out the front door.

"What in the world was that? Should we call the fire department?" I said, digging in my purse for my cell phone.

"It doesn't smell like smoke," Bryn said, sniffing near the doorway. "Let me take a peek inside and see."

Bryn took a couple of steps inside the building, craning her neck to see into the office.

"I know this sounds crazy, but it looks like it's gone," Bryn said.

I followed her back into her office and couldn't see a trace of the fog we'd seen just moments before.

"Smoke couldn't have cleared out that fast," Bryn said, shaking her head. "Plus, the smoke alarm didn't go off."

"It was thick around our ankles," I said. "Smoke doesn't act like that. Smoke rises. In fact, they say the safest thing to do in a smoke-filled room is to drop to the floor and crawl out."

"It's gone, the phone call is gone," Bryn suddenly said with disbelief.

"What?"

"The strange phone call," Bryn said. "In fact, all my messages have been erased. Crap."

The green message light I remembered seeing earlier when she played the call was no longer lit up.

I handed Bryn her purse, which was lying on the credenza behind her desk, and motioned for her to follow me out the door.

"It's just hard to believe I accidentally deleted all those messages. I'm always so careful. There were callback numbers on there that I hadn't written down," Bryn said.

"I don't think you accidentally erased them," I said. "But someone did, and that someone could still be hiding in the building. I don't think you should go back in there. I think you should call the sheriff."

"You may be right," Bryn said as we took a few more steps away from the building, closer to the street and the safety of passersby and neighboring buildings.

"Yes, I'm definitely not going back inside the

office today," Bryn said. She gingerly stepped onto the stoop and quickly locked the front door.

"I'm going home," she said. "Our housekeeper, Myrna, is there, and nobody comes around without her noticing. I'll talk to Pierce about what happened. He may want to have someone check the air ducts in the office. I'd feel foolish calling the sheriff if it turns out there's a simple, logical explanation for all this."

"Okay," I said. "And I can back you up as a witness about the phone call, since I heard it, too. I think you should drive straight home."

"Oh, don't worry," Bryn said. "I will."

Bryn got into her sports car and drove away, and I walked back to my office. I was dying to tell Di what Bryn had said and what had happened at her office, but Di doesn't like getting phone calls while she's working, so I decided it would have to wait until tonight.

I fought with my conscience about whether I should phone Dave about the phone call Naomi had overheard about the patents the day Morgan died. I convinced myself to wait one more day. I told myself it was only fair to allow Naomi time to tell the sheriff herself. In the meantime, I decided I would drive out to the greenhouse and talk to Dylan to try to better understand this manufacturing deal Morgan had proposed to Jasmine.

I drove to the nursery just a few miles outside the corporate limits of Dixie. A light wind rattled the trees lining the winding roads, shaking loose leaves in autumnal shades of gold, crimson, and sage that danced into the road and crunched beneath my tires. Green's Plant Center covers several acres, with saplings, young trees, small shrubs, and herbs planted in the ground and in containers. Annuals, seedlings, and more fragile plants are nurtured in two greenhouses. A simple shingled cottage is attached to the smaller of the two greenhouses and serves as office, sales counter, and home to Dylan and Jasmine.

Dylan was walking toward the cottage wearing a lightweight jacket and camo pants and carrying a wide shovel. As I pulled up the gravel driveway, he spotted me and waved. I parked and walked over to him.

"Hi, Dylan. Looks like you've been hard at work."

"Today I've been raking and mulching leaves," he said. "Just finished shoveling some leaves into the fall compost bin." He leaned the shovel against the side of the house and peeled off his thick gardening gloves.

"I'm sure you're carrying a heavy load right now, keeping the business going without Jasmine around," I said. "It can't be easy—for either of you."

"I'm okay. Working keeps me from going crazy right now. It's Jasmine I'm worried about."

I assured Dylan that there were a lot of people who were concerned about Jasmine and convinced of her innocence.

"I don't know if there are a lot of people who believe Jazz is innocent, but I know of at least two," he said. "Nell and Sindhu have brought by a mountain of food for me and have visited Jazz at the jail. I'm vegan, so I can't eat most of the stuff they bring over, but I appreciate the thought."

"I have a really hard time believing that Jasmine could have murdered Morgan," I said. "But I won't lie to you, Dylan. Things don't look good for her. That's why I came by. There's something I wanted to ask you about."

He invited me into the office area at the front of the cottage, and we sat down facing each other on bar stools on opposite sides of the sales counter.

"Jasmine told me she had turned down Morgan's proposal to manufacture her face cream. But did she ever sign any kind of document with Morgan? Something about exploratory or preliminary research or securing a patent on the formula? Anything?"

"She did sign a permission form for a lab to test the formula to determine if it was safe for cosmetic use. Jasmine knew it was safe from using it personally for almost three years, including two years of lots of customers using it with no adverse effects. But she liked the idea of having its safety confirmed by a lab," he said.

"Are you sure this didn't give Morgan some legal rights beyond just the testing?" I asked.

"Yeah," he said. "I looked over the details real close—I actually took two years of pre-law classes before we moved to Dixie. It was a pretty straight-forward form."

"Nell told me Morgan kept after Jasmine about manufacturing the face cream, didn't want to take *no* for an answer," I said.

"Yeah, she'd back off and then come in from another angle," Dylan said. "She even offered to give part of the proceeds to some 'Save the Planet' charity of Jasmine's choosing.

"Then just a few days before the retreat, Morgan came by and brought Jazz a big basket filled with organic chocolates and candies and apologized for being such a pain. She said she understood and respected Jasmine's decision and that she wouldn't bring it up again. She sounded sincere, but Jazz and I obviously still had our doubts."

I fell quiet for a long moment, and Dylan offered me a cup of tea, which I accepted. While he prepared the tea, I mulled over everything Dylan had said as well as what Naomi had overheard Morgan saying, and tried to make some sense of it all.

Chapter 18

I made it home in time to whip up some spaghetti carbonara for supper. Larry Joe likes it—honestly, he likes anything with bacon in it. So I thought it might soften the blow of my leaving him to eat supper by himself. And I hoped that with his mouth full he wouldn't be able to quiz me about what I was up to, since I had a guilty conscience and wasn't very skilled at putting on a poker face.

I tossed a salad to go with the pasta and ate a few bites of the freshly prepared spaghetti dish, then set the table for Larry Joe. As the clock ticked toward five-thirty, I was beginning to think I'd have to just leave him a note. But about that time he came through the kitchen door.

"Hey, hon. I smell bacon," he said with a smile. I was retrieving a glass for his iced tea when he slipped up behind me and wrapped me in a bear hug.

He washed his hands at the kitchen sink while I plated up his dinner.

"Aren't you eating?" Larry Joe asked after noticing

only one plate on the table and assuming, of course, that it was his.

"I'm afraid you're on your own for supper tonight," I said. "I'm going to change clothes and drive to Holly's. I'll probably go by Di's, too. But I won't be late."

While I didn't out-and-out lie to Larry Joe, I wasn't exactly being truthful, either. I was going by Di's, and technically I also planned to drive past Holly's house on my way home.

After changing into my burgling clothes, I grabbed a Diet Coke from the fridge and gave Larry Joe a quick kiss before heading out the door.

Di was waiting on her front deck when I pulled into the driveway. She walked over and got into the driver's seat of her car, so I killed the engine, walked over, and got into the passenger's seat of her Buick.

"I think my car will be less conspicuous in Daisy's neighborhood," she said.

I found it hard to believe that her vintage jalopy would be inconspicuous in any neighborhood, but I took her word for it.

"I started having misgivings earlier today about snooping around Daisy's house," Di said. "I actually decided just to knock on her front door and ask her to join me and some other yoga chicks for coffee after class. Talk to her face-to-face."

"What happened?"

"Turned me down flat, saying she had to get home right after class. Brushed me off like I was a Jehovah's Witness, practically slammed the door in my face. She definitely acts like someone who's got something to hide."

Di drove quickly to Daisy's neighborhood. We wanted as much time as possible to snoop and still be long gone before she arrived home from yoga class.

We drove past her house and confirmed that Daisy's car wasn't in the driveway. Since she rarely ventures out, we knew this meant the coast was clear. Di parked just around the corner of Daisy's block. The corner house had a towering boxwood hedge. We reasoned this would hide the car, and even though it meant we had to walk past three houses to get to Daisy's place, we could duck behind a shrub or tree or even retreat into someone's carport in a pinch. If Daisy came home early or one of the neighbors caught a glimpse of us and decided to call the cops, at least they wouldn't have an easy time giving a description of the car or recording the license plate number.

It was twilight, with long shadows falling across the lawns and sidewalks. We didn't spot anyone out in their yards or on the sidewalk on either side of the street. Di grabbed a dark canvas tote bag lying on the seat between us, which she said contained a few tools she hoped we wouldn't need to use.

I was starting to wonder about Di's definition of peeking in through the windows.

Clad in dark clothing, we walked quickly and quietly to Daisy's house and darted into the backyard from the shady side of the house.

The blinds were all closed and the back door was locked. I was about to dig through our bag of tricks when we noticed there was a doggie door at the bottom of the back door.

After looking at each other for a moment, Di handed me the bag and dropped down on all fours.

"Wait," I whispered as I squatted next to her. "What if there's a watchdog?"

"I haven't seen or heard a dog since Daisy moved in," Di said. "This door must be from when the Woodleys lived here. Their dog, Boomer, died a couple years ago."

Di wriggled through the doggie door. Things were going fine until she got to her hips. She's slim, but her hips flared just enough to stop her from slipping through.

Di backed out and said quietly, "Let's try this again."

She turned around and started to slide through the opening, faceup this time. She still got caught at the hips, but was far enough through to reach up and unlock the deadbolt.

Di slid out, stood up, and turned the knob. She stepped inside the kitchen and I followed haltingly. I felt like a great big hypocrite breaking into Daisy's house after the scolding I gave Nell and Sindhu for searching Lucinda's room. But I didn't let a little twinge of conscience stop me.

I took a small flashlight out of the bag, but Di grabbed my hand.

"Let's not use any more light than we have to," she whispered. "Mrs. Roper might see it."

She tilted up the slats on the back door mini blinds just enough to let the last rays of the setting sun stream in.

Nothing looked out of place in the kitchen, only a few dishes stacked in the sink. I peeked in the refrigerator. Nothing unusual there: some takeout containers of Chinese food, probably delivered since she doesn't go out much; a couple of yogurts; and the wilted remains of a tossed salad.

The sparsely furnished living room housed a leather sofa, a television, and a coffee table with a laptop computer sitting on it. On the side table next to the lamp was a graduation photo of a young woman standing with an older man and woman I presumed to be her parents.

"Is that Daisy?" I whispered.

Di took a look at the photo.

"Yeah, her hair's a little shorter now," Di said. "But that's her."

We peeked into the first of two bedrooms, with an unmade bed and clothes strewn on the floor. The bathroom was bare, except for a tropical print shower curtain and a toothbrush lying on the pedestal sink.

In the back bedroom, empty boxes were tossed in the far corner. Along the wall directly across from the door, a long table sat below the window. This single window had both the blinds and lined curtains drawn, so we couldn't see much.

"Turn on the flashlight," Di said in a low voice. "I don't think much light is going to escape through that window."

I hung the bag on the doorknob and fished out the flashlight. Scanning the beam of light across the tabletop, we saw a few knife-like instruments, some straws, and some laboratory-looking glass tubes, along with gloves and tissue.

We both stepped forward to get a closer look. Then suddenly from behind us we heard an unsettling hissing noise. I spun around and spotted some boxes or cages draped in dark cloth.

Di and I made a hasty retreat, both of us squeezing through the doorway at the same time.

"Let's get out of here," Di said, breathily.

We were of one mind on that point.

Once in the kitchen, I doused the light and dropped the flashlight in the bag, and Di closed the blinds after a quick look out. We left and pulled the door shut behind us. We took a quick peek around from the corner of the house and then power walked to the car. Neither of us uttered a word until we'd driven three or four blocks away from Daisy's house.

"Was that a snake we heard?" I said, my heart still pounding in my chest. I couldn't believe I was having another close encounter with a snake just two weeks after doing battle with the one on Mama's porch.

"I don't know, but it sure sounded like one, and I wasn't about to hang around to find out," Di said.

"And what about all that equipment on the table? Maybe she defanged her pet snake," I said, groping for a plausible explanation to the implements we'd seen.

"That setup looks like some kind of ongoing project," Di said. "I'm pretty sure you only have to defang a snake once."

"I suppose snakes eat insects," I said, thinking about what Mrs. Roper had said about Daisy collecting insects from the yard.

"If they're big enough, they can eat whatever they dang well please," Di said.

I nodded and thought that over for an uncomfortable moment.

"We may need to give some more thought to this Daisy and Ted matchup," she added.

After we arrived at Di's place and said our good nights, I hopped in my car and started driving home. I was almost to my street when it occurred to me that I had forgotten to drive past Holly's house in the elaborate ruse I'd constructed to convince myself I wasn't technically lying to Larry Joe.

As I drove toward Holly's place I realized in all the excitement I had also forgotten to tell Di about what happened today at Bryn's office. I briefly considered driving back to Di's, but figured we'd both had a full day. I decided to just go home.

Larry Joe and I watched an episode of some renovation show on HGTV. I couldn't help noticing how they managed to finish remodeling a house in a matter of months instead of years.

We were both yawning and called it an early night. Larry Joe was gently snoring within minutes of getting into bed. I lay awake for the longest time before drifting off. During the night, a nightmare of that odd hissing sound menacing me from a dark corner woke me up from a sound sleep. I went downstairs and raided the fridge. After comforting myself with some leftover carbonara I went back to bed and finally fell into a fitful sleep.

Chapter 19

After a busy morning at the office on Thursday, I took time out to eat a quick lunch of tomato soup and a grilled cheese sandwich at the diner. As I was walking back across the square to my office, Dave came charging down the courthouse steps and called out my name in that bad-cop voice that let me know I was in trouble.

"Liv McKay, when are you going to learn to keep you nose out of my murder investigation?"

Before I could answer, he continued, "And just when were you planning to tell me about your little conversation with Naomi Mawbry and what she overheard outside Morgan's office?"

"Which is it, Sheriff Davidson? Do you want me to keep my nose out of your investigation or tell you what I find out?" I said, peeved that he wanted to have it both ways.

I could tell he was mad, because his nostrils were flaring.

"Maybe you decided not to tell me what Naomi had to say because if Morgan was going behind

Jasmine's back to patent her face cream, that would make things look even worse for Jasmine."

"Dave, I'll admit I'm not convinced of Jasmine's guilt. But unlike Nell and Sindhu I'm not convinced of her innocence, either. I certainly wouldn't try to hide evidence either way. I was just giving Naomi the opportunity to tell you herself," I said.

"That so?" Dave said. "It seems to me you—and Miss Souther—make up the rules as you go along depending on what suits you at the moment."

He made me so angry that I wanted to give him a good dressing down. But since he and Di seemed to be going through a rough patch in their relationship lately, I decided to go to bat for her instead.

"Dave, I went to talk to Naomi all on my own. I didn't discuss it at all with Di. So don't let your beef with me cause any distance between you and her."

"I don't have to. She does a pretty good job of that without any help from me," he said, the righteous indignation on his face suddenly melting into sadness. "Just leave the questioning of witnesses to me, okay?"

Dave abruptly ended the conversation and walked away. I was really starting to worry about those two.

Back at my desk I got down to work on my seemingly endless to-do list. Surprisingly, I didn't have the usual phone calls and interruptions, so I was able to tick boxes off my list at a furious pace.

I'd made it to the next-to-last item when the desk phone rang. It was Di.

"I tried to call your cell phone, but didn't get an answer," Di said. "When I drove past your office a little while ago, I saw your car parked out front."

"You called? How come I didn't hear it ring?" I said. I picked up the cell phone sitting beside my computer. It was dead.

"Oh, great," I said. "I forgot to charge it. What time is it anyway?"

"It's about five-twenty."

"I completely lost track of time," I said. "There's just so much to do before the fund-raiser. But I'm beat. If you're not busy, I'll wrap things up here and come over to your place. In all the excitement last night, I forgot to tell you about my meeting at Bryn's office yesterday."

"Sure," Di said. "Come on over."

I locked up the office and drove to the trailer park. Di opened her door for me and I walked in, plopped down in the recliner, and pulled the lever to put my feet up.

I briefly filled Di in on my conversation with Bryn, the weird fog that filled the room momentarily, and the erased messages.

"I don't think Bryn erased that message," I said. "I saw the green light on the answering machine showing messages after she played the recording. It was just an instant later when that mist rose up and we rushed out."

"I can't believe you and Bryn went back in the office after that," Di said. "What if that stuff was some kind of toxic gas?"

I hadn't even considered that possibility, but since it had been more than twenty-four hours, I figured I'd probably live.

"We have to work out what we're going to tell

Dave about Pierce and Lucinda—and what happened at Bryn's office," Di said.

"I have a headache and I'm starving. Why don't we talk about it over supper at Taco Belles," I said.

"Okay," she said. "Where's Larry Joe?"

"He's got a Jaycees meeting tonight."

"I'll drive since you've got a headache," Di said.

We climbed into the Buick and made the short drive to Taco Belles.

As we entered the restaurant, Di and I passed Mitzi leaving with a sackful of takeout containers. She just scowled as she walked by.

We snagged a back corner booth where we'd have relative privacy and ordered our usual—catfish tacos and mango slaw, along with margaritas.

"What about what happened at the chamber office?" I said.

"Let's start with what Lucinda told us. That might be less complicated," Di said.

"Okay," I said. "Assuming Lucinda was telling the truth, the real question is whether Pierce was telling the truth."

"Let's break it down and see what we've got," Di said. "A. Pierce was telling the truth. Morgan was just playing Lucinda to get what she wanted from her."

"Morgan manipulating someone to get what she wants is entirely believable," I said.

Di nodded.

"B. Pierce was lying. He and Morgan really were planning to get married, but now that she's dead he doesn't want anyone to know," Di said.

"That one doesn't ring true to me," I said. "Why wouldn't he admit it to Lucinda? And if he really was in love with Morgan, wouldn't he have seemed at least a little upset about her death?"

The waitress delivered our margaritas. We slurped the frozen beverage through our straws as we pondered for a long moment.

"Hmm," Di said. "Or, C. Morgan really believed she and Pierce were going to be married, but he never intended for that to happen."

"If C is the correct answer, then Pierce could have had motive to kill Morgan. If she was starting to believe her own fairy-tale version of things, and even saying so to a few select friends like Lucinda, he might have wanted to shut her up—permanently," I said.

"Especially with his political ambitions," Di said. "Scandal could hurt his chances of getting elected, or even getting a campaign off the ground."

"Right," I said.

The waitress returned with our platters and a squeeze bottle of chipotle tartar sauce.

"Of course," Di said, waving her fork in the air, "B would give Bryn a pretty strong motive for murder, if she found out Pierce was planning to dump her and marry Morgan."

"Although, for it to be a motive for murder, Bryn would have to actually care that her husband was fooling around, which I don't think she does," I said. "I don't pretend to understand it, but some marriages seem to work with that kind of arrangement."

"Okay. So it seems Pierce may have had more of a motive to kill Morgan than his wife did. But it was

Bryn, not Pierce, who had the opportunity to slip poison into her drink at the retreat," Di noted.

"I guess so," I said before taking another bite of my taco and mulling things over for a minute. "But Pierce could have hired one of the caterers to kill her. He's got plenty of money, and the bartender could have easily slipped poison into Morgan's drink."

"Or, maybe Nell's husband, Billy, killed Morgan because she was threatening to tell Nell about the two of them or because he found out about Morgan and Pierce and became insanely jealous," Di said.

"So basically we're right back where we started," I said, feeling frustrated.

"Pretty much," Di said. "We have plenty of suspects, but all the real evidence points to Jasmine."

"No, no, no. . . ." My brain was suddenly racing, new possibilities darting through my head. "If we factor in what happened at Bryn's office this afternoon, *all* the evidence doesn't point to Jasmine."

"You think Lucinda made that phone call to Bryn," Di said.

"Not only do I think Lucinda left that phone message, I think she sent one of her lackeys to erase the message. Think about it, Di. That message had been sitting on Bryn's answering machine for over a week. Why would someone decide to get rid of it at that very moment?"

Di thought for a minute and said, "Because she played it for you?"

"Exactly," I said.

"So what, you think Lucinda had Bryn's office

bugged or something?" Di said. "How would she know?"

"I don't think the office was bugged," I said. "I think the answer is far simpler than that. We confronted Lucinda about her meeting with Pierce. After that, I think she told someone on her payroll to keep an eye on us. I don't know if one of her goons was eavesdropping or if Lucinda just got worried when they phoned and told her where I was. But either way, she decided it would be a good idea to make sure that recorded message was erased. I have no idea how they managed the instant smoke or whatever it was, but it was obviously meant to drive Bryn and me out of the building—which it did. That gave someone just enough time to slip in through the back door and erase the messages."

We ended supper with more questions than answers and decided to go back to Di's to continue our conversation.

We got into Di's car and pulled onto the road headed for Sunrise Mobile Village, and I was asking Di if Dave had mentioned anything new about the case recently. Just then, I felt something furry brush against my hand. I looked down at the seat between us and saw the biggest, ugliest, hairiest spider I'd ever seen in my life. It was the size of a baseball. I jumped as high as someone wearing a seat belt can jump and pressed myself against the passenger door.

"Di, there's a tarantula right next to you," I said in a high-pitch whisper.

"Don't be ridicu . . . oh, sweet Jesus!" Di yelled as the giant spider climbed onto her leg. Both of us shrieked as she careened into oncoming traffic. Then she jerked the steering wheel hard to the right and drove headfirst into a ditch.

The car was lodged, headlights down, taillights up. We each scrambled out of our respective doors. I clawed at the steep embankment, trying to pull myself out of the ditch and as far away from the monster spider as I could.

On her side of the car, Di had managed to escape the ditch by climbing up over a culvert. She was standing in the driveway of Dixie Savings and Loan, screaming into her cell phone.

"Get over to the bank right this minute. Bring a shotgun—and call a tow truck," she yelled, sounding as crazy as I'm sure we looked to passersby.

Moments later, Dave and Ted pulled into the bank's well-lighted parking lot. While Di was trying to explain to Dave what happened, Ted grabbed a rope from the trunk of the cruiser. Following his instructions, I tied it around my waist. After making sure the spider was nowhere in sight, I steadied myself against the side of the car and took one big step up, followed by a series of tiny steps up the embankment as Ted tugged on the rope.

I walked over and stood beside Di just in time to hear Dave say, "Now you know it couldn't possibly have been a tarantula. Fishing spiders can get a pretty good size, but they're not poisonous. And any spider can startle you if it climbs up on you."

"Do not treat me like some hysterical female," Di said, her eyes flashing with anger. "I am telling you, it was a tarantula. Liv saw it. Tell him, Liv."

"I swear, Dave. It was as big as your fist."

"I'm sure it seemed that way," Dave said patronizingly. "Did you two by any chance have drinks with dinner?"

Di's eyes shot daggers in Dave's direction.

"Ted, would you kindly drive Liv and me home? I'm sure your boss here can wait for the tow truck."

Ted looked over to Dave.

"We'll all wait for the tow truck," Dave said. "After he pulls it out of the ditch, we need to see if the Buick is drivable."

Di threw her hands up in the air, walked up to the bank steps, and sat down. I joined her.

"Insinuating I'm drunk. He's got some nerve," Di muttered.

I decided silence was golden on this one.

The tow truck arrived. Dave blocked off the lane next to the ditch with a couple of orange cones retrieved from the trunk of the patrol car. Ted directed traffic, allowing a few cars at a time to pass in one direction before switching the traffic flow.

The tow truck driver attached a winch to the back of Di's car and hoisted it from the ditch. He then backed into the bank parking lot and lowered her car onto the pavement.

Ted got in the car and turned the key, which Di had left in the ignition. After making an awful grinding noise, the engine fired up. He jumped out of the car, fetched a cardboard box from the cruiser, and went back to Di's car. Ted's head disappeared as he leaned across the front seat. In a moment he stood up, walked over to Dave, and showed him the contents of the box.

Dave took off his hat and raked his fingers

through a mop of wavy dark hair. He took the box from Ted and walked over to where Di and I were sitting.

"This look familiar?" he said, lowering the box for us to peer inside. After a quick peek, we both recoiled.

Di jumped up and said, "I hope that'll teach you to doubt my word, Sheriff Davidson."

"Yes, ma'am," he said.

I took another peek at the spider from a safe distance. "We could have been killed."

"Actually, Ted has a keen interest in insects and spiders," Dave said. "He's always watching those nature documentaries. He says tarantulas rarely bite, and their venom isn't dangerous to humans."

"I'll keep my distance all the same," Di said.

Ted was lying underneath Di's car, his legs sticking out, while the tow truck guy took a look under the hood.

"Doesn't look like there's any damage to the undercarriage," Ted said, standing up and brushing off the seat of his pants.

"Things look all right under the hood, too" the truck driver said. "They built 'em solid back in the seventies."

The body of Di's Buick Riviera is vintage 1972, albeit not in mint condition. But the engine is newer and completely rebuilt with only 77,000 miles on it courtesy of Di's ex-husband, who's currently cooling his heels in the Texas State Penitentiary.

Di asked the tow truck man what she owed him,

and he told her it had already been taken care of. She gave Dave the faintest of smiles.

The sheriff asked the guy if he'd mind dropping Ted off at the sheriff's office.

"Ted," Dave said, handing the box over to the deputy, "take our little friend back to the office and put him in that old terrarium Terry used to keep her turtle in. I'm going to follow Di's car to make sure these two make it safely home," Dave said in an ominous tone.

Chapter 20

Di pulled onto the gravel pad in front of her trailer and parked next to my SUV. Dave pulled in behind her.

Once inside, I collapsed into the recliner and Di flopped down on the sofa. Dave remained standing, his lips pursed together tensely.

"The thing that concerns me most, ladies," Dave said, "is that tarantulas aren't exactly indigenous to this area."

Di interrupted him.

"Really? That's what concerns you most. Not the fact that Liv and I could have both been killed?" she said, looking like she was ready to burst into flames.

"I know you had a fright, but I told you tarantula bites aren't deadly to humans," he said from his high horse.

"Forget about the spider, bites or no bites," she said. "When that thing attacked me, I lost control of the car. Fortunately, we ended up in a ditch instead of having a head-on collision with oncoming traffic.

That could have killed both of us—and maybe even some other people."

"You're right. And I am very thankful that no one was injured," he said. "But the fact remains, that spider did not stroll out of the woods and climb into your car. Which means somebody put it there," Dave said, his eyes darting from me to Di and back to me.

"And my best guess is that it was intended as some kind of warning," he said in an accusing tone. "I think you better tell me what you two have been up to lately."

Di and I looked at each other blankly, then suddenly our eyes widened.

"Of course," I said. "We know exactly who put that giant spider in the car, don't we?"

"Yeah, we do. But something tells me you're not going to like it," Di said, looking at Dave.

After a beat, Dave said. "Well . . . who was it?"

"Lucinda Grable," Di said.

Dave threw his hands in the air and paced back and forth for a moment.

"Lucinda Grable, Lucinda Grable," he said. "Everybody in this town is obsessed with Lucinda Grable. Can I ask why Lucinda would want to put a tarantula in your car?"

"Well, to be precise," I said, "it wasn't Lucinda herself who put the spider in the car. It was that lapdog assistant of hers, Mitzi."

"That's right," Di affirmed. "We saw her at the restaurant tonight."

"Even so," Dave said. "What reason would Lucinda or her assistant possibly have to want to frighten you?"

"Because she knew we suspected she was involved somehow in Morgan's death," Di said.

"And how did she know that you suspected her?"

"Because we told her, in so many words," Di said.

"And when and where did you have this conversation?"

"Tuesday in her hotel suite," Di said.

Before Dave could say anything else, I jumped in. "Look, Dave, we saw Lucinda meeting with Pierce Davenport at Red's. It was all very cloak-and-dagger. They slipped in the side door and into the small private dining room. We told her that we saw her."

"And you two just happened to be at Red's when they showed up?"

"No," I said. "We just happened to be in the strip shopping center across the street when they showed up."

That was a bold-faced lie. But I wasn't about to throw Nell and Sindhu under the bus at this point.

"And from your vantage point across the street, you could see that Pierce and Lucinda went into the little private dining room in the back of the restaurant?" Dave said, shifting into interrogation mode.

"No, Mr. Smarty Pants," Di said. "After we saw them go in, I walked across the street and went inside the restaurant to take a good look. Just to be absolutely sure it was them."

"Even if she did meet with Pierce, how does that prove she had anything to do with Morgan's death?" Dave said.

"It doesn't prove anything," Di said, jumping up from the sofa. "But it does *suggest* that Lucinda may have had other reasons for coming to Dixie besides speaking at the PWAD retreat. It also suggests that maybe Lucinda didn't come as a favor for her dear old friend Morgan, out of the goodness of her heart. And it might also explain why she's still hanging around town like a bad cold after you've told her she's free to leave. If she wants, she could always fly back in for Morgan's funeral after the medical examiner releases the body."

Dave looked like he was holding his breath, and Di had that familiar expression on her face like she'd said all she had to say. I intervened.

"Dave, you said yourself that tarantulas aren't native to this area," I said. "Nobody in Dixie walked into the woods and scooped up a tarantula. But the globe-trotting Miss Grable could have easily procured one. In fact, a big hairy spider crawling across a tombstone is just the kind of creepy thing they'd do on her show."

"Yeah," Di said. "She may even have a spider wrangler on staff for all we know. And tell him about that weird fog that just suddenly came up in Bryn's office," she said, motioning toward me. "Fog hugging the ground is another special effect they'd use on her ghost show."

"Fog?" Dave said, exasperated. "What the hell is she talking about?"

I explained what happened at Bryn's office with the fog and the voice mail.

"Dave, Bryn told me she was going to call you," I said. "But she wanted to talk to Pierce about it first. I bet he talked her out of it, probably afraid the publicity would make him look foolish."

"Well, I think maybe I should go have a little talk with Bryn *and* Pierce," Dave said.

"Hah, of course you do," Di said. "You're willing to talk to anybody and suspect everybody except Lucinda Grable."

"If I don't have all the facts in this case maybe it's because *some* people are withholding evidence," Dave said.

"And maybe there's *some* evidence you just refuse to look at," Di said. "Maybe you're a little too comfortable with the evidence against Jasmine and you've stopped looking elsewhere."

If we were in a cartoon, steam would have been coming out of Dave's ears at this point.

"So now you're telling me how to do my job? It so happens that Ted and I are still working like crazy, tracking down leads—every real lead. Not that I owe you an explanation."

"Oh, so you don't owe me any explanations, but I owe you an explanation about every single move I make and everybody I happen to talk to."

Dave walked over to the door and grabbed his hat off the dining table.

"Everything having to do with this murder investigation *is* my business," he said, turning to face Di. "And I will question anyone who sticks their nose into the investigation or harasses witnesses. And I will lock up anybody who tries to play detective for interfering in a criminal investigation—and that includes you two," he said before leaving.

As soon as Dave had gone, Di took off her shoe and hurled it at the front door.

"Oooh, he makes me so mad," she said, clenching her fists. "I can't believe he's more concerned about our talking to Lucinda than about her putting a freaking tarantula in my car. He's such a . . ." Di searched a moment for the right word before giving up and walking over to the kitchen.

She stood on tiptoe to reach into the cupboard above the fridge and pulled out a bottle of rum. She then grabbed two cans of Diet Coke from the refrigerator and two glasses from the cabinet beside the sink. She sat a can and a glass on the little table beside my chair. She fixed her own drink, adding three fingers of rum before slamming the rum bottle down next to my glass.

I was reluctant to have a drink before driving home, but decided I could do with just a splash to steady my nerves.

"I wonder if Dave will even question Lucinda about the Godzilla-sized spider she had Mitzi put in your car," I said.

"I bet he does," Di said, taking another swig. "She'll deny it, of course. And he'll believe her—unless he just happens to spot a spiderweb the size of Tokyo in her hotel room."

Di plopped down on the sofa before adding, "Lucinda's definitely up to something, but I guess it would be a pretty big coincidence for her to use the same rare poison to kill Morgan that Jasmine just happened to have growing in her greenhouse."

"Yeah, I know," I said. "I told Nell the same thing when we visited Jasmine on Sunday. . . . Wait a minute! Who says it has to be a coincidence?"

"What do you mean?" Di said.

"Morgan was all hot to manufacture Jasmine's anti-aging cream, right? So she could have told

Lucinda about it, could've even told her the secret ingredient."

"That's true," Di said. "If Morgan thought she'd gotten her hands on something better than Botox, she certainly would have bragged about it."

"We should probably mention this to Dave," I said.

"You can tell him anything you want," Di said. "I'm not talking to that man until I hear an apology."

Chapter 21

I hung out at Di's a bit longer before heading home. Larry Joe had made it home from his meeting and was making himself a sandwich when I walked into the kitchen from the garage.

"Hey, honey," I said.

He put down the knife he was using to slather peanut butter on bread long enough to give me a quick hug and kiss.

"Wasn't it a dinner meeting tonight with the Jaycees?"

"Yeah, but they served salmon, which I don't much care for. You know I'm a catfish kind of guy. So I'm still hungry."

"You been working late or hanging out with Di?"

"A little of both. Actually, we had an accident—but don't worry. We're both fine. In fact, there wasn't any noticeable damage to Di's car."

Larry Joe sat down at the table with his sandwich and a glass of milk and I filled him in on the spider incident and the car going into the ditch, which I figured he'd hear about anyway. Then I gave him a very abbreviated version of our conversation with Dave."

"I agree with Dave," Larry Joe said.

Why does this not surprise me?

"So you don't believe Lucinda is involved, either?" I said.

"I don't know. I don't give two hoots about Lucinda," Larry Joe said. His face was red, but I could tell he was trying not to raise his voice. "I care about you. I think Dave's right that this spider business was intended as a warning. I want you to heed that warning and keep your distance from anything having to do with Lucinda and the whole murder business. Dave wears a gun and a badge—let him handle the rough stuff."

"I guess so," I said.

"I mean it," he said firmly. "We've been down this road before. You had the very best of intentions when those Farrell boys got killed, but you still ended up with a rifle pointed at your head. You have to promise me to stay clear of this whole mess. If you don't, I swear I'll enlist my mom and your mama to follow you around until Dave wraps up this investigation. And you know they'd do it."

It was an ugly threat. The thought of being stalked by my mother and mother-in-law forced me to quickly promise I'd stay clear of trouble.

"Okay," I said. "If I should happen to hear anything, I'll just pass the information on to Dave. What he does with it is his business. At least my conscience will be clear. Besides, the Halloween fund-raiser is the day after tomorrow and I've got a hundred things to do."

"And Morgan's funeral is tomorrow afternoon," he said.

"Oh, poo. I'd forgotten all about Morgan's funeral," I said. "Make that a hundred and one things."

Larry Joe put his plate and glass in the dishwasher and followed me into the den. We switched on the TV to watch the news. Just after a recap of national news headlines, footage of a reporter talking to Pierce Davenport came on.

"Reporting from Nashville, I'm Ross Kelp here with Pierce Davenport where a campaign fundraising dinner for the governor will be held tonight at seven o'clock. Mr. Davenport, I won't keep you, because I see guests are already making their way into the reception hall for the cocktail hour. But word on the street has it that longtime state senator Rick Cromwell will not seek reelection and that you plan to run for his senate seat. Can you confirm this for us?"

"Well, Ross, Senator Cromwell hasn't officially announced his retirement, so that kind of conversation would be premature. I can tell you that if my party were to ask me to run for an elected position, I'd certainly give it careful consideration."

"I heard Cromwell's in poor health," Larry Joe said. "Sounds like we may have a senator from Dixie in the state house next time around."

"I'd be more excited if was someone other than Pierce Davenport," I said.

After the commercial break, one of the Memphis reporters came on screen, broadcasting live from Dixie.

"Look, honey," I said to Larry Joe, who was scrolling through e-mail on his phone. "They're in front of Sindhu and Ravi's hotel. You can see Dave and Ted in the background."

A reporter holding a microphone said, "Celebrity ghost hunter Lucinda Grable, who hails from Dixie originally, has been staying at this hotel in her hometown. Tonight she had quite a scare. According to witnesses, a dark-colored SUV with tinted windows tried to run down Miss Grable as she was walking across the parking lot around nine o'clock tonight.

"Her assistant, Mitzi Tanner, said Miss Grable was too upset to speak with us. And Delbert County Sheriff Dave Davidson said he had no comment at this time.

"The couple behind me, Dell and Sandra Bowen, say they witnessed the incident. Mrs. Bowen, can you describe for us what you saw?"

"Yes, sir. Me and Dell had just gotten back from having dinner with friends. We were getting out of the car when all of a sudden, one of them big SUVs revved its engine and raced across the parking lot going straight at some lady. She screamed and jumped off to the side, falling on the pavement. He never slowed down and just kept going on out of the driveway.

"Of course, we ran over to see if the lady was okay. It was only then we saw who she was. We just love Lucinda's TV program. Don't we, Dell?"

Dell nodded.

"Did you get a glimpse of the driver or the license plate?" the reporter asked.

"No, sir," she said. "It all happened so quick. And all we were thinking about was checking to see if the lady was okay."

"Did Ms. Grable seem injured?"

"I don't think nothing was broken. But she was scraped up some. I reckon she'll be pretty sore tomorrow."

"Thank you, Mrs. Bowen. Reporting live from Dixie, this is . . ."

I muted the sound.

"I'm going to call Di."

"Don't you two start scheming," Larry Joe said. "Remember your promise."

"I just want to know if she saw the news report."

I walked to the kitchen to retrieve my cell phone from my purse. Larry Joe walked past me, announcing he was going to bed and giving me one more look of admonishment.

I hit speed dial.

"Hi, Di. . . ."

"I saw it, too," she interrupted.

"Are you thinking what I'm thinking?" I asked.

"That it's a shame she wasn't badly injured?"

"How about that Lucinda was never in any real danger. That she staged the whole thing?"

"Actually, that thought had crossed my mind," Di said.

After a short conversation with Di, I went upstairs to bed. Larry Joe woke up just enough to mumble something unintelligible as I crawled under the covers.

Chapter 22

Before I fell asleep, I had decided I would stop by the sheriff's office on my way to work the next morning to tell Dave my theory that Morgan could have shared the name of Jasmine's secret face cream ingredient with Lucinda, giving her the perfect opportunity to set Jasmine up for murder. And while I was at it, I'd give him my take on Lucinda's phony somebody-tried-to-run-me-over drama—not that he was likely to listen.

Dave saved me the trip by showing up on my doorstep a little after seven AM and caught me still wearing my bathrobe.

I invited him in and he followed me to the kitchen, where I offered him a cup of coffee.

"No thanks, Mrs. McKay. I just have a couple of questions for you."

I've learned from experience that whenever Dave calls me ma'am or Mrs. McKay, it means it's official sheriff's business, not a social call.

I poured myself another cup of coffee. "Sure, what would you like to know, sheriff?"

"Where were you around nine last night?"

"Let me see. I got home from Di's about eight-thirty or so."

"Was Larry Joe at home then?"

"Yes, he was. He's already left for work this morning, but you can call and ask him yourself. After I got home, Larry Joe and I sat in the kitchen talking while he ate a sandwich. For the record, it was peanut butter. Then we went into the den and watched TV. I'm guessing this line of questioning has something to do the incident at the hotel we saw on the news."

Dave nodded and then had the nerve to ask, "Mind if I take a look at your SUV?"

Oh, he makes me so mad.

"Help yourself. It's parked in the garage. You can have a CSI team go over it if you like, to look for traces of Lucinda's blood. Please tell me she bled."

"I'm just doing my job, Liv," Dave said.

I turned my back to him and opened the fridge to get some milk for my coffee. I hoped the blast of cold air would cool the anger I felt flushing my face. I was sitting at the kitchen table, clanking the spoon noisily against the mug as I stirred my coffee when he came back into the kitchen.

"Can you eliminate me from your inquiries, or should I call my attorney?"

"I know you and Di don't have much use for Lucinda, but an attempt was made on her life. I have to investigate."

"Oh, honestly," I said in complete disbelief of Dave's gullibility where Lucinda was concerned. "Nobody tried to kill her. It's obvious Lucinda staged the whole thing to deflect suspicion off herself."

"Obvious, huh?" Dave said. "Enlighten me."

"Why would Lucinda venture out without her security guys? Have you asked yourself that? I'm not even sure she goes to the bathroom without an entourage. I haven't seen Lucinda go anywhere by herself since she got here. Now suddenly she's wandering around by herself after dark?"

"I have been asking the questions. You and Di just don't want to believe the answers.

"Lucinda was going out to meet her personal trainer to fool around. We confirmed he's been staying at a nearby hotel. She gave her staff the slip because she says she believes that one of them has been selling information about her love life to the tabloids. I know Nell and Sindhu believe Lucinda was involved in Morgan's death, but they both have alibis for last night. Sindhu and Ravi were at the elementary school for their daughter's play—lots of witnesses, and two of Nell's neighbors were at her house watching their favorite talent show on TV. Everyone from the retreat—Billy and his crew, Bryn, Winette, and the Wythe sisters—have alibis. In fact, you and Di have the weakest alibis in the bunch, so don't push your luck," he said, red-faced.

"You forgot to mention Jasmine, Sheriff. She has an airtight alibi, being locked up in your jail and all," I said.

"That she does. But Dylan doesn't happen to have an alibi," Dave said coolly.

"So Jasmine *and* Dylan are cold-blooded killers, while Lucinda is just a sweet, innocent darling?"

"The driver may or may not have intended to kill

Lucinda. He or she may have just wanted to deflect suspicion away from Jasmine by making it look like there's still a killer on the loose," Dave said. "Isn't that your theory about Lucinda, that she staged the attack to deflect suspicion from herself? Good day, Mrs. McKay," Dave said before stomping out through the front door.

Larry Joe had taken a tie and jacket with him when he left for work so he wouldn't have to come by the house on his way to the church. I followed his cue and dressed for the day in the navy blue pantsuit I planned to wear to Morgan's funeral.

I had just stepped out of my car in front of the bakery when Nell hollered to me from the salon door.

"Hey, Liv. Wait up."

She started walking toward me in a hurry, and I met her on the corner.

"I s'pose Sheriff Dave asked about your whereabouts last night, too?"

"Yeah. He stopped by first thing this morning."

"He came to my place last night. I guess that makes me suspect numero uno," she said. "I was fortunate to have an alibi, since I didn't know I'd be needing one."

"Me too. What do you make of this attempt on Lucinda's life?" I said.

"I think it's a bunch of hooey," Nell said. "It's funny how murder and mayhem seem to follow her around like a hungry hound. What about you?"

"I tend to agree. I can't help but wonder if our diva staged the whole thing."

"She's good at arranging things, all right," Nell said. "Sindhu had spotted her going out to meet some beefcake guy at about the same time the past few nights."

"Dave said she was meeting up with her personal trainer for some hanky-panky, but she was trying to hide it from her entourage because she thinks one of them has been selling information about her personal life to the tabloids," I said.

"Hah. I bet she feeds information to the scandal sheets herself, or maybe lover boy is the one doling out the information."

"If someone did try to run her over, her boyfriend could be the one who let that someone know what time she'd be in the parking lot."

"You know Dave thinks *that someone* is Dylan," Nell said. "I guess the sheriff wants to lock him up along with Jasmine so he'll have a matched set. I don't think anybody except Dave actually believes Jasmine is guilty. Even Bryn Davenport, who's always seemed a little snooty to me, called and offered to contribute to Jasmine's defense fund. After the Residential Rehab fund-raiser we may need you to help us plan a fund-raiser for Jasmine, unless Dave comes to his senses."

"I hope Dave catches the real killer, whoever that may be," I said. "But at the moment I can't think about another fund-raiser. I've got an endless list of things I need to do before the mystery dinner to-morrow night."

As soon as Nell walked away, I realized I had forgotten to tell Dave what I'd meant to tell him this morning before he dropped by and ruined my day.

I called the sheriff from my mobile, but it went straight to voice mail. Either Dave was busy or he wasn't taking calls from me. Either way, I left a message briefly laying out my theory that Morgan may have shared the name of Jasmine's secret face cream ingredient with Lucinda, giving her the perfect opportunity to frame Jasmine. It would be up to Dave to follow up, if he could find the time between kissing Lucinda's backside and trying to find a way to arrest Dylan.

I finally made it from the sidewalk into the bakery to make sure pastries would be delivered to each of the event sites first thing in the morning. I wanted all our volunteers hopped up on caffeine and sugar and ready to work.

"Hey, Liv," Renee said as I walked through the door of Dixie Donuts and More.

"Hey, girl. I just wanted to check with you on doughnuts for each of the event sites in the morning."

"We're good to go. We'll have a mix of doughnuts and muffins," she said. "Fred will make deliveries to the church gym and the country club before seven AM. Someone's coming by to pick up pastries for the work crew out at the farm, and Winette is stopping in to pick up boxes to take to her office for the planning committee."

"Perfect," I said. "Renee, I really appreciate that you and Fred are donating breakfast, not just for tomorrow, but for several of the planning meetings and even the town-wide kickoff meeting. You've been very generous."

"We're glad to do it," she said. "Our schedule doesn't allow us to volunteer with Residential Rehab, so this is a small way we can help out. And I think we've picked up a few new customers who happen to like our muffins even better than the diner's, which is flattering. But I wouldn't even try to compete with Mabel's pies."

"You've got the market sewn up on doughnuts and decorated cakes, and the diner has pies covered. So I guess the two of you can divvy up customers when it comes to muffins. Everybody wins.

"And speaking of muffins, I ran out the door without breakfast. Let me have one of those large blueberry muffins."

"You're in luck," Renee said. "I've got some just out of the oven."

I couldn't resist taking a bite out of the warm, fresh muffin as soon as I got in the car. I drove the whole block and a half and parked in front of my office.

Winette called to me from the front door of Sweet Deal Realty.

"Liv, have you got a minute? I think we may have a bit of a problem."

Great. I felt a case of indigestion coming on and I'd had only one bite of my muffin. I followed Winette into her office.

"What's up?"

"I know we already gave Felix a final count for the dinner, but this morning I have four more people who want to come. Could you ask Felix if he has enough food to accommodate four more diners?"

I breathed a sigh of relief.

"*Whew*, you had me worried for a minute. Felix always orders a bit extra, just in case. But four more people willing to pay a hundred dollars apiece to benefit RR? I'll give them my and Larry Joe's dinners if that's what it takes."

"If it comes to that, I'll share my dinner with you," Winette said with a laugh. "I'll call those folks back and tell them we can accommodate them—that is, if they can drop their checks by my office sometime today."

"I'll call Felix and give him the heads-up. We've got less than thirty-six hours til showtime."

"Ooh, don't remind me," she said. "I'm already developing a nervous twitch. Just look at my left eye," she said, turning the left side of her face toward me slightly. "I look like a crazy woman."

I finally made it up to the office, but I was having a hard time concentrating. I blamed Dave for that. I really wanted to talk to Di, since the sheriff had insinuated he had already questioned her, but I hated to call her while she was working. I finally texted and asked her to call me if she had a chance. Seconds later, my cell phone started buzzing. I picked up.

"Hey, I suppose Dave gave you the inquisition, too," she said. "I made him stand on the front porch to talk to me. Told him he'd need a warrant to come in."

"Are you at work?" I asked.

"No. I heard Lucinda was going to eulogize Morgan, and I thought that was too good to pass up. I called Legs Findlay and asked him to fill in for me. He's retired and always up for the chance to play postman for a day."

"Legs?" I said.

"If you'd ever seen him in Bermuda shorts, you'd understand the nickname," Di said.

We compared notes on our respective interviews with Dave.

"He had the nerve to ask to look at my SUV, like he thought I may have tried to run Lucinda down," I said. "And he didn't seem to appreciate my suggestion that Lucinda staged the whole thing."

"Yeah, he didn't much like it when I mentioned that, either. Actually, Dave's theory seems to be that Dylan may have stolen or borrowed a dark SUV for the evening. There were acceleration marks on the hotel parking lot where the SUV gunned it toward Lucinda. Likely the only reason Dave hasn't already arrested Dylan is that the tires on his SUV don't match the tread marks shown in the photos. So Dave checked your tires. And I'm sure he checked Nell's, as well," Di said.

"Dave was kind enough to tell me that you and I have the weakest alibis among the usual suspects. I was at home with Larry Joe. But presumably a husband might lie to cover for his wife."

"The only reason I have any alibi is that after you left I went for a walk to clear my head. My neighbor waved to me as I was coming back to the trailer around nine. But she couldn't be exact about the time."

"Dave told me Nell and Sindhu's alibis," I said. "I wish I knew what the other alibis are."

"I can tell you that. I quizzed him after he said my alibi was pretty weak. Winette was at some real estate association meeting. She and Mr. Sweet carpooled and didn't get home until after nine-thirty. The Wythe sisters were at home, but the lady who helps take care of Miss Annabelle didn't leave until about eight forty-five. Billy and his crew were catering an event in Hartville until something like ten o'clock. Oh, and Bryn always calls her mom at nine on Thursday nights. Her housekeeper says she brought Bryn a cup of tea just as she was dialing the number," Di said.

I told Di I'd see her later at Morgan's funeral, then forced myself to get to work on my long to-do list. I put some coffee on and listened to voice mail while I savored the rest of the muffin. Fortunately, no bad news. Of course, if there were problems I'd rather hear about them today than tomorrow.

I phoned Felix to tell him we had four more for tomorrow night's dinner. He mumbled that was fine and hung up. Our Cajun chef had his hands full with a dinner tonight at the country club. It would have been more convenient for me if the country club didn't have a dinner tonight so we could start setting up today. But since they're donating the space and Felix and his staff are donating their time for the fund-raiser, it's definitely better for the country club not to forgo revenue two nights in a row.

Almost all the food, materials, and labor for the Halloween fund-raiser were being donated. Just thinking about how much money we'd be able to raise for Residential Rehab and how many people would be helped made me feel good, despite my anxieties about being able to get everything done in time.

I fielded phone calls and marked off and refined my checklists all morning. At twenty-five minutes until eleven, I made a quick stop in the ladies' room and put on some lipstick before going to the funeral. I drove to Dixie Community Church, the nondenominational church I've attended since childhood. The main parking lot was full, so I had to park in the overflow lot.

I didn't see Larry Joe's car when I pulled in, but he walked around from the side of the building and fell in step with me as I approached the front.

Mama waved at us and elbowed Earl to scoot over. The rest of the people on the pew scrunched together to make room. Larry Joe reached across Mama to shake hands with Earl, and we all settled in and listened to the organist play traditional hymns.

"I hope they don't play 'Precious Memories,'" Mama said to me in a stage whisper. "I always boohoo when I hear 'Precious Memories.'"

For everyone's sake, I hoped they didn't play "Precious Memories." Once Mama gets started, she can boohoo as loud as any paid mourner.

There wasn't a viewing before the service. I wondered if that was because the funeral home couldn't get that horrible expression off Morgan's face.

I looked around at the congregation. I couldn't see everyone from where I was sitting, but with her unusual hair color it wasn't hard to pick Nell out of the crowd, even from behind. Billy was sitting on one side of her and Sindhu was on the other side. I saw Miss Maybelle seated near the front of the church. Again her hair, a white cloud, served as a beacon. She appeared to have left her sister at home, no doubt with a sitter. Probably a prudent decision, seeing as Miss Annabelle is given to outbursts at inopportune moments. Out of the corner of my eye, I spied Winette. Just about everyone from the retreat was present, except Jasmine. I didn't see Bryn, but that didn't mean she wasn't there. I couldn't locate Di in the crowd, either. However, the church was packed, including the seldom-used balcony.

At straight up eleven, the funeral director and his assistant began rolling Morgan's white lacquer casket down the center aisle. The organist played "Amazing Grace" as Morgan's parents, Randall and Rose Robison, along with a few relatives, walked slowly behind the coffin. Mr. Robison and another man were on either side of Morgan's mother, gripping her by the elbows. It looked as if they were all that was keeping her on her feet.

Mama grabbed my hand and held it tightly. I knew she must have been thinking about how difficult it would be to lose my sister or me.

One of the cousins read a letter written by Morgan's parents as a tribute and farewell to their only child. My heart went out to Morgan's folks, but I was having a hard time thinking about anything except Mama's death grip, which was beginning to cut off my circulation.

There was a wave of whispers across the sanctuary as Lucinda walked up to the pulpit. She recited a perfectly composed script about her fond memories of Morgan as a childhood friend and former roommate, and how glad she was that they had the chance to reconnect before Morgan's untimely passing. Her speech hit just the right notes of warmth and affection with a touch of humor. It sounded as phony as her breast implants to me, but maybe my personal encounters with Lucinda had prejudiced me a bit.

Mama eventually let go of my hand to dig around in her purse for a tissue. Earl gallantly passed her his monogrammed handkerchief.

The pastor's comments about Morgan were clearly drawn from her parents and not from any personal knowledge. But then a funeral isn't the time or place to speak the unvarnished truth about the deceased.

Pastor Caleb Duncan ended with a comforting prayer and the organist started playing the recessional. Pallbearers, designated by a white rose in their lapel, walked alongside the coffin. Morgan's parents and relatives followed solemnly behind it.

Everyone stood quietly until the last family member had filed out of the auditorium. The preacher announced that the graveside service would be a private, family-only affair.

After Brother Caleb's comments, a whir of whispers quickly escalated into the roar of normal tone conversations, except for Mama and a couple of other women, whose normal speaking voice was always a few decibels above most people.

"Liv, why don't you and Larry Joe stop by the house for lunch. I've got a cold cut platter, some potato salad, and an apple pie."

Mama's homemade pie was tempting, but we told her we had to get back to work.

"We offered, of course—the church ladies—to fix lunch for the family," Mama said. "But they were having it catered, or some such. Honestly, I don't think Rose is going to make it through the graveside service. She could barely stand upright. She needs to go home and lie down. Bless her broken heart.

"I'm so excited about the mystery dinner tomorrow night, hon," Mama said, quickly changing gears. "Is there anything I can do to help you get things together for the fund-raiser?"

I thought about that offer for a nanosecond before replying, "No. I don't think so. With Holly and Winette's help, I believe we're in good shape."

"Wait til you see my costume. I haven't even let Earl see it yet," she said, looking over at Earl.

I think he was trying to look excited, but it's hard to tell with Earl.

Larry Joe and I made our way out of the church, speaking to everyone and stopping for hugs and handshakes along the way.

Larry Joe gave me a quick kiss on the cheek and we parted ways at the bottom of the church steps. I caught a glimpse of someone waving at me. It was Di.

"Hey," I said. "I didn't see you inside the church."

"I got here late and ended up sitting in the balcony," she said.

"That was some performance Lucinda gave, huh?"

"Yeah, unfortunately, she didn't look like somebody who'd just been run down by a car. I had hoped to see some contusions," Di said.

"I know, me too. I guess that's pretty awful of us," I said as we started strolling toward the parking lot across the street.

"I don't feel awful about wanting to see Lucinda roughed up a bit after what she put us through with that tarantula business," Di said before suddenly grabbing my arm.

"Well, looky who's chatting up Miss Daisy over there."

I turned to look in the direction Di had indicated and spotted Deputy Ted, all smiles, having what seemed to be an animated conversation with our wallflower, Daisy.

We walked in their direction.

"Maybe we shouldn't interrupt," I said.

"Are you kidding?" Di said.

"You're right. I'm dying to know what's going on."

Chapter 23

"Hi, Ted. Hi, Daisy," Di said, before introducing Daisy to me.

"Hey, Di," Daisy said. "Ted and I were actually just talking about y'all. I'm afraid I owe you two a huge apology."

"I can't imagine why," Di said.

"As we were walking out of the church, I happened to overhear Ted telling the sheriff he needed to go by the office to feed the tarantula," Daisy said. "And since one of my pet tarantulas went missing yesterday, I asked him about it. He told me the whole story about how Tango, that's his name, somehow ended up in your car and spooked you so bad that you ran off the road."

"So the tarantula belongs to you?"

"Yes," she said. "I'm so sorry. I've been racking my brain trying to figure out how he could have ended up in your car. The only thing I can imagine is that he must have climbed into your mailbag yesterday while we were talking on the porch. When

I didn't see him right away, I thought he was hiding under the dresser. He does that sometimes.

"And I'm sorry I rushed you off so rudely yesterday, Di. But I had a couple of my spiders out of their containers and I don't like to open the door when they're loose. But it's hard to imagine he could have traveled all the way to the front door that quick. I guess Tango hitched a ride on my shoe without me realizing it. Sorry about all the trouble."

"Well, it obviously wasn't your fault," Di said. "It gave us quite a scare, that's for sure. But Ted explained how tarantulas aren't deadly to humans. And there was no real damage to the car."

"I'm so glad no one got hurt. Please let me treat you ladies to lunch," Daisy said. "It's the least I can do. Ted and I were fixing to go over to Taco Belles. Why don't you join us?"

"We don't want to intrude," I said.

"No, really," Ted said earnestly. "We'd love to have you join us."

Ted had a line of perspiration above his lip and the temperature was maybe in the upper 50s. So we agreed to go along.

Di and I took my car to the restaurant.

"Well, it looks like Ted has found someone who shares his odd spider obsession," Di said. "Who knew?"

"I know, I can't believe it. And Daisy the wallflower is suddenly all chatty," I said. "I wasn't sure if we should go along or leave them on their own, but Ted seemed to be pleading with us to join them."

"Yeah, I think he really likes her and has a case of awkward schoolboy nerves," Di said.

"I feel kind of bad with Daisy being all apologetic

about the spider getting out," I said. "We both know that tarantula didn't crawl into your mailbag."

"No. He must've crawled into that canvas tote bag when we broke into her house, which means he was in my car all night Wednesday and most of the day yesterday," Di said with a shudder.

"Do you think we should grab the check?" I said. "I don't feel right letting her buy us lunch after we broke into her house and unintentionally kidnapped her pet spider."

"I'm okay with her paying for lunch," Di said. "It *was* her pet tarantula that caused us to have a car accident, and it *is* thanks to us that she and Ted have gotten together, at least in a roundabout way. And let's face it, both of them would be hard up to find mates willing to put up with their peculiarities."

Ted and Daisy had already nabbed a table for four by the time Di and I arrived at the crowded restaurant.

It turned out Daisy has a license to import spiders, mostly for her own collection. But she also sells some of them and is a bit of a celebrity in the arachnid world. She writes for a spider journal, as well as runs her own blog. And I was actually right about her selling little Victorian-style insect and spider collections—apparently that's what's in the boxes the UPS guy picks up.

"Daisy, do tarantulas ever make any sounds? We certainly didn't hear anything in the car when Tango suddenly surprised us," I asked coyly, curious about the hissing sound we'd heard inside Daisy's house.

"Some do," Daisy said. "When they feel threatened they'll make a hissing sound as a warning for predators to stay away. But they don't have vocal chords. They produce sound by rubbing special bristles on their hind legs together, similar to the way crickets create sound."

"That's fascinating," Ted said.

Daisy's definitely an odd girl, but Ted was all moony-eyed over her, obviously smitten.

"It must have been fate or something that brought me to the funeral today," Daisy said, giving Ted a shy smile. "It's embarrassing to admit, but I only went so I could get a look at Lucinda Grable in person. I never even met Morgan. Is that awful of me, crashing a funeral?"

"Believe me, most of the people at the funeral weren't any closer to Morgan than you," I said, wondering silently if anybody had really been close to Morgan.

Our meals arrived at the table, and I knew Ted must have it bad for Daisy. I'd seen Ted plow through a hefty plateful on several occasions. Today, he barely touched his food.

"I'm sorry I always have to hurry off right after yoga class," Daisy said to Di and Ted, but mostly to Ted. "I take part in an online forum for serious spider enthusiasts every Wednesday night. Being live on the webcam still makes me a little nervous, so the yoga session helps me relax."

"It's impressive how you've built a career around your passion for spiders," I said.

"Yeah, I'm really lucky," she said. "I make a little money with the writing and a little with the spider and collection sales. I also sell venom to some medical research teams at a couple of universities."

"Wow, that's wonderful," Ted said, still looking as if he were under a hypnotic trance.

"What kind of medical research?" I asked.

"They've discovered that peptides from some varieties of spider venom are effective in treating chronic pain. There's also promising research that a certain protein in spider venom could be used to treat muscular dystrophy. I was a biology major and know a few people who are now doing graduate work in medical research."

"So small amounts of spider venom can be used as a painkiller?" Ted asked.

"Not exactly. There aren't any human trials yet, at least not for the researchers I supply," Daisy said. "And the venom I collect isn't sterile or licensed for clinical use. They're studying the effects of different venom compounds. Most of these could then be replicated synthetically."

"Wow," Ted said.

Di and I decided to leave when they ordered dessert. Daisy grabbed the check.

"Di," she said as we got up from the table. "I'd really appreciate it if you didn't mention my spider collection to the neighbors, especially Mrs. Roper. The spiders are no danger to them, but I know from experience neighbors can get pretty unpleasant about it. And if they complain to the Woodleys, I could end up having to move."

"No worries," Di said. "You learn all kinds of things when you deliver people's mail. I make it a policy to keep people's private business under my hat. And I don't talk to Mrs. Roper any more than I have to."

Daisy and Ted, who had just met an hour earlier,

were sharing a dessert as we left. Afterward they were planning to go by the sheriff's office to collect Tango.

With any luck they'd have the whole afternoon to get acquainted. I had phoned Dave on the way to the restaurant to inform him that Ted was on a date with a real live woman and he should not under any circumstances be called away for work. Dave seemed so surprised that I had a feeling he'd comply.

We drove back to the parking lot. I pulled up beside Di's car and turned off the engine.

"You know this means Lucinda didn't have anything to do with putting that tarantula in your car," I said.

"Yeah. But that doesn't mean she's not fooling around with Pierce or that she wasn't involved in Morgan's murder," Di said, obviously still fuming over our conversation with Dave the previous day.

"So doesn't the sweet little romance blossoming between our awkward wallflowers inspire you at all to work things out with a certain handsome sheriff?"

Di gave me one of her trademark deadpan expressions.

"Look," I said, turning to face her. "If you don't want to tell me what's going on with you and Dave, that's fine. At least be honest with yourself—and with him. Every time it seems like things are going really well between you two, you suddenly push him away. Can't you see that?"

"Yeah, I can see that," Di said.

I hadn't expected her to admit it, so I wasn't sure what to say. We sat silent for a long moment before I had to ask.

"Why?"

"You really want the truth?"

"Of course."

"Dave and I have been pretty low key as a couple so far. But if our relationship becomes serious—and public—people are bound to find out that my ex is in prison. How will that look for Dave, especially when he runs for reelection?"

"Di, your ex-husband being in prison in no way makes you guilty of anything!"

"That may be true in theory," she said. "But this is a small town, Liv, and you know perfectly well that some people just won't see it that way. Jimmy Souther was convicted of armed robbery. He's a thief. And if word about that gets around, what it means in real life, my life, is that certain people in Dixie will be taking inventory of the silverware whenever I leave their house."

Di sniffed. I could tell she was close to tears. And I've rarely seen her cry.

"Please at least talk to Dave about this and let him know what's going on in your head," I said.

"I can't talk to him about this—and you'd better not say a word. I mean it."

"Don't worry. It's not my place," I said. "But you can't let your past, or more specifically your ex-husband's past, determine your future."

In a few seconds, Di started laughing.

"That sounds like something you read in a fortune cookie," she said between giggles.

"What if I did? It's still good advice," I said, trying to sound indignant before bursting into giggles along with Di.

Di got out of the SUV and climbed into her car, and I started to drive back to my office.

I noticed I had a text message from Holly. She said Mr. Crego had picked up the screaming lady from her house. He was doing a daylight run-through and wanted us to come over to see how everything looked. I phoned Holly.

"I'd love to see how everything looks for the hayride, but do you think we can spare the time to go out to the Crego farm?"

"Of course we can," Holly said. "We should treat the fund-raiser events like we would any other party. And we'd check every detail, wouldn't we?"

"Yes, we would," I agreed.

"Besides it's awfully generous of Mr. Crego to host the teen event," Holly said. "He wants to show off his hard work, so I think we should let him."

"You're absolutely right, Holly. I'll swing by your house to pick you up in about fifteen minutes."

Homer Crego helped us into a long wagon pulled by a tractor. Holly and I took a seat on a couple of hay bales. Mr. Crego climbed in with us while his teenage son, Robby, started the tractor.

As we approached a copse of trees a spotlight suddenly came on, illuminating a homemade sign that said ENTER AT YOUR OWN PERIL.

"Of course, all this will stand out and be a lot scarier when it's good and dark," Mr. Crego pointed out.

The tractor turned onto a trail that went about one hundred feet into the woods. The next spot-light that popped on lit up a skeleton hanging from a tree. As we neared the skeleton, a ghost came flying toward us on a zip line. Even in the daylight it startled me, which brought a big smile to Mr. Crego's face.

We emerged from the woods near the edge of a field, where a creepy scarecrow was affixed to a pole. As we got closer the scarecrow suddenly spun around, revealing several arrows lodged in its back.

We neared an outbuilding with a narrow porch. A spotlight switched on, revealing the screaming lady. Holly and I knew what to expect, but it would be a chilling surprise for a wagonload of kids in the darkness.

Mr. Crego explained that after the outbuilding with the screaming lady, the tractor would turn around and head back toward the campfire.

"The kids will probably think that's the end of the frights. So when we get to about here," Mr. Crego said, motioning to the barn just up ahead on our left, "my brother-in-law, who'll be wearing a Jason mask, will come running around from the far side of the barn, cranking up a chain saw."

"Oh my, Mr. Crego," I said. "You've done a wonderful job of setting up the haunted hayride. I think the teens are going to love it."

"Yes," Holly added. "I saw a demonstration of how the screaming lady works and it seemed pretty complicated to me. I'm most impressed with how you rigged up the flying ghost and spinning scarecrow on your own."

He beamed.

"That was pretty simple mechanical stuff. But that old lady leaping out of the rocking chair really puts it over the top. Even Robby said it's pretty cool—and that's high praise coming from a teenager," he said. "I thank you ladies for spending the time and money to get this animated prop for us."

On the drive home I told Holly how glad I was that she had insisted we go out for the demonstration.

"It's obvious that Mr. Crego has put an awful lot of time and effort into this."

"So have we," Holly pointed out. "And tomorrow night it's showtime."

Chapter 24

I dropped Holly off at her house and drove straight to the office to get to work. I needed to make sure everything was coming together. Tomorrow. That word sounded almost as scary as the screaming lady.

Since the town council had officially changed the date for trick-or-treating to October 30, I saw a number of costumed tots running from business to business on the square to collect treats. It was still sunny, but most of these preschoolers would be heavy-lidded by the time darkness fell.

I pulled up in front of my office just as a miniature Batman and pint-size pirate strolled up and wandered into Sweet Deal Realty. Winette, who had left the door propped open to encourage roving trick-or-treaters, picked up a large bowl filled with candies and walked over to the costumed youngsters.

She leaned over and lowered the bowl to the right height for them, inviting the children to take a piece or two of candy. Of course they grabbed all the candy their tiny hands could hold before looking up and reciting the sweetest-sounding thank you.

I stepped back to let the kids run out the door and rejoin the weary-looking man waiting for them on the sidewalk.

"Aw, they're just precious," I said to Winette as I walked in.

"Yeah, we've had a steady stream of little ones the past hour or so," Winette said. "Folks know that the businesses on the square always have candy to hand out. Kids can score a bagful of candy in short order, and parents can get it over with quickly and go home. It's a win-win situation for young families— but I'm not getting much done. I'd go home to work, but there are lots of kids in my neighborhood, too. I expect the doorbell to ring nonstop until I turn out the lights."

"Larry Joe's on his own with the trick-or-treaters," I said. "I'm going to wrap up some stuff in the office and then head over to Holly's to put some decorations together for the mystery dinner. Winette, you'd better turn your porch light off early and try to get a good night's sleep. Tomorrow's going to be a long and busy day."

"Yes, indeed. And I suggest you take your own advice, Liv."

I went upstairs, locking the street door behind me. Partly because I didn't want to be interrupted by little costumed beggars and partly because I didn't have any candy to hand out and I couldn't bear the thought of tears.

I spent a couple of hours making phone calls, touching base with all the team leaders and members of the planning committee. Then I loaded everything I would need from my supply closet into the car, so I wouldn't have to stop by the office in the morning.

I drove to Holly's place and we ordered pizza delivery before getting down to work on decorations for the dinner tables. We put together Clue-themed embellishments to place in and around the live flower arrangements that would be delivered tomorrow to the country club.

Each floral arrangement would sport a wooden floral pick with a pair of game cards of Clue characters glued back to back. We had found some fun, vintage game cards from the 1950s on eBay, featuring colorful drawings of the usual suspects.

At the base of each arrangement, we'd place a couple of items related to the featured character. There would be a pair of evening gloves and a veiled hat for Mrs. White, a couple of books and a brass microscope for Professor Plum, rhinestone-studded cat-eye glasses and a small jade peacock statue for Mrs. Peacock, and so on.

We were interrupted a few times by the doorbell. Holly, who almost always looks like she's wearing a sixties costume anyway, would slip on a witch's hat to greet the trick-or-treaters at her door and distribute candy. I stood a few feet behind her in the entry hall to get a peek at all the cute costumes. Early on we had a few young kids dressed as princesses and lions and one precious little lamb. As the hours went by, the kids got taller and the costumes turned to mostly vampires and zombies. Holly finally extinguished the porch light to signal that the candy store was now closed.

We ended the evening by going over the work list for the big day—it was distressingly long. But that's the nature of our business. So many things just can't be done ahead of time.

It was late by the time I left Holly's house and headed for home. With a few exceptions, the houses along the way were dark and the streets and sidewalks were clear. I did pass one convertible filled with teenagers playing loud music and wearing Goth costumes, or at least I assumed they were costumes.

When I pulled into my driveway I decided not to open the garage door. I worried the noise might wake Larry Joe, who was likely fast asleep by now.

We always turn off the porch lights before bed, so it was dark as I went up the front steps. I was fumbling with the keys, trying to find the one to the front door, when I felt something brush against my arm.

I turned my head and found myself nearly nose to nose with a disfigured face staring at me. I screamed and backed away, tumbling down the steps and landing on my backside. The figure seemed to remain motionless as I scrambled to get to my feet and make a run to the car.

The porch light suddenly lit up and a shirtless Larry Joe dashed across the porch and down the steps, still zipping up the blue jeans he had hastily pulled on over his boxers when he jumped out of bed.

"Liv, are you all right?" he said, rushing over to me.

He clasped my hands and helped me to a standing position. Wordless, I looked past him to the porch. I could still see a sleeve mostly hidden by the porch column.

"What?" Larry Joe said, following me as I walked haltingly back to the porch.

On closer inspection and with the benefit of the porch light, I saw a dummy wearing a Freddy Krueger mask lashed to one of the porch columns.

Okay, so we do live on Elm, and Mama likes to refer to our house as the Nightmare on Elm Street. But I didn't think this prank was Mama's handiwork. Somebody else apparently shared her warped sense of humor.

"Huh, I didn't even notice that when I rushed out the door. I guess I was so focused on you and seeing if you were okay," Larry Joe said.

Larry Joe and I went into the house.

"Did you have many trick-or-treaters tonight while I was gone?" I asked.

"Quite a few," he said, "including some teenagers. My guess is that one of the older kids came back and installed Freddy after I switched off the porch lights. Pretty appropriate decoration for our house when you think about it."

"I'm too tired to think about it," I said as I wearily ascended the stairs to the bedroom.

* * *

I must have fallen asleep well after midnight, with my time line and fund-raiser notes strewn on the floor beside the bed. I woke up before the alarm went off at six.

I was already showered, dressed, and sucking down coffee when Larry Joe came down to the kitchen just after six-thirty. He grabbed me by the waist and pulled me up against him.

"Breathe, Liv," he said, gently kissing me on the forehead. "You have covered every detail of this event. . . ."

"Events, plural," I interrupted.

"Events, plural," he said. "Everyone is eager to pitch in, and it's going to be great."

I looked up at my husband's dreamy brown eyes and baby-face dimples and enjoyed the view for a moment before the sheer panic of reality kicked in again.

"Thanks for the vote of confidence. Now I gotta run," I said. "You have your to-do list?"

"Yes, ma'am. I'll leave the office no later than three o'clock to get my chores done."

"You're a keeper," I said, then gave Larry Joe a quick buss on the lips and hurried out the door.

At seven AM at command central, otherwise known as Sweet Deal Realty, we were still waiting for a couple of folks to arrive. I stirred creamer into my coffee and looked over the muffins and doughnuts on offer, or what was left of them. Some men were standing on the far side of the room chatting, their paper plates piled with pastries. I had run out the door without any breakfast, and my stomach was starting to growl.

"Ooh, some of these muffins are still warm," Dorothy said.

"Did you just eat the last pumpkin spice muffin?" Bryn asked, furrowing her brow. "Those are my favorite."

Dorothy gave a sheepish grin and mumbled "Sorry"—with her mouth full.

"Here, Bryn, take one of these blueberry muffins," Winette offered, sliding a box in her direction. "They're delicious, and I think they're still warm."

"Thanks, but I'm allergic. Blueberries make my throat swell up."

"That very same thing happens to my little grandson, Luke, if he eats anything with peanuts in it," Holly noted. "In fact, he has to carry one of those EpiPens everywhere he goes. I never realized before how many things have peanuts in them."

"My son Lester can eat anything—and does," Dorothy said. "The only thing he's allergic to is hard work."

Winette clapped her hands to get everyone's attention.

"Speaking of work, we all need to get to our assigned areas to make sure everything that needs to happen for tonight's festivities happens," she said, rallying the troops.

I handed out checklists to the planning committee members to take with them to their assigned areas. Holly, Winette, and I would be roving among the various venues to troubleshoot any problems that arose.

After going over the schedule and answering a couple of questions, the committee members started filing out the door.

Holly and I helped carry food out to Winette's vehicle. Her car loaded with several grocery bags of marshmallows and chocolate bars and a couple of ice chests filled with hot dogs, Winette headed out to the Crego's farm to check on arrangements for the teen hayride and bonfire.

"Holly, why don't you go on over to the country club? There's so much going on there, what with the dinner, the dance, and the play. I'll go by the church gym to check on the children's Halloween festival and join you later."

"Awlright, darlin'," Holly said.

She turned to leave and I suddenly blurted out, "Holly, what are we forgetting?"

I realized my hands were clammy and felt certain I would break out in hives at any moment.

"Don't worry, Liv. We've got this," Holly said with enviable poise. "Everything has been meticulously arranged. And you, Winette, and I will make sure the plan is executed to the letter. Nobody would dare mess with us."

After inspecting the Presbyterian Church gym and checking up on the volunteers for the children's festival, I started to feel a little better about things. The kindergarten teacher in charge of the kids' event had all her workers divided into pairs or "buddy teams" to make sure no one could wander away from their duties unnoticed. I wouldn't have been the least bit surprised to see them walking single file, holding on to a line of string.

I arrived at the Dixie Country Club a few minutes

before eight AM. The apparent chaos gave me an instant headache. It was eleven hours til showtime and the only things that had been set up were the tables.

The florist brought in the flowers for the table centerpieces, and Holly and I began placing the Clue-themed decorations in and around the arrangements. A couple of the ornaments had come apart in transit. I dug into my bag of tricks and realized I'd forgotten to pack a glue gun. I asked the carpenter who was working on erecting the sets if he had one I could borrow. He looked at me like I was crazy, waved a pneumatic nail gun in my direction, and said, "Would this work?"

I thanked him for the offer and told Holly I would drive back to the office to get the glue gun and anything else I thought we could possibly need.

"Don't worry about things here, darlin'," Holly said. "We really are in good shape."

Whether or not it was true, I appreciated her saying it. As I was about to leave, my cell phone rang. It was the team leader at the church gym.

"The teenage volunteers setting up our booths and games have burned through all the doughnuts, muffins, and bagels already, even though I thought we had enough for days. One of them was even desperate enough to dip into the basket of fruit on the table, although the rest of them turned their noses up at the suggestion of something healthy. It's a long time until lunch, and I don't want their energy levels to drop off," she said. "Is there any way you could have someone deliver extra goodies to tide us over?"

"I'm just heading into town, so I'll take care of

it," I said, thinking how she was used to giving snacks to kindergarten students whose tastes and appetites were a bit different from teenagers.

I parked on the square and ran upstairs to my office. I tossed into a file box the glue gun, extra glue sticks, an additional stapler, some magic markers, and several other things I thought might come in handy.

I stowed the box in my SUV and was about to get in the driver's seat when I spotted Di and Dave coming out of the diner. Di waved me over.

"You look worn out already and it's only eight-thirty in the morning," Di said. "Be sure you make time to eat so your blood sugar doesn't bottom out on you."

"You do look kinda frazzled," Dave added.

"I've been swilling coffee and eating doughnuts since the crack of dawn. I don't think blood sugar's my problem," I said.

"I'd better get back to the office," Dave said, giving Di's arm a discreet little squeeze before sauntering down the block.

"So you and Dave had breakfast together. Does that mean he gave you an apology?"

"We both apologized. I did say some pretty nasty things to him the other night," she said sheepishly. "But don't go making a big deal out of it, okay?"

"Okay."

"I know you've got your hands full today. Anything I can do to help?" Di asked.

"Actually, you could make a delivery for me, if you wouldn't mind."

I explained how the students had eaten a day's

worth of doughnuts already. Di fell in step with me as I started walking toward Dixie Donuts and More.

"Although I can't really criticize the kids, grown folks were plowing through the muffins at the planning meeting this morning like it was their last meal."

Renee said hello as we entered the shop. "What can I do for you?"

"The teenagers out at the church gym are bottomless pits," I said. "Could you add some more doughnuts and muffins to my tab?"

"For the kids, I'll give you three dozen on the house," she said. "Just tell me what you want."

I looked in the display case and started picking out an assortment, a half dozen of these, a half dozen of those. Renee started packing up my order, and even though I should have paced myself on the caffeine, I ordered a coffee to go.

I paid for the coffee, and Di and I started walking back down the block. I thanked Di for offering to make the delivery and told her to help herself to a muffin or a doughnut.

Then suddenly it struck me. I guess the huge volumes of caffeine I'd imbibed had finally made it to my brain. I turned to Di, almost spilling my coffee in the process, and said, "I know who killed Morgan!"

Chapter 25

After making this startling declaration, I absently set the bag filled with bakery boxes on one of several benches lining the square before crumpling onto the bench myself.

"What? Who? How?" Di said, covering all the bases except for "When?"

I shared my epiphany with her.

"Wow," she said. "You have to tell Dave about this right away."

"You're right."

We put the bakery bag in Di's car and hurried across to the sheriff's office.

I started telling Dave my story, and while I was talking something else that didn't register at the time suddenly came to mind. For a change, Dave seemed genuinely interested in the information I was giving him instead of dismissing me as a nut job.

"Problem is," I said, "I don't know if there's any way to prove it."

"Let me worry about that," Dave said. "Ted and I will get right on this and see what we can dig up."

He started to walk away, but I called out, "Dave, if possible please don't arrest anybody until after the mystery dinner tonight."

Dave opened his mouth to object, but I cut him off.

"I know it may not be a reasonable request, but it is for charity and it would be a shame if anything threw a wet blanket on the fund-raiser at this point," I said with imploring eyes.

Dave wouldn't promise anything, but told me I needn't worry since he had no evidence to make an arrest right now. Then he reminded me there was still a pretty strong case against Jasmine. I swear he was like a broken record.

Di and I walked out of the sheriff's office.

"I'll ride with you out to the church," I said. "Maybe we can think of some way to help Dave out."

"Loathe as he is to accept help from us, he seemed to jump on what you told him."

"I know without a doubt who killed Morgan," I said. "But proving it is another matter entirely."

Di and I drove to the church gym. By the time we delivered the doughnuts, we had hatched a plan we hoped would trap a killer.

The first and most crucial step was to catch Lucinda before she left town, even though I knew Dave's head would probably explode if he knew we were talking to her. I had no idea what time her flight was scheduled to depart, but I knew she wasn't an early riser by choice. It was 9:20 AM when we arrived at the hotel.

"Do you actually think we can talk Lucinda into this? Why would she ever agree to it?" Di said.

"Your lack of confidence is inspiring," I said. "I'm depending on Lucinda's ego. She loves an audience, and I'm hoping that performing in front of the home crowd will be an enticement she can't pass up."

"You really believe that?" Di said.

"Yes. I have to. Because if she doesn't agree to play along, it's game over."

I was a little worried when I didn't spot one of her goons standing guard in the lobby. I waved at Ravi as we walked to the elevator, and he shot me a weak wave and a worried look.

Di and I got off the elevator on the third floor, and two guys from Lucinda's entourage stopped us halfway down the hall to her room, telling us we couldn't see Lucinda without an appointment.

That was good news. At least we knew she hadn't left for the airport yet.

The more insistent they were that we leave, the louder Di got.

"You might as well take your hands off us," she said. "We're not leaving until we speak to Lucinda. And despite what she may think of us, she'll want to hear this."

Mitzi stepped into the hallway. The disgusted look on her face told me she was ready to give us what for. But to my surprise Lucinda stepped out right behind her.

"I'll handle this," she said, waving them all away before turning toward us.

"I had a feeling I wouldn't make it out of town

without seeing you one more time," Lucinda said, glaring at me.

"That's because you're psychic," I said, immediately regretting that I sounded so antagonistic.

She started to turn away, and I said, "I'm sorry, Lucinda. Please hear me out. I know who killed Morgan."

"You do?" she said with a genuine look of surprise.

"Yes. But we need your help to prove it."

Di and I briefly laid out our little hare-brained scheme and crossed our fingers that Lucinda would buy it. To our surprise she seemed amenable and invited us into her sitting room to discuss the details of what we wanted her to do.

"It's a crazy idea. But I suppose I owe it to Morgan to do what I can to bring her killer to justice," Lucinda said in that imperious tone I'd come to find so unendearing.

She called Mitzi in and instructed her to change the airline tickets for the two of them to a Sunday departure.

"The rest of the team can fly out as scheduled," she said. "But since we're packed, go ahead and book us for tonight at a hotel closer to the airport under your name. I don't want to risk getting waylaid one more night in this town."

So far, so good.

Next up, I needed to go to the high school and enlist Mrs. Cooley's help. I felt badly about abandoning Holly. Di volunteered to go to the country club and help Holly in whatever way she could.

"Do you want me to tell Holly what you're up to?" Di asked.

"No. Just tell her some other things came up," I said. "As big and spread out as tonight's events are, she'll have no trouble believing that."

Di dropped me off at my SUV and loaded the box with the glue gun and other supplies into her car before driving to the country club. I hoped Mrs. Cooley would be receptive to the plan. Our plot to trap the killer would fall flat without some help from the murder mystery performers.

On the drive over to the school I toyed with the idea of calling Nell to tell her that the sheriff was finally on the trail of the real murderer. But I thought better of it, knowing Jasmine wasn't in the clear just yet.

Since it was Saturday, the school office was closed and the main entrance was locked. I drove around to the side of the building, where several cars were parked and a side door was propped open. It was the door to the auditorium.

Mrs. Cooley was once again in the front row, running the actors through their scenes. When she saw me cutting through rows of theater seats as I made my way down front, she called out "Cut" and told the kids to take five. She stood and started walking toward me. We met in the main aisle.

"I'm a little surprised to see you here with everything you have going on today," she said. "Is everything okay with the sets? A couple of the dads volunteered to oversee the construction and setup, and I thought that was probably a better idea than having the students do it."

"Oh, everything with the sets seemed to be coming

along nicely when I left the country club," I said. "That's not why I'm here."

I tried to explain the confusing situation as clearly as I could and hoped she'd agree to her necessary part in the plan.

"Basically, you'd only need to rewrite a few lines in the next-to-last scene," I said. "I jotted down the gist of it here," I said, handing her one of my earlier checklists with notes scribbled on the back of it.

"Of course, you'd be the one to write the actual dialogue, since you wrote the script to begin with."

She seemed skeptical, but took the paper and read over the notes.

"It's pretty eleventh hour for the students to learn new lines. . . ." she said.

"I really wouldn't ask if it weren't so important," I said. I held my breath as she mulled it over.

"Are you sure the sheriff will be okay with this? I wouldn't want to put the students or their parents in an awkward situation."

"I understand, and I accept complete responsibility," I said. "Besides, none of the lines the students will be acting out will be directly related to the murder—Morgan's murder, that is. We're just changing the trajectory of the story a bit to set the stage for our star performer."

"I suppose so," she said, reading over my notes again. "Okay, if it helps bring a killer to justice, I can hardly refuse. I'll write it so Ryan and Megan— Professor Plum and Mrs. Peacock—have the new dialogue. Neither of them will have any trouble learning a few new lines. But I don't think I'll tell the students the reason for the changes. It would just make them more nervous."

"Oh, I agree completely. Thank you, Mrs. Cooley. Thank you so much," I said. "Call me on my cell if you have any questions or problems. I'll put the additional props you'll need on the set. What time do you think you all will arrive at the country club?"

"The kids will be in costume and on the set by five forty-five for a final run-through."

"Great," I said.

I hurried to my car and made one more quick stop to pick up the necessary props before driving back to the country club.

When I pulled into the parking lot, Winette was walking toward her car. I waved to her. I believed it was best that as few people as possible knew about our catch-a-killer plan, but I felt Winette was one of those few people who needed to know. After all, she would be the emcee for the evening.

I outlined the basic idea, and Winette listened with a pained expression.

"*Mmm-hmm.* I know it would be a waste of time to try to talk you out of this," she said as she opened the driver's door to her car. "You should probably make sure the sheriff will be on hand tonight, just in case."

I thought about her parting comment as I watched her drive away. But I couldn't imagine what could go wrong with the plan.

Di, who had volunteered to help Holly in my stead, came over as soon as she spotted me.

"Is Mrs. Cooley on board?" she asked quietly.

"Yes," I said. "All systems are go. Have you seen or heard from Dave?"

"No," Di said. "But I don't really expect to until

tonight. Unless work intervenes, which is a real possibility, he plans to come to the dinner."

"Oh, good," I said. "Winette seems to think it would be a good idea for him to be around for the proceedings."

"Have you told anyone besides Winette and Mrs. Cooley—and Lucinda, of course," she said.

"No. I figure the fewer people who know, the better."

"Unless you need something else from me, I'm heading home," Di said.

"I think we're good," I said. "Thanks for pitching in. I'll see you tonight."

It was no surprise that Holly seemed to have things well in hand in the main dining room, so I checked in with Felix in the kitchen and then proceeded to the ballroom to see how preparations for the dance were coming along.

Harold and Kenny were affixing strands of twinkling lights to the underside of the catwalks and scaffolding near the ceiling of the ballroom. When most of the lights were dimmed, except for the spotlight aimed at the band performing onstage, it would look like a canopy of stars. White wooden folding chairs were arranged around the perimeter of the room in small groupings between white columns that were wrapped in ivy and strands of white lights.

I took a short lunch break to eat one of the sandwiches that ladies from a couple of local churches had brought by for the volunteers. I had to cajole Holly into sitting down for a few minutes to eat something. She's a force to be reckoned with when she's on a mission.

I moved back and forth between the dining room and ballroom. I spent a lot of time on the phone, fielding questions and putting out fires. Fortunately, there were no literal fires, although I double-checked with the chief of the volunteer fire department to make sure someone would be onsite for the evening bonfire out at the farm.

Dylan came into the ballroom pushing a cart loaded with planters and pots of blooming shrubs and flowers to add to the ones already lining the front of the elevated stage. Nell's son, Billy Jr., walked in just behind him and helped unload oversize pots of trumpet-shaped blooms of four o'clocks along with overflowing planters of sweet autumn clematis. The bounteous blooms, all white, would look even more beautiful tonight, bathed in the glow of strategically placed uplights.

"Dylan, the flowers and shrubs look amazing. And they smell wonderful, too," I said, breathing in the heady scents.

"Yeah, this variety of clematis is really pretty this time of year, and so fragrant," he said, gently cupping his hand under one of the star-shaped blooms. "And the four o'clocks will keep blooming like this until the first frost."

"Thank you so much, Dylan," I said. "It's so generous of you both to haul all these heavy planters in for just one evening."

Billy Jr. gave me a weak smile. I had a feeling helping Dylan out was Nell's idea, not his. But at least he didn't seem to be complaining.

"Glad to do it," Dylan said. "I've pitched in with RR a few times and have seen firsthand the amazing way they help people."

"Will I see you at the dinner tonight?"

"I'm still not sure yet," he said. "We'll see."

Just before five o'clock, Lucinda called and insisted I come by the hotel and help walk her through her part again. I didn't really have the time, but I couldn't risk having her flee the scene before showtime.

I stopped by my house for a few minutes on the way to the hotel to freshen up and to grab my costume. I discerned—rightly, as it turned out—that Lucinda would hold me hostage until it was time for the dinner.

Chapter 26

Guests were beginning to arrive for the mystery dinner in their Clue game-themed costumes when I pulled up beside the country club and parked in the employee parking lot. I was behind the wheel of my SUV, with Lucinda in the backseat just like old times. We climbed out of the car, and she gave me a wink before heading to the kitchen door. I felt a twinge of nerves in my stomach, but quickly dismissed it. The show must go on, I reminded myself.

I walked through the front door, greeting some of the dinner guests in the lobby before hurrying to the dining room. I paused only briefly to admire the Residential Rehab sign beside the doors.

Winette came up behind me and touched my sleeve. "I was beginning to wonder where you were. And I continue to wonder about your sanity. Are you sure you want to go ahead with this little scheme?"

"Sure as I'll ever be."

"Well, then, good luck," she said, doubtful. "It should be interesting, anyway."

"Oh, there you are," Holly said. "We're going to open the dining room doors to the dinner guests in less than ten minutes."

I hadn't had time to fill Holly in on our last-minute plans for the murder mystery and hoped she wouldn't feel slighted.

"Holly, I don't have time to explain now. But don't be surprised about anything . . . uh, unusual that may happen during the play. It's all planned, sort of."

She gave me a curious look, said "Awlright, darlin,'" then moved on to apprising me of some last-minute wrinkles that needed ironing out, like a new foursome of guests who'd showed up without reservations and being short a waiter.

Holly said she had already checked with the chef, who said he had enough food to accommodate a few extra diners. I quickly conferred with Winette to make sure she hadn't turned away any unregistered guests—I didn't think it would be fair to let in last-minute guests if others had already been turned away. She hadn't, so I advised the group they were welcome for dinner if they were prepared to hand over a check for the one hundred dollar donation per plate. I said this tactfully, of course.

I asked Holly if Kenny was still around. My go-to handyman had volunteered to take care of any last-minute carpentry needs that came up while erecting the sets for the play and decorating the ballroom for the dance. He'd been at it most of the day.

I spotted him double-checking some of the stage sets.

"Kenny, do you have plans for tonight?"

"Just planning to chill out and watch some lame horror movie on TV."

"I hate to ask, since I know you've already put in a full day. But would you be willing to stand in as a waiter? We have one who hasn't shown up. Since this is way above and beyond the call of duty, I'll pay the usual hourly wage if you can stay."

Kenny looked at me with puppy dog eyes.

"You hurt my feelings, Ms. Mac, thinking I'd accept money. I'm happy to wait tables or whatever, but only as a volunteer, right?" he said.

"I'm sorry, Kenny. I just didn't want to take advantage of your generous nature when you've already done so much. Go on out to the kitchen and Holly will find you a waiter's uniform that fits—more or less."

As he started to walk away, I called out, "Oh, and Kenny . . ." He looked back at me over his shoulder. "Thanks," I said.

He gave me a thumbs-up and a shy smile before heading to the kitchen.

I looked over to see that the dining room doors were open and guests were streaming in.

I stood dumbstruck for a moment, taking in the surreal sight.

When the planning committee decided to add a costume contest to the murder mystery dinner, we had tossed around a few ideas. We had discussed favorite movie characters or favorite detectives before settling on Clue as the theme. We reasoned that people could use ideas from the game or the movie as inspiration. It also gave us a chance to hand out more prizes. Instead of just one or two for best male and female costumes, it allowed us to give a best costume award for Mrs. Peacock, Colonel Mustard, and so on. We also decided to include awards for the butler and maid to bring it up to eight costume categories in all. Mrs. Cooley liked the idea so much that she decided to use the Clue characters in her murder mystery script as well.

This also let us have a bit of fun with the prize baskets. The award for the best Miss Scarlett, for example, included a gift certificate to a lingerie shop.

But the assortment of costumes I surveyed as the guests flowed into the room was more creative than I could have imagined. I spied one Mr. Green wearing a conservative green-gray suit, with matching fedora and vintage green patterned tie. I also noted a Mr. Green in a shamrock green polyester leisure suit with a wide seventies-style tie, and another wearing lime green lederhosen with a matching cape. Other characters sported similarly broad variations in their costume designs.

As if a spotlight were beamed on her, Mama swept through the door wearing a turquoise satin 1950s-style dress, with a fitted bodice and flared skirt, undergirded with petticoats, and matching turquoise pumps. Her hat was wildly festooned with feathers, including some peacock feathers. She also sported evening gloves, a matching purse, and a brooch fashioned to look like a jewel-handled dagger.

The look suited her personality perfectly.

Earl was in tow, wearing a brown suit with a peacock feather patterned skinny tie. A medal pinned to his suit pocket indicated he was supposed to be Colonel Mustard. But it was obvious to me that he was really just an accessory for my mother's arm.

Holly called my name, jarring me back to reality, such as it was. I scurried into the employees' locker room, slipped into a restroom stall, and quickly changed into my Miss Scarlett homage—a red A-line dress that showed a modest amount of cleavage. To accentuate my modest cleavage, I pinned a pearl brooch at the center of the neckline.

I hustled to my assigned table near the kitchen so I could check on things as needed. Larry Joe was already seated at our table, along with my in-laws and Di; there was an empty chair for Dave in case he made it for dinner. Larry Joe looked gorgeous in a tuxedo that rarely gets pulled out of the closet. He gave me a big smile that showcased both his dimples—a half smile only brings out one dimple, the left one.

"You look beautiful, hon," he said with a lusty look that set me to thinking about giving him an after-dinner treat.

I got settled in my chair just as Winette stepped up to the mike to welcome the guests and get things rolling.

Winette was also in character, but like me had kept it understated, since as organizers we were recusing ourselves from the costume contest. She wore a simple navy blue dress and a small, tasteful hat with a single peacock feather stuck in it.

"Welcome, everyone," she said. "We are overjoyed that so many of you have turned out to support Residential Rehab. Our major sponsors and donors are listed on your program. But I could not even begin to list all the volunteers and donors who have helped bring this evening to fruition, including the brave folks entertaining the little ones over at the church while we enjoy a grown-up evening here. Please join me in giving all these generous volunteers a round of applause."

After the clapping died down, Winette said in a solemn voice, "On behalf of the fund-raiser planning committee, we'd like to take a moment of remembrance for a member of our committee who is no longer with us. Morgan Robison was a young woman whose life ended tragically before her time. She and her family generously supported tonight's fund-raiser, as well as many other local charities. I'd like to ask everyone to join me in observing a brief moment of silence in her honor."

After an appropriate interval, Winette continued, "Thank you so much. Your first course will be served in just a few moments. Enjoy conversation with your fellow diners and look over your programs. As soon as the waiters have cleared the tables from the first course, the lights will be dimmed. That's your cue to turn your attention to the sets on my left and enjoy the murder mystery featuring students from the Drama Department at Dixie High School, under the able direction of Mrs. Dana Cooley."

More applause.

"Be sure to take notes and confer with your dinner companions between acts. After the third act, each table will take a vote and submit a card indicating their pick for whodunit. In the fourth act, the identity of the killer will be revealed and we'll all savor the moment over dessert."

Gesturing toward my table, Winette said, "And please welcome our hometown television celebrity,

Lucinda Grable, who is generously supporting our local charity tonight."

Lucinda, who had remained out of sight until Winette introduced her, stepped from the hallway just beyond our table and waved and nodded to the crowd before taking a seat beside me. She was wearing a long-sleeved red evening gown. The sequins framing the plunging neckline accentuated her cleavage, not that she needed any help on that front.

Holly, seated at a nearby table with some of her friends and neighbors, had on a rather *Breakfast at Tiffany's* inspired evening dress—in white, instead of black—with a double strand of pearls, elbow-length gloves, and Audrey Hepburn sunglasses. She even sported a glamorous, extra-long cigarette holder, displaying an unlit cigarette.

My in-laws were adorable as Mrs. White and Colonel Mustard in costumes Miss Betty had used her considerable seamstress skills to adapt to the theme. She wore a simply elegant boatneck white satin dress with a gauzy ruffle circling the neckline. She had customized a khaki suit jacket with service ribbons above the breast pocket for Daddy Wayne.

Like Larry Joe and me, Di had taken a more practical approach by wearing clothes she already owned. She had on a French maid's uniform, a leftover from Halloweens past.

Four wineglasses were lined up in front of each diner, along with a water glass and coffee cup and saucer. Gloved waiters in short tuxedo jackets poured a Chardonnay and then served pumpkin-ginger bisque as the first of a five-course meal. The play would be performed in four acts, one after each course, wrapping up with dessert.

My mother-in-law was a bit starstruck, babbling on to Lucinda about how much she enjoyed her TV show. Daddy Wayne didn't seem impressed and was even less impressed with the quantity of soup. He seemingly inhaled it in a few quick spoonfuls.

"I hope they're going to serve us something more substantial," he groused.

"They're serving dinner in courses, dear," Miss Betty said. "I'm sure you'll be filled up by the end."

"Maybe you should pace yourself, Dad," Larry Joe said.

"Should've eaten something before we came," he said, with a childish pout.

Larry Joe didn't have a lot to say, but his eyes kept wandering over to Lucinda, and it seemed to me they were aimed a bit lower than her face. If I'd been sitting next to him, he'd have a big bruise swelling up on his shin. *If he keeps this up*, I thought, *he's going to be sleeping on the sofa tonight.*

Just as the waitstaff finished clearing the soup bowls, the room lights were dimmed and a spotlight illuminated the library scene, where some members of the cast were already positioned. The others entered shortly from stage left, and we were introduced to each of the characters and learned something about them during the course of their conversation. The scene closed as the butler invited them into the dining room for dinner.

I was proud of the students.

As the spotlight was extinguished, appreciative dinner guests spontaneously burst into applause.

"Oh, Liv, I think they did a wonderful job with the kids' costumes," Miss Betty said.

"They do look good," Lucinda said. "Certainly better than anything the Drama Department had when I was at Dixie High. Speaking of which, the sheriff said it would be okay, so I walked around that little cemetery at the retreat center this afternoon," she said, turning toward me.

"Did your crew shoot some more footage out there?" Di asked.

"No, I was just hoping for some inspiration for tonight," she said.

We were interrupted by Dave, who slid into the empty chair next to Di. He was dressed like a sheriff.

Dave spoke to everyone and said he'd probably have to slip out again shortly. "Y'all look great," he said, with a polite nod to the rest of us before locking eyes with Di.

I filled the awkward silence by resuming the conversation with Lucinda.

"You didn't drive all the way out to St. Julian's by yourself, did you?"

"No, I was chauffeured by my former stalker, Sindhu. She's been dying to do something for me, so I let her drive me there."

"Stalker?" Dave said.

"Just starstruck," I interjected. "You know how silly some people act around celebrities."

Lucinda and I shared a knowing look before she continued.

"It was kind of creepy being out by the lodge again, but I hope Agatha will offer me some insight tonight," she said.

"Lucinda has agreed to take part in our little play tonight," I said, attempting to head off any more inquiries from Dave. "We thought it would be a real treat for the audience."

"Who's Agatha?" Larry Joe piped up.

Clearly it was a mistake for me not to sit within kicking distance of that man.

"A ghost," Lucinda said matter-of-factly.

That brought the conversation to a screeching halt. The waiters rescued us from the uncomfortable silence when they began serving the fish course.

Larry Joe's dad tucked into the bacon-wrapped scallops and had cleared his plate before everyone at the table had been served. My mother-in-law blushed, her white dress emphasizing the pink tinge of embarrassment that flushed up her neck and face.

Deputy Ted entered the room and waved to attract Dave's attention.

"Sorry, folks," Dave said. "I hate to eat and run, but duty calls."

"Can't you stay for the main course?" Di said. "You've barely eaten anything."

"Sorry. Maybe you could save me a doggy bag," he said, giving her a wink as he rose from the table.

As the spotlight cast a glow on the set for the second act, the characters were seated at a dinner table as the butler served soup. Colonel Mustard was trying to flirt with an unimpressed Miss Scarlett, and Professor Plum seemed extremely interested in the circumstances surrounding the recent demise of Mrs. White's husband. Mrs. Peacock and Mr. Green were playing it close to the vest, but the butler tossed out a couple of double entendres that let us know they were not as innocent as they tried to seem. The scene ended with all the actors racing from the dining room after hearing a loud crash from somewhere offstage.

Shortly after the house lights came back up, the servers started bringing out the main course.

"Well, it's about time," my father-in-law blurted out.

"Wayne, watch your manners," Miss Betty said.

Waiters sat plates of roasted root vegetables and green beans at each place and carved the prime rib from a cart, table side.

When they offered to serve Lucinda, she declined, saying she didn't care for anything.

"I'll take hers," Daddy Wayne said.

I noticed Lucinda closing her eyes, and I gathered she was preparing herself for her upcoming performance as she had done the night of the retreat.

The men were fully focused on their medium rare beef, so Di, Miss Betty, and I took turns surveying the room and commenting on various costumes.

I searched for some of the usual suspects, curious about their costume choices.

Nell was dressed up as Miss Scarlett, although her skintight miniskirt, red sparkly tube top, and boa seemed to suggest more two-bit hooker than upscale madam. Her husband, Billy, was outfitted as a pimp-inspired Mr. Green.

Sindhu looked stunning in a predominately red silk sari, offering a classy, exotic spin on Miss Scarlett, while Ravi channeled Professor Plum in a tweed jacket with a purple ascot and matching pocket square.

Bryn was wearing a white satin strapless evening gown with matching shawl and a diamond necklace that looked like it should be locked up in the Tower of London. Pierce was wearing a tuxedo tailcoat, but could in no way be mistaken for a butler. The handsome couple looked as if they might be on their way to the opera.

Jasmine and Dylan were also in the audience. I hoped that seeing Jasmine out of jail would be unsettling without prompting our killer to bolt. Jasmine was also dressed as Mrs. White, except her version featured a white-on-white embroidered tunic with a white denim skirt and a wreath of white flowers in her hair. Dylan looked a bit like a wayward cast member from *A Clockwork Orange* in a white button-front shirt, white jeans, and tan suspenders, except his bowler hat was green instead of black.

"Am I seeing things, or is that Dorothy from *The Wizard of Oz* sitting by the door in the back?" Di asked.

"It certainly is," I said. "Maybe she didn't quite understand the theme."

"I guess there's one in every crowd," Di said.

I noticed the mayor and other costume judges strolling from table to table, taking notes.

"It'll be interesting to see who the judges pick for best costumes," Di said.

"I don't envy their job," Miss Betty said. "Did you see Connie and Chester Menster? I think it's cute they decided to swap roles."

After she pointed out where they were sitting, I couldn't help but giggle at the sight of Mrs. Menster, who's maybe five feet tall, dressed in a tuxedo blouse with tie and black pants and her taller-than-six-foot husband wearing a cheap wig and a thrift-shop sleeveless red dress that accentuated his hairy-as-gorilla arms.

Daddy Wayne, who had finally lifted his head from the feeding trough, turned to see what we were talking about.

"Chester looks like a damn fool," he said a little too loud for my mother-in-law's comfort.

After the main course had been cleared away, the lights were dimmed and the play opened with all the actors in the library, searching the room. After finding no explanation for the crash they heard at the end of Act 2, the entire cast proceeded to the kitchen through a secret passage that had been pointed out by the butler.

The actors discovered the maid's body on the kitchen floor. Next to her was a large silver platter along with a scattered mess of food and broken dishes that must have made the crashing noise when she dropped the tray. The victim's lips and tongue were blue, so they suspected poison. Mrs. Peacock spied a bowl of mouth-watering blueberries on the counter and started to take a bite. Professor Plum yelled, "Don't eat those. They're poisoned."

The scene ended.

Lucinda suddenly stood with a faraway look in her eyes and began speaking to some unseen spirit. The spotlight was once again illuminated and bounced erratically across the room before landing on Lucinda. A hush fell as the confused audience wondered whether this was a continuation of the play.

Lucinda revealed the spirit to be Agatha, the same ghost that "spoke" to her at the cemetery the night of Morgan's death. She channeled Agatha, the ghost we had heard on the recording, who was now talking about the blueberries, but Lucinda seemed perplexed. "The blueberries are from tonight's play. Please go back to the night of the retreat." But the childish voice persisted, saying, "She couldn't eat the blueberries."

Nell stood up and hollered, "There were blueberries at the retreat—in one of those teas." I couldn't actually see her in the darkness, but there was no mistaking that voice.

"Who couldn't eat the blueberries?" Lucinda asked the ghost.

Glassy-eyed, Lucinda picked up the blueberries from the stage set and walked to Bryn's table, holding out the bowl to her. Agatha's shrill voice accused, "You didn't eat the blueberries. You gave them to the smiling lady." Bryn jumped up, screaming, and knocked the dish from Lucinda's hands, shattering the crystal bowl and scattering the blueberries across the table and onto the floor.

"I insist you end this charade right this minute, Winette," Bryn called out. "I think it shows extremely poor taste to incorporate Morgan's murder into the script."

Winette looked over to me in the dim glow behind the spotlight, and I tried to discreetly hold out my hand in a gesture that said "Wait."

Lucinda collapsed onto a chair and seemed to start emerging from her trance. The lighting tech killed the spotlight and brought up the house lights. But a tense audience seemed to have grown suspicious of Bryn.

"I remember serving blueberry-hibiscus tea to Bryn, as well as Liv and Morgan and a couple of other women at the retreat," Jasmine said. "So why would the ghost say she couldn't drink it? I don't understand."

"Because Bryn is severely allergic to blueberries, that's why," Dorothy chimed in. "She said so just this morning at the planning meeting. "Liv, Winette, Holly, y'all were there. Y'all heard her say so, remember?"

"This is ridiculous," Bryn said, with the wild eyes of a cornered animal. "Jasmine would say anything to cast suspicion on me or anyone else. The sheriff's got her dead to rights. She's already been charged with Morgan's murder, or have you all forgotten that?"

Pierce stood up and called for cool heads. "I think everyone's getting carried away by tonight's murder mystery and a stellar performance by our celebrity psychic here. But please, folks, let's remember this is all just scripted fiction." He reached over and touched Bryn's hand in a silent admonishment to keep quiet.

Pierce started to say something else to the crowd, but Dylan interrupted him, talking loudly. "I remember showing the hemlock water-dropwort plant to Bryn before the garden tour that the chamber sponsored this spring. She asked me all kinds of questions about it. That's *not* fiction."

Dave walked into the room, and Pierce said, "Thank goodness you're here, Sheriff. Imaginations are running wild, and things were beginning to get a little out of hand."

Dylan took a couple of steps toward Dave. "Yeah, I'm glad you're here, too, Sheriff. That plant the poison came from, the one your deputy confiscated. It was always kept under a bell jar so animals couldn't accidentally eat any of it. There shouldn't be anybody's prints on it except for Jasmine's," he said emphatically. "Can plants be dusted for fingerprints?"

An eerie silence fell over the room as everyone waited for Dave's answer.

"Actually, yes, in some cases they can," Dave said. "In fact, a forensics expert from the FBI field office in Memphis did just that. He managed to get a clear thumbprint from the root of the hemlock water-dropwort plant stored in the evidence room. And it's a perfect match to a thumbprint we retrieved from a wineglass cleared from Bryn Davenport's table after the first course this evening."

The silent pall over the room erupted into gasps and waves of chatter.

Dave walked directly to Bryn's table as deputies Ted and Eric moved toward the table from either side.

Pierce, shifting into attorney mode, jumped up and protested. "This is outrageous. If the district attorney pursues this case against my wife, I'll tear it apart in minutes. Don't you dare underestimate my reputation."

"Your wife, your reputation," Bryn suddenly exploded. "That's rich. You don't care any more about me than you did that two-bit floozy, Morgan, even though you'd been sleeping with her for the past two years, and your secretary—and God knows who else."

Pierce's face reddened as he ran his index finger inside his formal collar and nervously twisted his neck.

"Sheriff, I implore you to admit my wife to the hospital for psychiatric evaluation," Pierce said quietly. "She's been under a tremendous strain, and I'm afraid she may be a danger to herself."

Bryn scooped up a shard of broken glass and lunged wildly at her husband. She missed slashing Pierce's face by mere inches as Ted grabbed her shoulders and jerked her back.

"Ted, I think you better cuff Mrs. Davenport and Mirandize her," Dave said.

"You're crazy if you think I'm going to let you lock me up in some loony bin," Bryn yelled at Pierce. "You're the one who should be dead. I should have killed you. . . ."

She was still shouting at Pierce as Ted and Dave led her away. Pierce pulled his cell phone from his pocket and started to walk away.

"Not so fast, Pierce," Dave said. "That thumbprint we retrieved from the poison plant didn't belong to your wife. It was yours."

"You can't be . . . this is j-j-just . . ." the usually eloquent Pierce stammered.

"And another interesting thing. We found a fragment of the blouse Miss Grable was wearing when she was run down the other night. It was caught on the side-view mirror of a dark SUV also belonging to you."

You could have heard a pin drop in the room.

"Pierce Davenport, I'm placing you under arrest

for attempted murder and for conspiracy to commit murder," Dave said as he snapped handcuffs around Pierce's wrists.

"Eric, read Mr. Davenport his rights."

Dave walked behind Eric as he led Pierce out of the building.

After a few more minutes of chaos, Winette took the microphone and instructed people to take their seats and asked for quiet.

"Our drama students have worked so hard and done such a good job, I know none of us wants to miss the big reveal. If someone from each table will write down the table choice for the killer in the play, I'll come around and collect them. As soon as they've all been turned in, we'll dim the lights for the final scene."

The unveiling of Miss Scarlett as the killer was a little anticlimactic after Mrs. White, aka Bryn Davenport, and her husband had just been dragged away in handcuffs. But the students did a nice job with the finale, and the audience gave them a grateful round of applause.

Lucinda, who wasn't accustomed to being upstaged, tapped me on the shoulder and told me her ride had arrived to take her to her hotel in Memphis.

"Thank you, Lucinda, for playing the part tonight," I said sincerely. "Bryn's emotional confession in front of half the town is certainly icing on the cake."

"I'm glad I could play a small part in finding justice for Morgan. I especially enjoyed the part where the high and mighty Pierce Davenport suffered utter humiliation," Lucinda said with a weary smile. "I can't believe he tried to kill me."

Actually, it wasn't that hard for me to imagine someone wanting to kill Lucinda, but I didn't say so.

Lucinda made a less than grand exit through the side door.

I wasn't terribly surprised when Mama was announced as the winner for the best Mrs. Peacock costume. The audience was wildly enthusiastic when Chester Menster was awarded the best Miss Scarlett prize. I was just happy the judges didn't give it to Miss Fake Bosoms Grable, since Larry Joe had been nearly hypnotized by her silicone implants all evening.

However, I thought the judges' shining moment was awarding the Mrs. White and Mr. Green awards to Jasmine and Dylan. Everyone viewed it as a gesture of the town's support for Jasmine, who had been unjustly jailed after being framed for murder. Jasmine burst into tears when the audience gave her a standing ovation.

All the McKays gathered around to congratulate Mama on her win. She was clutching her trophy like an Academy Award.

Despite the tense drama of the arrest, everyone was so relieved to have Morgan's killer in custody that the mood was festive. The alcohol flowed liberally from the cash bar, and folks were just as generous in opening their wallets for the silent auction. The fund-raiser for Residential Rehab was a resounding success. Several people told me that they thought we should make this an annual event. That was not something my brain could even begin to process at that moment.

As we made our way to the ballroom for the dance, I caught a glimpse of Di making a discreet exit. It looked as if this wouldn't be the night that Dave and Di finally made it onto the dance floor at the same time after all.

When I had finished off a glass of wine, added to what I'd already imbibed with dinner, I accepted Larry Joe's offer for a spin around the dance floor. As the music began, I kicked him in the shin for good measure.

"*Ouch.* What was that for?"

"That's for staring at Lucinda Grable's chest all during dinner."

"Aw, Liv, I couldn't help but notice. But you know you're the only woman in the world for me," he said, flashing me a smile framed with dimples on both sides.

"I'm not quite ready to forgive you," I said. "But I'll think about it."

Larry Joe and I danced until our feet hurt. But we cut off our alcohol consumption by ten-thirty since we felt certain we would need to give somebody a ride home. In fact, after the hayride crew shuttled the kids back to town, a number of teens ended up being the designated drivers for their parents. Those with young children had left right after the dinner to pick up their tots from the Halloween carnival at the church hall.

Winette took charge of assigning drivers to everyone who needed a ride home.

Our plans had included lining up a few designated

drivers, but we had woefully underestimated how many we'd need.

Larry Joe drove his mom and dad home around one AM while I shuttled Mama and Earl to their respective abodes. Mama insisted she wasn't tipsy, but said her feet hurt too much to drive.

Chapter 27

Larry Joe and I fell into bed bone tired and didn't stir until well after noon. My guess was that the congregations were a bit sparse at most of the churches around Dixie this fine Sunday.

After putting on a robe and slippers, I stepped onto the front porch to retrieve the Sunday newspaper. This turned out to be a mistake on my part.

Edna Cleats waved and yoo-hooed to me from the end of her driveway before barreling across the street toward me. I stepped down from my porch and into the middle of the front yard to avoid having to invite her to come inside.

"Oh, Liv, I see you and Larry Joe are finally up and at 'em," she said.

I happened to know my early-rising neighbor thought sleeping in was akin to sloth.

"I heard y'all had big excitement at the mystery dinner, what with Lucinda Grable being visited by a ghost and the Davenports getting arrested."

"It was something, all right," I said. If she was interested in details, she was going to have to drag them out of me. I wasn't really in the mood to be chatty. I thought about suggesting that she call my mama for details, but I decided that wouldn't be Christian of me. Then again, Mama had practically pushed me into the fangs of a serpent on her back porch.

"Well, while you all were whooping it up, dancing and drinking, I was among the brave souls at the church hall looking after the children.

"I tell you they were a rowdy bunch. Not bad kids, just overexcited from too much candy. I had one little preschooler with a cone of cotton candy in her hand get away from me and make a beeline to the bouncy house. I went running after her, thinking what a nightmare it would be if she and those other kids bouncing around were to get cotton candy in their hair.

"By some miracle I snatched her back just before she climbed inside. I managed to keep her out, but I lost my balance and tumbled headlong into the bouncy house myself. Oh, my word, there must've been a dozen kids jumping and somersaulting in there. Just when I'd start to get my balance, a gaggle of kids would land beside me, shifting the floor, and I'd end up on my tushy again.

"Thank goodness the kindergarten teacher finally leaned inside, clapped her hands, and instructed the kids to exit single file, or I don't know if I ever would have made my way out."

She barely took a breath before continuing. "I had such a sick headache by the time I made it home last night, I had to take a half a Valium to calm my nerves.

"Mr. Winky and I plan to take it easy today. We'll

probably just snuggle up on the sofa and watch some old movies."

Mr. Winky is her cat. The Newsoms swear he's the one that keeps setting off their car alarm by jumping up on the hood in the middle of the night, but Mrs. Cleats flatly refuses to believe Mr. Winky could do such a thing.

"Mrs. Cleats, I really appreciate you and the other volunteers who ran the festival and looked after the kids while their parents were at the dinner. We raised a lot of money for Residential Rehab, and you were a key part of making that possible."

"Now, hon, I don't need any thanks or recognition," she said. "I've never been one to seek the limelight. I prefer to work quietly behind the scenes where my good works are known to God alone."

I resisted a strong urge to say *Amen.*

"You should get some rest," I suggested. "I'd better go inside and make some breakfast for Larry Joe and myself."

"You might as well move on to lunch at this point," she said with that judgmental tone that made it hard for me to love my neighbor—even if it was Sunday.

Larry Joe had already made the coffee by the time I came into the kitchen with the paper.

"You have a nice chat with Mrs. Cleats?"

"About as nice a chat as I ever have with Mrs. Cleats," I said. "She was telling me about all the good works she does that nobody except God knows about."

"Just God and you, right?" he said with a smirk.

"Uh-huh."

"Since you had such a jam-packed day yesterday,

why don't you sit down and read the Sunday paper while I whip us up some French toast," Larry Joe said.

I flipped through the sales circulars and drank coffee while Larry Joe gathered bread, milk, eggs, and the skillet.

"Oh, Liv, after Mr. Crego dropped off the teenagers at the country club, I talked to him a bit while you and Winette were matching up kids with driver's licenses to take their parents home."

I could smell the cinnamon and vanilla extract as he began frying the toast.

"Seems they had a bit of excitement out at the bonfire," Larry Joe said. "Apparently some junior high kid managed to set his pants leg on fire when a flaming marshmallow fell off its skewer."

"Oh, my goodness. Was he hurt?"

"No. In fact, a senior high school cheerleader flung herself against him, knocking him to the ground, and rolled them both over a couple of times in the dirt to put out the fire. Mr. Crego said by the time he made it over to check on him, the boy was smiling from ear to ear with firelight glinting off his metal braces. Catching fire was probably the best thing that happened to that kid all night."

"Good for him," I said. "Mrs. Cleats got knocked around in a bouncy house by some preschoolers hyped up on sugar."

"Good for them," Larry Joe said.

He slid a plate of French toast in front of me and gave me a kiss before sitting down across from me at the table. He's pretty sweet, so I decided to forgive him for eyeing Lucinda at the dinner.

As Larry Joe got up to refill our coffee cups, the landline rang.

"It's your mama," Larry Joe said, glancing at the caller ID.

"I might as well talk to her," I said. "She probably wants to tell me that there weren't many people at church this morning."

"Hi, Mama."

"Lord love a duck, Liv, you'll never guess what Earl Daniels did to me this morning."

I wasn't sure if I wanted to know, but after a pause I asked, "What?"

"He was clearing the toilet paper off the trees in my front yard and—"

"Your yard got rolled last night?"

"Yes it did, and so did half the other houses in the neighborhood. I guess after the hayride a bunch of the teenagers decided to cap off the night by wasting toilet paper," she said. "But that's another story. Anyway, Earl was up on a ladder pulling the paper off the tree and I came out on the front porch to check on him. I walked over by the ladder, and all of a sudden this little snake drops out of the tree and lands on my shoulder.

"I flicked it off and went running. I was all the way over in the Rowland's yard when I heard Earl hollering, 'It's not a real snake, Virginia.' I turned around and he's standing on the ground, laughing his fool head off. He bent over and picked up this rubber snake and started waving it at me."

I was trying very hard not to laugh. But it was difficult to do with Larry Joe practically doubled over in his chair laughing, since Mama talks loudly enough for anybody in the room to overhear her part of the phone conversation.

"I tell you I was madder than a wet hen. I

grabbed the rake that was leaning against the side of the house and went after him with the stick end of it. And he ran, too. I think he knew he'd be in for it if I caught up to him. The very idea. Earl Daniels is going have to make this up to me if he ever expects to sit down to supper at my table again. I even thought for a minute about putting some ex-lax in his gravy, but I decided to be the bigger person and turn the other cheek."

At this point, Larry Joe slapped his napkin over his mouth and ran out of the room.

Mama's call waiting beeped, and she told me she had to let me go. Just in time, too, because I don't think I could have bit my lip to hold back the laughter another second without drawing blood. The image of Mama chasing Earl around the yard while turning the other cheek just about pushed me over the edge.

After clearing away the dishes, Larry Joe and I got dressed and decided to take a stroll through the neighborhood. It was a sunny day with perfect, long-sleeve temperatures. We held hands and shuffled through piles of leaves that had gathered in patches along the sidewalk. Nobody on our street seemed to have gotten their yards rolled, but on the street just behind us we saw a couple of people clearing away toilet paper from trees and shrubs. The dummy with the Freddy Krueger mask scared me half to death Friday night, but at least he was easier to clear away than reams of dew-dampened toilet paper covering a towering oak tree.

After our walk, Larry Joe and I snuggled up on the sofa in the den and put our combined brainpower to work on the Sunday crossword puzzle.

Around three, Di called and invited us to come over to her place for supper at seven.

"Dave said he's going to fire up the grill and throw some T-bones on the flame to celebrate putting Morgan's real killer behind bars."

Di said she would be contributing baked potatoes and a tossed salad to the menu. I said we'd bring beer and wine.

Chapter 28

By the time we arrived at Di's, the temperature was beginning to drop outside. So when Dave pulled the steaks off the grill in front of Di's trailer, we all headed inside to dine at the kitchen table.

Dave looked more relaxed than I'd seen him in weeks.

"So did you two fix Ted up with that odd little spider lady?" Dave said, eyeing us with that bad-cop look he puts on for interrogations.

We told him the truth in a slightly deceitful way.

"I barely know her," Di said. "She's in my yoga class."

"I'd never met her until Friday at the funeral," I said.

"Hmm," Dave said, unconvinced.

"Dave, you know Ted joined the yoga class only as a last-ditch effort to meet women," Di said. "You should be happy for him that he's found someone."

"I suppose," he said. "But I didn't much enjoy him telling me how great it felt to have a tarantula crawl across his bare chest."

"*Eww,*" Di said.

"So he's already gotten bare-chested with Daisy?" I said, a little surprised that either one of them would move so quickly.

"I'd rather not think about Ted's bare chest right after I've eaten," Larry Joe said.

Di and I shared a knowing look before I began clearing away the dinner plates while Di put some coffee on. After filling our coffee mugs, she dumped a bag of trick-or-treat candy onto the table.

"They had this marked down when I ran by the dollar store today," she said.

I had avoided saying anything about the events of the previous evening to Dave, since I wasn't sure I wanted to hear what he thought of our little stunt, using the play to rouse a reaction out of Bryn, à la Hamlet. I was trying to think of a way to bring up the subject casually when Larry Joe saved me the trouble.

"So, Dave, it sounded to me like Bryn confessed to killing Morgan, but you said you found Pierce's fingerprints on the poison plant. What's the deal? Who killed Morgan, and why?" Larry Joe asked.

"The two of them were in on it from the beginning," Dave said. "This was a carefully planned murder. Morgan refused to fade away quietly. According to Bryn—who's been talking nonstop since her arrest—Morgan had threatened to go public about the affair if Pierce didn't file for divorce. Pierce couldn't afford that kind of scandal, since he was planning to start campaigning for the state senate as soon as Senator Cromwell announced his retirement. Word on the street has it that Pierce was being groomed for a run at the governor's office in a few years. And I think Bryn liked the idea of being Tennessee's first lady as much as Pierce liked the notion of being governor."

"But why kill Morgan at the retreat?" I asked. "Pierce could have killed her quietly pretty much anytime."

"That's just it. They needed the murder to happen in such a way that Pierce wouldn't be suspected, and at a time when Jasmine would be. They probably started hatching their murder plan shortly after Bryn first learned about the highly poisonous plant while making arrangements for the garden show back in the spring. She and Pierce just had to wait for the right time."

"I admit, I never suspected Bryn," Di said. "I was convinced Lucinda was the killer after that tarantula episode, until it turned out the spider belonged to Daisy."

"Yeah, me too," I said.

"Y'all *wanted* to believe it was Lucinda. So did a lot of other folks," Dave said.

"Listen, even before the spider I figured if it wasn't Jasmine, it had to be Lucinda. She was in the best position to get her hands on some of that hemlock water-dropwort, since she'd recently been to Europe. And then that attempt on her life seemed like the kind of phony dramatics Lucinda would come up with," I said.

"Right," Di said, turning to Dave. "And how were you always so dang sure the attempt on Lucinda's life was genuine?"

"I knew the attack was the real deal because I saw her right after the incident. She was scraped up and bleeding, and crying real tears. Lucinda may be on

TV, but she doesn't strike me as the type to do her own stunts.

"I should've dug deeper into Bryn as a suspect early on," Dave said. "Pierce was the only one we knew for certain was having an affair with Morgan—Bryn and Pierce both admitted as much to me."

"I still don't understand who did what to who and when," Larry Joe said, throwing his hands in the air.

"Okay, here's the way it went down yesterday," Dave said. "When Liv told me she remembered that she and Bryn got blueberry tea at the same time at the retreat, and yet Bryn had just said she has a severe blueberry allergy, that moved Mrs. Davenport to the top of my list of suspects."

"And while I was telling Dave about the allergy, I suddenly remembered something Lucinda had mentioned when Di and I talked to her about her meeting with Pierce. According to her, Pierce had said something like, when he first heard about Morgan's death he had thought it was ironic that someone who was such a health nut died from drinking herbal tea. It dawned on me that even if he guessed Morgan had been poisoned, he couldn't possibly have known that the poison was served in the tea. Nobody knew that until a few days later, when the medical examiner gave the test results to Dave. And that was the day Dave arrested Jasmine."

"I'd known something was fishy when *someone* finally got around to telling me about the mysterious fog and disappearing voice mail nonsense in Bryn's office," Dave said.

"Liv, I think when you called and said you

needed to talk to her, Bryn got worried you might be onto her. She knew some people in town were already convinced of Jasmine's innocence, so she decided to use the fog machine and voice message to cast suspicion on Lucinda."

"It worked," I said.

The miniature candy bars lying on the dining table were calling out to me. I picked up a Butterfinger and unwrapped it.

"I needed to dig up some physical evidence against Bryn," Dave said. "Then I recalled reading in a forensics journal that fingerprints can sometimes be retrieved from plants, so I called in a favor from a friend who's a forensics expert at the FBI field office in Memphis.

"While waiting for those results, it occurred to me that if Bryn had killed Morgan, she was also a good suspect for the attempt on Lucinda's life. So I decided to take another run at the housekeeper to see if Bryn's alibi held up."

"Hang on a minute," Larry Joe said. "I understand why they wanted Morgan out of the way. But why kill Lucinda?"

"Because they didn't know how much Morgan may have shared with Lucinda about Pierce," I said.

"And they couldn't risk Lucinda possibly deciding to leak some of that information to the tabloids after Pierce announced his candidacy, especially if Lucinda suspected that Pierce, or Bryn, was somehow involved in Morgan's death," Dave said. "Now where was I?"

"You were going to interview the housekeeper again about Bryn's alibi," Larry Joe said.

Larry Joe never pays this much attention to the thread of the conversation when I'm talking to him, I thought.

"Right," Dave said. "The maid, Myrna, stuck to her story about bringing tea to Bryn while she was on the phone with her mom—and phone records confirmed there was a twenty-six-minute call to a Virginia number. So I had Myrna go through the whole evening again, pressing her about anything that might have seemed unusual. She remembered taking the kitchen trash out to the garbage can in the garage and thinking it was odd to see Mr. Davenport's Mercedes there. She said he normally drives the Expedition only on hunting or fishing trips. I quickly wrapped up the interview with her and took a quick peek through the garage window on my way out. I could see that the big SUV parked inside was indeed a dark color with tinted windows like the one that tried to run down Lucinda. I figured if it wasn't Bryn who tried to run Lucinda down, it could be Pierce. I called the judge to get a warrant before taking a closer look at the SUV. I wanted to be sure we did everything by the book."

"Bryn drove that SUV to the retreat," I said. "I can't believe I didn't think of that earlier, since she usually drives that little sports car."

"Wait a minute," Larry Joe broke in again. "Pierce was in Nashville at a dinner for the governor the night Lucinda was attacked. Liv and I saw the TV reporter interviewing him."

"That puzzled me, too, at first," Dave said. "But when we reviewed the news video, the reporter had said the cocktail hour was about to begin. That would have made it an hour before the seven o'clock dinner. Pierce could have put in an appearance during cocktails and still have driven from Nashville to Dixie in less than two and a half hours—putting him in town in time to run down Lucinda. We're going through security camera footage from the hotel where the dinner was held, trying to nail down when Pierce left the building.

"I'm not sure how Pierce knew about Lucinda's little nine o'clock appointment. But he could have paid someone to keep tabs on her," Dave said.

"Actually, I think I know how he got hold of that tidbit," I said. "Nell said Friday that Sindhu had told her about Lucinda's nightly dates. Nell also mentioned that Bryn had called and offered to make a contribution for Jasmine's defense. I'm sure that was just a pretext for Bryn to pump Nell for information. And in my experience you don't have to prime the pump to get a flood of gossip from Nell."

Dave took a notepad from his shirt pocket and scribbled something down.

"I'm going to need to get formal statements from you and Di and Nell, and the rest of the women from the retreat," Dave said.

"We didn't have fingerprints on file for Pierce or Bryn," he continued. "But I figured I could retrieve prints from their wineglasses at the murder mystery dinner. I didn't want to alert them to our suspicions before we'd taken a look at the SUV. We had a forensics tech from Hartville standing by to go over the vehicle as soon as the couple left the house. Fortunately, neither of them had been at home when I'd questioned the housekeeper earlier in the day.

"The tire treads on the Expedition were a perfect

match to the acceleration scuff marks we found in the hotel parking lot. Even better, there was a tiny fragment of Lucinda's blouse snagged on the side-view mirror.

"The waiters at the country club were already wearing gloves, which was perfect for gathering the evidence. As soon as we confirmed the fingerprint match, we headed back to the country club. I didn't expect the commotion you and Lucinda had orchestrated," Dave said, looking directly at me. "But Bryn's confession certainly beefs up the case against her. And she just kept on talking, even after being advised of her rights. Her biggest concern seems to be making sure Pierce gets put away."

Dave relaxed his shoulders and leaned back in his chair.

"Wow, what a twisted mess of politics, murder, and scandal," Larry Joe said. "I bet the media will be camped out in Dixie when the trials begin."

"I expect so," Dave said. "Especially when our celebrity ghost hunter takes the stand."

"Oh, joy," Di said. "We can look forward to Lucinda coming back to town."

My cell phone went off. The ringtone let me know it was Mama. I looked over to Larry Joe.

"You might as well take the call. You know she'll just call back."

"Hello."

Mama started talking a mile a minute as soon as I answered.

"Liv, grab your suitcase and get over here. I'll be waiting on the porch in fifteen minutes."

"Mama, what are you talking about?"

"Your sister's on her way to the hospital to have the baby."

"Oh, okay," I said. "We could probably wait and leave in the morning."

"Liv, the baby's early," Mama said, emphatically. "She shouldn't be in labor for at least another week."

"Calm down, Mama. I think they can go a week or two in either direction," I said. "I'm sure there's nothing to worry about. What did Emma say when she called?"

"That's another thing," Mama said. "I didn't talk to Emma. Hobie called. When she went to the hospital with Lulu, Emma called me. It worries me that she didn't get on the phone herself."

"Mama, I . . ."

"Liv, you can come with me or not, but I'm too worried to just sit around here twiddling my thumbs. I'm packed and I'm hitting the highway in the next thirty minutes."

"Okay, Mama," I said. "I'm on my way."

All eyes were on me when I ended the call.

"Is something wrong with your sister or the baby?" Larry Joe said.

"I don't think so, but Mama insists on leaving right away. I can't let her drive all the way to Charlotte by herself," I said. "Guess it's a good thing we slept in today."

"We'd better head home and get your suitcase," Larry Joe said.

I promised Di I'd let her know as soon as we heard anything about Emma and the baby.

Epilogue

Mama was rocking baby Trey, Lulu was sitting on my lap, and my little sister was sitting beside me on the sofa with her feet propped up on the ottoman. Hobie was in the study, either catching up on work or hiding from Mama.

Emma clicked the remote to the right channel just as the intro music for *P.S. Ghost Encounters* started playing.

Lucinda was standing in a graveyard, bathed in soft light, fog swirling at her feet.

"Do her breasts look that huge in person?" Emma asked.

"Like perky melons," I said.

"Mine don't even get that big when I'm breast-feeding."

"Shush," Mama said. "Look, they're showing a picture of Lucinda in that little cemetery at St. Julian's."

The camera slowly pulled back to a wider view

to show the ladies of PWAD huddled around the tombstones.

"Look, there's Miss Annabelle and her sister," Emma said.

"Is that you, Liv, standing next to Winette?" Mama said. "What's wrong with your eyes?"

"If I ever see Lucinda, I'm going to kill her," I said.

Our star stood there looking glamorous and everyone else looked like a normal human being. But my eyes were glowing like a creature in the woods. And I looked like a hunchback from that angle. *I'm probably the only one who thinks I look hunchbacked,* I thought.

"Why are you all hunched over?" Mama said. "Did you drop something?"

Emma was laughing so hard, she grabbed a pillow and pressed it against her stomach to protect her cesarean stitches.

"Aunt Liv looks funny, huh, Mommy?" Lulu said.

My precious niece tilted her head back and gazed up at me with that sweet little face. I couldn't help but smile, despite my televised deformity.

Just as they cut away to a commercial, we could hear a recording of Miss Annabelle saying, "Was that the dead cat talking?"

Emma doubled over with laughter and Mama cackled, her body shaking so violently it woke up the baby.

Tips for Hosting
a Murder Mystery Dinner

While the murder mystery dinner in the book is a large-scale event, a smaller, more intimate gathering can be just as much fun. And themes can be selected to make the dinners perfect any time of year—not just at Halloween.

One of the pluses of a murder mystery dinner is that it ensures guests are engaged throughout the evening, even if they don't know each other. This helps eliminate awkward silences and the all-too-common scenario in which some guests become wallflowers because they don't dance, for example.

STEP 1: PLANNING THE "MURDER"

The simplest way to put together a murder mystery is to buy a kit. Most of these kits, which can be purchased online or in department stores, include the script, instructions for running the mystery, clues, costume ideas, and even invitations.

These may be used as is or, with a little effort, may be customized for specific groups.

For instance, a murder mystery in which the

victim is the unpopular CEO of a company could be easily adapted for a party of coworkers to make their boss the "victim." If the boss is a likable, good-natured sort he or she might even be included on the guest list and play the victim at the party!

Really ambitious hosts can even opt to write their own scripts.

STEP 2: SENDING OUT INVITATIONS

Send out invitations at least a month before the party to give guests time to look over their character descriptions and backstory. (Over the course of the dinner, characters will receive additional clues about their character and details about the murder to reveal). If it's a costume party, guests will also need ample time to assemble their outfits. And be sure that guests RSVP so that you know all the roles for the mystery are covered.

STEP 3: PLANNING THE DINNER

Most murder mystery dinners are arranged in "scenes" that happen between courses. If hiring a caterer, the host will need to ensure that the courses are served in concert with the progress of the mystery. If hosts are making and serving the dinner themselves, even more careful planning is needed.

Keep it simple. Have appetizers ready before guests arrive. Let guests pour their own drinks. Serve the main course as a buffet, and if possible have desserts already arranged on a table. Having as much of the dinner ready ahead of time allows the hosts to enjoy the party.

If the group comprises close friends, hosts may even decide to make it potluck.

STEP 4: SETTING THE STAGE

For most people, a murder mystery dinner at home will likely mean limiting the guest list to between six and ten people. This is also the number of characters in most murder mystery kits.

Dinner guests must be at a table or tables in the same room or in adjoining rooms open to each other, so everyone can be in on the action. Use table decorations that fit the theme of the script, which can be anything from *The Great Gatsby* to a 1970s disco. The host may stage the crime scene in a different room and have the guests "commute" between dinner courses to view evidence at the appropriate point in the story. White masking tape can be used to create a chalk body outline, and shoes pressed into flour or baby powder can be pressed onto a dark rug to provide footprints.

STEP 5: LET THE PLAY BEGIN

After the guests have arrived and had a few minutes to greet each other, get things rolling. It's the hosts' job to prompt the next scene, keep the action moving, and keep the story on track.

But above all, relax and have fun. Unless you hire actors for the evening, some of the characters will inevitably forget or flub their lines. Make sure all the necessary clues to solve the murder are revealed, and laugh together at any missteps.

After the murderer is revealed, guests will want to look back over the way things unfolded and whom they suspected at various points of the story, so allow time for this, perhaps over coffee or cordials.

Tips for Hosting a Riverboat Gambler/Casino Party

At a casino party, with a riverboat gambler theme or not, there should be at least three games on offer, perhaps more, depending on the size of the guest list and the venue. Choices ensure there is something for everyone.

Invitations should indicate the style of the party, whether Casino Royale formal or Las Vegas strip casual, so guests can dress accordingly.

While we usually think of a casino party as adults only, it can also work for family gatherings. Bingo is a good multigenerational game—even youngsters can play or help an older relative keep track of the numbers.

Play card, roulette, and dice games with chips that can be cashed in for small prizes, such as books, novelties, or costume jewelry. The host may create a stockpile of prizes by hitting garage sales or scoring some great finds on eBay. Gift cards or a bottle of wine also make great prizes. And casino parties are a perfect fit for fund-raisers. Guests receive chips in exchange for donations to the chosen charity.

THE EQUIPMENT

Roulette wheels may be purchased online, starting at as little as $20 and going up to a few hundred dollars for more deluxe models. Poker chips and blackjack boards are also available, often in sets and very affordably priced.

Bingo sets can be purchased inexpensively, but can also be downloaded and printed out on home computers and printers.

Professional model game sets and games tables can also be rented from party supply stores. (This often adds delivery and retrieval costs.)

THE DETAILS

Set the stage, starting on the front porch. Fashion a gangplank, and hang netting and buoys along the porch railing. Stencil "Mississippi Queen" or "Gambling Hall" onto a square of plywood and brush the dried paint with steel wool to give it a weathered appearance.

Continue the theme inside, draping food tables with fishing nets and placing small nautical items here and there. Search and find vintage riverboat scenes online and available for free download. Enlarge and print images and hang them on the wall in frames you already own. Perhaps swap out some framed family photos for riverboat-themed images for the evening. Or haunt flea markets or rummage sales to find some inexpensive paintings with river or nautical scenes—or even dogs playing poker for a fun, kitschy touch.

WORD TO THE WISE

If you scatter playing cards as decorations on the food and beverage tables, be sure to use cards with different color backs for the card games, so sly card-sharps don't win hands with something stashed up their sleeves!

Engagement Parties

WHO?

These days more couples are throwing their own engagement parties, traditionally hosted by the bride's parents. But there's no reason a couple can't have it both ways. They may host their own engagement party for friends and have the parents host a gathering for family. It's mainly a chance for some of the important people in the couple's life to get acquainted.

WHEN?

Engagement parties are typically held six to eleven months before the wedding—relatively soon after the proposal, but before the crunch of wedding preparations.

INVITATIONS

In the book *It's Your Party, Die If You Want To*, since Rachel wanted the riverboat gambler theme to be a surprise for her fiancé, the invitations didn't give it away. However, if you're not trying to keep the theme under wraps, you can have fun with the invitations. Maybe you could include something like "This pair is a winning hand," along with photos of the happy couple in costume. Or "Rachel and Mark hit the jackpot and fell in love."

BONUS TIP

For larger parties of any kind, hosts can actually save money by hiring an event planner. Paying for a few hours of a professional planner's time upfront is often enough to keep an event on track and on budget, saving an inexperienced host or planner significant time and money—and making the party a success!

Catch up with Liv and Di from the beginning!
Don't miss

Death Crashes the Party

On sale now!

Chapter 1

Monday was a scorching August day that had turned into hell for me when the Farrell brothers crashed a party that already had disaster written all over it.

I was repeating the dreadful details for the umpteenth time to Sheriff Eulyse "Dave" Davidson.

At 10:00 a.m. I met yet again with the Erdmans to continue negotiations for their fortieth-anniversary party. Making all Mrs. Erdman's peculiar dreams come true, while still pacifying her husband, was a complicated balancing act—like spinning plates on poles. This is a skill every good party planner must learn.

Mrs. Erdman, her red hair sticking out in barbed curls, sat on a chintz sofa in the couple's expansive living room. We discussed every tedious detail of a moonshine- and magnolias-themed party. Mr. Erdman sat in a recliner, paying scant attention to anything that didn't require personal effort on his part.

In a nutshell—the Erdmans being the nuts—she wanted an elegant party with frills, fancy foods, and elaborate decorations. Mr. Erdman wanted to wear comfortable clothes and drink lots of liquor. So he and his buddies would sample generous servings of different whiskeys, including moonshine from his cousin Vern's still. The ladies would dress as Southern belles, sip mint juleps, and listen to a Dixieland band on the veranda. The men, at the insistence of Mr. Erdman, would be dressed as bootleggers. Picture *O Brother, Where Art Thou?* We finally ironed out a major wrinkle when Mr. Erdman acquiesced to one dance with his wife. Hopefully, the other husbands would follow suit.

Mrs. Erdman's most recent vision for the party—and she'd had many—included ice sculptures. She wanted a giant forty perched atop a 1973 Plymouth Barracuda carved in ice, which would be displayed on the buffet table, with icy bare-butted cherubs to either side. The Barracuda was the car they took on their honeymoon. Not sure about the cherubs, but ours is not to reason why. After consulting with the ice sculptor, I now had to figure out how to store 250 pounds of ice—in August—so it wouldn't melt before the party. Although the Erdmans had two refrigerators with freezers in their kitchen, they were nowhere near large enough to accommodate the sculptures.

Mrs. Erdman offered that they had a deep freezer in the garage, which stored her husband's bounty of venison and catfish from his hunting and fishing exploits. She assured me that any game left in the freezer could be given away to friends and neighbors to make way for the sculptures. Mr. Erdman didn't dispute her assertion. I followed them into the garage, with tape measure in hand, to make sure the freezer could contain the ice sculptures.

"And . . . well, you know what happened next."

"Humor me," Dave said, with absolutely no sympathy for the day I was having. So I went through it—again.

I opened the freezer to measure the interior. Unfortunately, what we beheld was the frosty remains of Darrell Farrell, staring up at us like a fresh-caught walleye.

Mrs. Erdman screamed and ran back into the house. Her rotund husband stood for a moment, stunned. I backed away from the freezer, looking at a still slack-jawed Walter Erdman, trying to think of something to say. Instead, I tripped, knocking over a big green garbage can, and found myself sprawled on top of Darrell's very dead brother, Duane, who had toppled out with the trash. He was wearing what for the life of me looked like a Confederate uniform.

Walter Erdman screamed like a young girl and ran across the three-car garage and back into the house. I'd never seen anyone haul that much ass in one load. The Erdmans, who had the nerve of a bad tooth, had left me to deal with the problem at hand, despite the fact that it was not my house and it was definitely not my party. I dialed 911.

After phoning the police, I went into the house to let my clients know the sheriff was on his way. I found Mr. Erdman in his study, stretched out on a leather sofa, staring at the ceiling and clutching a bottle of Scotch. Sobs from the hallway indicated Mrs. Erdman had locked herself in the powder room.

"I went to the entry hall and sat on the stairs, waiting to open the door when you arrived."

The only fortunate aspect of this tiresome inquisition was that Sheriff Dave was conducting it in the air-conditioned comfort of the Erdmans' roomy kitchen, appointed with gleaming commercial-grade appliances and marble countertops. I helped myself to a Diet Coke from the under-counter fridge stocked with bottled water and soft drinks.

"Dave, you want something to drink?"

No, ma'am. I'm good."

Presumably to emphasize that this was official business, Dave made a point of calling me "Mrs. McKay" and "ma'am," instead of "Liv," despite the fact that we'd long been on a first-name basis. Tall, lean, and not bad looking, our normally genial sheriff could, nonetheless, present an imposing demeanor when he had a mind to.

"I know you didn't ask me, Sheriff Davidson," I said, following his cue on formality, "but, despite the fact the bodies were found at their house, which would naturally make them prime suspects, I can honestly testify that the Erdmans were both completely shocked by the discovery."

"Can't rule anything or anyone out at this juncture, but I take your point," he said.

After he finally stopped probing my brain for details, I had to ask, "Dave, do you have any idea why Duane was wearing a Confederate uniform?"

"He and his brother were both involved with one of those Civil War reenactment units," he said. "As to why he was dressed out in uniform, I can't say. They've got some big reenactment event coming up in a few weeks." He went on. "Now, let me ask you a question, Ms. McKay. You seem to keep your ear to the ground. Do you have any idea who might have had a reason to kill the Farrell boys?"

"Seems obvious to me, Sheriff," I said. "It must have been some damn Yankee."

Dave did not seem at all amused.